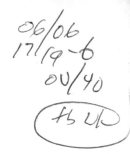

THE OTHER
Megan

Robbi McCoy

Bella
BOOKS

2016

Bella Books, Inc.
P.O. Box 10543
Tallahassee, FL 32302

Printed in the United States of America on acid-free paper.

First Bella Books Edition 2016

Editor: Katherine V. Forrest
Cover Designer: Judith Fellows

ISBN: 978-1-59493-498-8

Other Bella Books By Robbi McCoy

Acknowledgments

As always, I am thankful for the love and support of my best friend and life partner, Dot. For this book especially, which did not come easy, she got into the muck up to her elbows and helped me through it. Thank you, darling, for reminding me of the definition of "romance."

To Sara Guadarrama, *muchas gracias, mi querida amiga*. Your help was critical, and I'm grateful for your generous donation of time.

To my editor, Katherine V. Forrest, thank you once again for your expertise and your enthusiastic encouragement. As many have said and many others have agreed, myself included, Katherine is *always* right. To everyone else at Bella Books, thank you for the professionalism and the quality production. You have made my books the best they could be.

About the Author

Robbi McCoy is a native Californian who lives with her life partner and cat in the Central Valley, equidistant between the mountains and the sea. She is an avid hiker with a particular fondness for the deserts of the American Southwest. She also enjoys gardening, culinary adventures, travel and the theater. She is recently retired from her career as a software specialist and web designer and is enjoying a life of leisure with an occasional spurt of writing.

Dedication

To my sweetheart for all the life-expanding places she has made me travel, and for providing a loving sanctuary at home.

CHAPTER ONE

"Extra crispy or original recipe?" Jaye asked, walking into the front room of their house.

Willie had been peering intently through her glasses at the computer screen. At the sound of Jaye's voice, she jerked in her chair, banging one knee on the underside of the military-style metal desk.

I've got to learn to quit taking her by surprise, Jaye reminded herself. That woman has one hell of a startle reflex.

"What?" Willie swiveled to face Jaye. She rubbed her knee, blinking as if she couldn't focus.

She probably hasn't taken her eyes off the screen for an hour, Jaye thought. "Sorry, I didn't mean to scare you."

Willie waved a hand dismissively. She wore a white, short-sleeved shirt and cotton pants, one pant leg rolled up to the knee and the other all the way down in typically indifferent Willie fashion. Her taupe-colored hair was carelessly collected at the back of her head in a ponytail as usual, making her narrow face look even narrower. In spite of the bobby pins tucked into her hair at strategic points, several wisps had escaped and blew around her temples and neck in the breeze from the electric fan. Yes, Jaye marveled all over again, actual bobby pins. Willie must be the only twenty-six-year-old on the planet to use them. Before meeting Willie, she would have assumed bobby pins had gone the way of typewriter erasers and were no longer even being manufactured, but Willie had assured her they were, and, in fact, so were typewriter erasers. Jaye suspected Willie had had the same hairstyle since the age of seven.

She looks so unassuming, Jaye observed fondly—mild, maybe even timid. But her appearance was deceptive. Under that unexceptional façade was a strong woman of conviction. Within her breast beat a heart of boundless passion. Willie's passions, however, seemed not to extend beyond the cerebral. She was an ascetic, devoting her life to the service of others, specifically, providing free dental care to the island locals. If she possessed unrealized physical longings, she kept them well concealed.

"What did you say?" Willie asked, focusing her light, piercing eyes fully on Jaye.

"I asked which you preferred, extra crispy or original recipe?" Jaye paused at the counter containing several days' worth of mail.

Willie smiled, stretching her thin mouth even thinner. "Original recipe."

"Extra crispy for me. With biscuits and mashed potatoes and gravy."

"As long as we're fantasizing, can we order a cherry pie with that?"

"Why not? I don't think they have cherry pies at KFC, but that's sort of beside the point, isn't it?" Jaye began pulling junk mail out of the pile to throw away. "You know, I've never actually been to a KFC."

"Then how do you know you like extra crispy?"

"That red and white bucket was a mainstay at lesbian potlucks. Never failed to show up."

Willie laughed. "Don't lesbians like to cook?"

"Oh, sure. Some do, some don't. You've got one that doesn't, unfortunately for you. Just now I was peering hopefully into our fridge thinking about dinner. It looks like we've got some of that plantain lasagna stuff left, the thing Isabel Sanchez brought."

"Pastelon, yeah." Willie stood up and stretched her thin arms over her head, setting off a popping sound in her shoulders. She was about five seven, very angular and lean to go along with a nervous temperament. "Southern fried chicken sounds really good for a change, doesn't it?" she said. "Do they even have KFCs in the islands?"

"Yes, actually, a few. The closest one is on Grand Cayman."

"And how do you know that?"

"I looked it up on the Internet the last time I had this craving."

"That's kind of a long way to go for dinner. Plus we don't have a boat."

"It's funny what you end up missing, isn't it? I never would have guessed fried chicken."

"What else do you miss, Jaye?"

Willie's tone drew Jaye's attention from the mail. The look on her face suggested she was asking a serious question.

"Not much, to be honest. I have everything I need here. Other than better equipment, of course. And maybe air-conditioning. Yes, air-conditioning would be awesome. The X-ray machine is down again, by the way, if you want to call the guy. But on a private level, I don't miss much. This," she raised her arms to encircle the space, "is my personal paradise."

They both looked around the room, with its mismatched furniture, health and hygiene posters, water-damaged ceiling acoustical tiles, scuffed up linoleum floor, counters piled high with boxes of gauze, face masks and disposable gloves and the wall of painted white cupboards bulging with more of the same. Then they looked at one another and both burst out laughing.

Willie walked over to the far end of the room where a long table served as her craft area. This was where she made her birdhouses. A shelf suspended on the wall held several finished ones. On the table were others in various stages of completion, along with bark and wood scraps and other items she had foraged to add interest and whimsy to the avian domiciles. This was one of Willie's projects to keep her nervous hands and mind occupied. Willie was a chronic insomniac. It was not uncommon for Jaye to wake up at any time of night and find the neighboring bed empty. She didn't normally go looking for Willie, not anymore, as she knew there was nothing wrong. Early on, before she knew Willie's habits, she would get up to see what the matter was and would find Willie at three in the morning sitting contentedly at her work table gluing together strips of wood.

"So I guess it's pastelon tonight," Jaye said.

"It was pretty tasty," Willie remarked, her attention distracted by a bark house with a thatched roof she had been building the night before. She looked it over critically, then turned to face Jaye. "Who was here this morning?" she asked.

"Matteo Florenza."

"How is he?"

"About the same. He can't keep anything down. Still has a temperature."

"Poor guy. Do you think he needs to see a doctor?"

"Not just yet. I'm sure it's the flu. He just has to get through it, but if he doesn't turn the corner by tomorrow, then, yes, he might need more than tea and sympathy."

"Jaye, dear, you're giving him much more than tea and sympathy. You're running a medical clinic in the jungle, treating everything from paper cuts to stage four cancer. You're like the MacGyver of nursing."

"Still, there's only so much I can do. It'd be so much better if we could lure a doctor out here permanently."

"Not likely. The jungle doctors want to go where the action is, the front lines." Willie said it like she too would like to go where the action was. "This is a pretty tame assignment compared to some places in Africa."

Tame, right, Jaye repeated silently. No dodging gunfire and bottle rockets during the workday. That was true. The only real crime in Isla Santuario was generally what spilled over from drug trafficking in South America. The Caribbean island was situated on a route conveniently located between the drug cartels and their customers in the United States. Criminals used it as a transfer point or a cooling-off zone. Santuario used to be a quiet, safe and relatively unspoiled tropical island, Jaye had been told, but recently, two industries were propelling it into prominence: tourism and drug trafficking. As the pressure increased in the old hot spots in Mexico and South America, more and more drug lords were discovering the new sport of island-hopping their wares, using Isla Santuario as overflow parking for the mainland. Along with drugs came crime, something the government tried to keep from being widely publicized so as not to hurt the growing tourist trade.

Still, Jaye had been in the peaceful village of Tocamila six months already and nothing alarming had happened at all, for which she was grateful. She didn't need to be dodging gunfire to feel like she was contributing. It was challenging enough working in isolation on a shoestring budget.

Willie yawned and cast a weary smile Jaye's way, then took off her glasses and rubbed the bridge of her nose.

"Do you have a headache?" Jaye asked.

"Yes. How do you always know when I have a headache?"

Jaye shrugged. "I'll get you some aspirin."

Willie shook her head. "No, I'll wait till after dinner. I haven't had much to eat today. It's taken me all day to digest that huge feast from last night." Jaye recalled Willie's visit to a local family the night before, to follow up on a tooth extraction. She'd been gone for hours, though the home was less than a quarter mile away.

"How is little Mariana?"

"Healing nicely. No sign of infection. She'll be fine. But I have to remember not to make house calls at supper time. Her grandmother—great grandmother, actually—insisted I stay, and served up everything in the pantry and, I'm not lying, the barnyard as well."

"What'd she make?"

"Roast chicken, pork tamales, cassava fritters, pigeon peas, a very spicy soup and a kind of honey cake with coconut for dessert. It was delicious."

"Didn't you bring me any?"

"Sorry." Willie looked contrite. "She was very lively, Mariana's grandmother, and full of humor. She had no teeth. Not a single one. I asked her if she wanted dentures. She said no, thank you! She hadn't had any teeth for the last twenty years, she said, and had suffered no ill effects from the lack of them. She said she could bite clean through the leg of a mature billy goat with her gums."

Jaye laughed. "I hope she didn't mean a *live* billy goat."

"I didn't ask. We all had a good time. They laughed a lot and I'm sure they laughed at me some of the time, the way people find foreigners funny. I didn't mind being the entertainment. And it was kind of nice, you know, having dinner with a family for a change. Not that I don't like meals here with you. But it's been a long time since I sat down to a meal with a real family— kids, parents, grandparents." Willie smiled wistfully.

Jaye understood that she was thinking about her own family in Seattle, and how long it had been since she had been a comfortable part of it. Willie and the rest of the Willett family no longer communicated. "Philosophical differences" was the explanation Willie gave. It had something to do with money, as Willie's family was quite wealthy and Willie had some sort of moral conflict with that. *I wouldn't mind being rich myself*, Jaye thought, momentarily reminded of her own hardscrabble childhood with an unmarried mother who was rarely around and not much good when she was. Jaye was sure she could be both rich and happy. In fact, she wouldn't have minded if Willie claimed some of her family's wealth. The money would make a huge difference out here. But it wasn't Willie's way and Jaye had to respect that.

"What else do they have at lesbian potlucks?" Willie asked.

Jaye looked up from the invoice she had opened. "Lesbians."

Willie frowned. "No, no, you know what I mean. What dishes? What do lesbians eat?"

Jaye raised one eyebrow, giving Willie a meaningful look until Willie's eyebrows both shot up in understanding. She burst out with a choking chortle, then clamped her hand over her mouth and shook her head emphatically, giggling into her palm like a teenager.

Jaye dumped a pile of junk mail into the recycling bin, smiling. When Willie recovered herself, tears of merriment sparkled in her eyes. Her face was flushed pink. In some ways, Willie was an ancient sage. In others, an innocent child.

"God, Jaye," she said, trying to remove the smile from her face, "my mind would never have gone there, believe me."

"Oh, I believe you!"

Willie sat down in front of the computer and put her glasses back on.

Jaye was almost certain that sex was not something Willie thought much about. She didn't ever talk about it and seemed to have no interest in dating. If she had a sexual history, she never referred to it. Casual high school dating of boys was about all she'd ever mentioned. Jaye didn't find it hard to believe that Willie might be a virgin. That part of life simply didn't matter to her.

Jaye herself was on hiatus from romance. After leaving Lexie, she had wanted nothing to do with it. Her heart had gone numb. She needed a friend so much more than a lover. And she had found a wonderful friend in Willie.

She had everything she needed here, a comfortable home, friends and meaningful work. If she had been raised like Willie, with all the luxuries, maybe this lifestyle wouldn't be so easy to take, but Jaye had lived in worse places than this. Much worse. This was home now and she was happy.

"Quinoa salad," she announced, recapturing Willie's attention.

Willie snorted. "Seriously?"

"Yes. At least in the group Lexie and I ran with. Quinoa salad. Somebody always made that."

"Interesting. Was Lexie into stuff like that?"

"No. She was the meat-and-potatoes type. And beer. We always brought beer and wine to potlucks. She wanted to be sure they wouldn't run out."

Willie gave her a knowing nod. She knew all about Jaye's history with Lexie.

Hearing a car door shut outside, they turned simultaneously toward the front of the building. Jaye walked over and opened the front door to see Paloma's red hatchback parked beside the guava tree. The hatch was up and Paloma herself came into view a moment later carrying a cardboard box that nearly hid her face entirely. But over the edge of the box Jaye could see her large sable eyes, set deeply into a smooth cocoa-colored face. Paloma's mahogany hair was pulled back and twisted into one long braid. She wore khaki shorts and a blue, short-sleeved cotton blouse, the usual woven reed flip-flops on her feet.

When she reached the porch, Jaye held the door open for her. "We didn't expect to see you today. It's Sunday. Your day of rest."

"Day of rest?" Willie interjected, leaping over to take the box from Paloma's arms. "What a concept!"

"I thought you'd want to start getting everything ready for Tuesday," Paloma said. "There's more."

"I'll help," Willie offered, dashing out the door.

"You're right," Jaye said. "We can inventory and put this stuff away today. There won't be much time otherwise. But it's a shame you had to drive all the way out here on your day off."

"I don't mind. It gave me an excuse to get away from my family. Sundays at home are like you would not believe." Paloma laughed her easy laugh, dimples forming in both cheeks. "Everybody comes. Grandma, Grandpa, aunts, uncles, cousins. Babies crying and everybody talking at once. And Papa, he never turns off the TV. With two dozen people in the house, he turns up the volume so he can hear his soccer match, so everybody talks even louder. Every Sunday this happens, every Sunday after Mass, and they all stay until their supper has been digested and almost everybody has been insulted in one way or another."

Jaye laughed. "Sounds lovely. I'm sure they're missing you today."

"Oh, I know!" She shook her head with mock sadness. "I was so sorry to have to tell my mama I would miss our family day because I was on a mission of mercy for the clinic."

Jaye caught Paloma's typical sarcasm, a trait she particularly enjoyed in the young woman. Paloma was Willie's assistant, studying to be a dental hygienist. She was ambitious, intelligent, spirited and confident, and they were both delighted to have her on the team. For her part, she was grateful for the opportunity, attributing her selection to her excellent English. For whatever reason Global Dental Relief had chosen her, it had been a win for everyone.

Willie staggered in under the burden of another large box and set it on a counter beside the first one.

"Will you stay for dinner," Jaye asked Paloma, "since you're missing out on the feast at home? We're having pastelon."

"Don't worry," Willie assured her, "Jaye didn't make it. One of the village women did."

"No, thank you," Paloma said with an awkward look of embarrassment. She tried to mask it with an unsuccessful casual smile. "I'm meeting someone."

"Oh, really?" Willie grinned at her. "So you used us as a smokescreen with your mama. Well, thank you for the delivery. I'm glad it was you picking this stuff up in Punta Larga and not me. Was it a madhouse?"

"There are a lot of students there." Paloma rolled her eyes, though she herself was a student.

"Nothing crazier than swarms of drunken young people," Jaye said with a shudder.

"Weren't you ever a student on spring break?" Willie asked.

"Never like this bunch. I didn't have the money to go to some snazzy tropical island resort. And I'm sure I never mooned anybody from the back of a convertible."

"Nor did I. I spent my spring breaks reading in splendid isolation."

"Why does that not surprise me?" Jaye remarked.

"What is *mooned*?" Paloma asked, her round face sincerely innocent. Her English was perfect, but the idioms did sometimes trip her up.

Jaye glanced at Willie, who was already looking at her with a challenge on her face.

"Do you want to show her?" she asked, grinning. "It would make more sense coming from you, since you're a nurse."

"Like this requires some technical medical explanation?" Jaye asked sarcastically. She shook her head and turned to Paloma. "Mooning," she explained, "is showing your bare bottom to the moon, but in this case, it's usually done in the daylight and intended to shock innocent bystanders."

Paloma looked surprised, then covered her mouth and giggled. At nineteen, such things could still startle her. Jaye and Willie smiled at one another. Paloma went out to get the last box.

"For the record," Jaye said, "I never mooned anybody, but I did flash a boob now and then."

"I have a feeling you're concealing a shockingly wild youth," Willie said wryly.

Jaye said nothing, but grinned to herself. Compared to Willie's youth, it probably was shockingly wild. She took a pair of scissors and sliced through the tape on the supply boxes.

"That was nice of her to bring this stuff out," Willie said. "Save one of us a trip tomorrow morning."

"It was nice, yes, but it sounds like she had an ulterior motive."

"Right. She's meeting someone. Do you know anything about that?"

Jaye shook her head. "It's the first I've heard of it."

"I wonder why she didn't want her mother to know."

"Young people like their privacy. Besides, her family is so conservative. Maybe they wouldn't like it. Maybe the guy's not their idea of a dream husband."

Willie shrugged. "She's a good kid. Works hard. Studies hard. She's the only one of her family who's going to have a college education. She'll end up supporting her parents, you wait and see. You'd think nobody would have the slightest objection to whatever she does after how her brother turned out."

Willie was referring to Paloma's younger brother Eddie, who had been swept into a drug trafficking operation at the age of fifteen, nearly two years ago. Eddie's conscription by the *narcos*, as Paloma collectively called the drug traffickers, was a source of pain and shame for the entire Marra family. They lived in fearful anticipation of their son's early demise.

"Obviously, she trusts us," said Jaye, "so don't give her the third degree."

"Don't worry. I won't pry. But wouldn't you like to know?" Jaye nodded.

Paloma returned with the last box and Jaye took it from her.

"We're going to be in it up to our necks Tuesday," said Jaye, "so I hope you'll be here bright and early."

Paloma nodded. "Of course."

Willie approached Paloma, placing a hand on her shoulder. "We don't need you tomorrow, though. Have fun tonight."

"Bye, Jaye," Paloma said with a wave.

Jaye winked at her, then Willie walked her out. Jaye opened the boxes to inspect the contents. If her supplier had come through, there would be enough syringes, alcohol prep pads and everything else to meet the anticipated need for their big inoculation day.

As she unpacked the supplies, ticking them off her mental list, she was only vaguely aware of voices outside. She took little notice until she heard the sound of a man hollering emphatically, then a woman's scream. That was Willie!

Jaye dropped a box of adhesive bandages and flew to the door. She flung it open to see a Jeep parked a short distance along the driveway. She froze in the doorway, processing the scene. There were three men, all of them wearing military-style fatigues and black face masks, at least two of them armed with assault rifles. Paloma lay on the ground beside her car, unmoving. Two of the men were running toward the Jeep. The third was dragging, nearly carrying Willie in the same direction, moving too fast for her feet to keep up. She struggled, but the man was huge, his progress unimpeded by her thrashing.

"Jaye!" she called, her voice panicked, her eyes wild. "Help!"

Wakened from her momentary paralysis, Jaye sprinted after the men as they all leapt into the open Jeep, pulling Willie in with them.

"Stop, stop!" she yelled, still running toward them. One of the men shoved Willie to the floor and out of sight.

Another turned around in the vehicle and aimed his AK-47 directly at Jaye. She stopped immediately, expecting a spray of bullets to tear through her body. The Jeep lurched forward, the rear tires spinning momentarily in mud ruts, before the vehicle shot toward the road. The man with the gun kept it aimed levelly at Jaye. All she saw of him was his dark, hard eyes fixed on her. She watched helplessly as they reached the main road where they were swallowed up by a screen of thick vegetation.

She ran to Paloma and took hold of both her shoulders, turning her so she could see her face. "Paloma!" she cried. "Paloma!"

Her eyes were shut and Jaye was stricken with the thought that she was dead. She scanned her body for blood, signs of bullet wounds, but saw nothing. She was about to check for a pulse when Paloma moaned and opened her eyes, focusing on Jaye.

"Did they take her?" she asked weakly.

Jaye pulled her to a sitting position and held her close to her body. She answered reluctantly, trying to stem the flood of chilling thoughts cascading down upon her. "Yes."

CHAPTER TWO

"Ho'in the house!" yelled Mickey, lifting his arm over his curly auburn head to point toward the door of the bar. His voice, deep and resonant, could be heard even through the throb of the hip-hop beat and the roar of conversation, laughter and shrieking that pervaded the room.

Megan followed his gaze to see Heather Price enter the cantina, rocking a nearly nonexistent bikini, her straight blond hair reaching down below her shoulder blades where it swayed from left to right as she walked with a pronounced side-to-side hip flip. She glanced over and stuck her tongue out at Mickey. He grinned with satisfaction. Megan rolled her eyes. She knew Mickey was hot for Heather, but she was out of his league. He knew it too, but that didn't stop him from dreaming. Mickey was cute in a boyish way, but he couldn't have played the leading man in anything other than a screwball comedy. He was the Alfred E. Neuman type, complete with a red mop and freckles, with a complexion so afraid of the sun that he practically painted himself white with sunblock before they hit the beach.

Mickey was one of Megan's best friends from USC. His buddy Gavin was also here, wearing his usual red and gold Trojans ball cap. Megan wondered if he slept in that cap, as she had never seen him without it. Gavin was more classically handsome than Mickey and a startling contrast to him. He was slim and dark-complexioned with close-cropped black hair, his ebony eyes set off beautifully by long, thick eyelashes. Gavin usually had no trouble landing chicks, but when he had recently turned his attention toward Megan, he had met an unexpected challenge. She had resisted. That had confused him. He wasn't used to being turned down.

Yeah, he was cute, cool and all that, but she just wasn't that into him, so why start something? But how do you know, her roommate Nicole had asked her, if you won't get to know him? She just knew, she said. Besides, she was tired of the dating scene. Too much drama. She was happy now just having a group of friends to hang out with—her crew—most of whom were here in beautiful Punta Larga with her. Nicole was back at the hotel, but Mickey, Gavin and Lisa were here, determined not to let the night go to waste.

The Blue Parrot Cantina was tonight's hangout. After a day of swimming, kayaking, scuba diving, volleyball and baking on the beach, the sunburned kids all packed into the bars and nightclubs to dance and drink. Most of them still wore their swimming suits: baggy, colorful trunks for the boys and scanty two-pieces for the girls. Megan wore an oversized chambray shirt over her black and white print halter top and low-rise bottom. Both the boys were shirtless, Gavin's smooth, muscled, hairless chest a stark contrast to Mickey's pale, fleshy one with its covering of whitish down.

Lisa's costume was a neon green bikini with a filmy sarong of turquoise tied low around her waist like a belly dancer, carefully orchestrated to show off her dangling rhinestone navel piercing. Everything about her radiated health and youth. She was magnificent, bronze, tall and muscular. Lisa was the star of the women's basketball team, a gleaming Amazon with chestnut hair and blue eyes. After an hour of pounding tequila shots,

Megan had to admit that Lisa's smooth stomach decorated by the sparkling ribbon of rhinestones had enough sheer erotic power to make her dizzy. Holy crap, what's she doing to the boys? Megan wondered. Or, maybe more to the point, what's she doing to the other girls who swung her way? Megan glanced around the room, casually checking to see if there were any likely looking women checking Lisa out. No doubt Lisa was keeping a watch out for the same.

The bar was decorated with wood and plastic versions of its namesake, blue parrots of varying sizes hanging from the ceiling or perched wherever they could find a foothold. One clung to the top of the flat-screen television mounted in the corner. The TV was on, but couldn't be heard over the din of the partiers. The parrot attached to it had its head cocked to one side as if surveying the rowdy bar patrons. From that perch, the parrot had a view of the entire space.

Mickey threw a ping-pong ball to Lisa and she caught it handily in an empty cup. Rows of tequila shots sat on the table waiting for someone to miss the ball. Lisa tossed the ball to Megan and she caught it. She turned to her right and tossed the ball to Gavin. He missed and the ball bounced along the floor. "Shit, Gavin!" Megan whined.

"Drink!" Lisa hollered gleefully, then ran after the ball. She tripped over her sarong, but managed not to fall.

Mickey laughed. "Bro, I don't think you've caught one in the last half hour."

Megan nodded vigorously. "I know, right? Is he really on the baseball team?"

"What the hell?" Gavin objected, his nose shining under the hot overhead light. "That's a fucking ping-pong ball, not a baseball! And this is a fucking Dixie cup, not a glove!" Yep, he was hella drunk. All of the sweetness had been pickled out of him. "You wanna play with a glove and baseball, you'll see what I can do. I'd be a hundred percent sober right now and you'd all be on the floor puking your guts out."

"Drink," Lisa reminded them, returning with the ball.

Megan and Gavin both downed a shot of tequila. Megan had lost count, but she knew she was well past buzzed. The only thing that had saved her so far was her ball catching skills. She wasn't a big drinker, normally, but this was the biggest party of the season and drinking was the number one sport.

Last night's game had been different. Nicole had been with them, and the five of them had gone from one bar to another ordering a different drink in every one. They had to be real drinks, and the nastier sounding, the better. That game had been more fun than this one, she had to admit. The drunker they got, the funnier the drinks sounded. They'd gone from bar to bar asking for buttery nipples, a piece of ass, bald pussy, screaming orgasm and red-headed slut, which then became Mickey's name for the night. It suited him so well Nicole had clung to it throughout most of today, giggling herself silly every time she'd called him "Red-headed slut!" Too bad she'd decided to opt out of tonight's festivities. She was probably sleeping peacefully right now back in the room. Megan had tried to persuade her to come along tonight. This was party week, after all. Who but a nerd like Nicole would want to sleep through it? As a pre-med student with a 4.0 GPA, Megan had to work hard to avoid the nerd label herself, so she wasn't about to spend any time here with her head in a book. But as the tequila slithered down to her stomach, she had to admit that the cloud-like sumptuousness of her hotel bed would feel blissful right now. Observing Gavin's eyes, she could tell they wouldn't be at this much longer anyway.

When it was Megan's turn again, she instructed Gavin, "Hold your cup still. Don't move and I'll toss the ball in it." The strategy worked. He finally caught it. Or rather, he didn't miss it.

"Whoo hoo!" he cried, then made a bad toss to Mickey on his right. The ball hit the floor again.

"Dude!" Mickey moaned. "You're killing me."

The two of them drained a shot of tequila each. Gavin was swaying and his eyes were half closed. Megan readied herself for her next turn. Lisa's toss was good, but Megan's balance was faulty. The ball bounced off the lip of her cup.

"Drink, drink, drink!" Gavin ordered with glee. For once, he was not the loser.

Megan swallowed a shot, then Lisa did the same. Some of it missed her mouth and ran down her neck. She wiped it off with the back of her hand and giggled.

Megan felt but didn't hear her phone ring. She pulled it from her shirt pocket to look at the screen.

"Is it your boyfriend?" Gavin taunted, knowing she had no boyfriend.

"No, it's my mom."

"Your mom?" Gavin bared his teeth in a half snarl, half grin. "Hey, everybody, Megan's mommy is calling her! Aren't you going to answer it, Megan? Don't you want to talk to your mommy?"

She wagged her head at him defiantly and turned off her phone, but not before seeing that it was nearly one thirty in the morning. It was eleven thirty in California. Why would her mother be calling this late? Gavin's mocking kept her from answering now, but she'd check her messages later. Hopefully, she wouldn't need to call her mom back, as she didn't want to talk to her when she'd been drinking. Not that her mother was so naïve she expected sobriety from her twenty-one-year-old daughter during spring break. Still, there was no point making a show of being wasted.

"Hey, look at that!" Mickey yelled, pointing at the television.

Megan followed his finger to the screen with the parrot on top. She leaned into the table to steady herself. She was stunned to recognize her own face on TV. It was her Facebook profile photo, the one from her trip to Disneyland. Nicole had taken that photo after they'd come out of Space Mountain. Megan's face was flushed from excitement and her hair was windblown, but in a way that made it look like a Hollywood stylist had spent hours on it. In fact, after that picture had been taken, she'd asked her stylist to imitate the look. Her smile, genuine, truly happy, was one of her best. That photo had been her profile pic for six months already. She'd felt some pressure to change it, but so far, no more recent photo had bested it. She didn't want to let it go. It was an awesome pic, but what was it doing on TV?

Under her photo was the headline: "American Megan Willett abducted in Isla Santuario."

"That's me!" she said, laughing. She spun around, catching the eyes of each of her friends in turn. "How'd you do that?" she asked. "How'd you get that on TV?"

Gavin laughed so hard he started snorting and had to sit down.

"Did you do that, you red-headed slut?" she asked Mickey.

He shook his rusty mop, looking genuinely bewildered. She turned back to the TV where her photo had compressed to a small box in the corner while a handsome-looking Latino man talked over it. She was frustrated she couldn't hear what he was saying because of the noise in the bar. It was a good joke. She wanted to hear the story that went with it.

"Where'd you get that dude?" she asked her friends. "He looks just like a freaking newscaster! What's he saying?"

None of them answered. Gavin shrugged. When Megan looked back at the screen, her photo was gone and the story was over.

"Nobody's gonna 'fess up?" Megan complained.

They all looked at her blankly. She was surprised nobody was claiming credit for the prank. Maybe it had been Nicole's doing. It didn't seem possible, though, for Nicole to have whipped this up without somebody else's help, or at least their knowledge. And Nicole really wasn't the pranking sort. That would be Mickey's department, but he would never have been able to keep a straight face this long if he were responsible.

"Whose turn is it?" Lisa asked, drawing Megan's attention from the TV.

Gavin looked nearly green and had both his arms wrapped around his stomach.

"Maybe it's time to quit," Megan suggested. "This dude's gonna hurl."

Mickey peered into Gavin's face, then took hold of his arm, rushing him to the bathroom.

Megan glanced back at the television where the local weather report had come on. Warm and sunny tomorrow and the next day with a chance of afternoon showers.

Lisa twirled in place, letting her sarong billow around her long legs. Then she laughed and started singing along with the cantina soundtrack. Megan noticed that her gaze kept returning to the end of the bar. She followed it to see a young woman in a sleeveless top and shorts leaning against the bar and watching Lisa's dance. She was cute with wavy brown hair, a turned-up nose and a confident smile. Lisa twirled again, smiling back at the young woman, then tripped over the hem of her sarong and fell against Megan. The girl at the bar laughed and Lisa did too, letting Megan pull her to her feet.

"Let's go," Megan said, noticing the boys returning.

Lisa recovered her balance and threw a kiss to the girl at the bar before following the boys out of the cantina. Megan waited until the girl's pleased smile faded before going after them.

CHAPTER THREE

Jaye positioned a chair silently beside the hospital bed where Paloma lay sleeping. She looked peaceful, but her left cheek was swollen and purple. She had a fractured sternum where the butt of a rifle had been driven into her chest. That was the blow that had knocked her to the ground, her punishment for trying to prevent Willie's abduction. Jaye was so sorry she had not gone outside with Willie this afternoon. Maybe she could have been of some help, though how she couldn't imagine.

While they had waited for the ambulance, Paloma had described what she'd seen. Jaye had been rerunning the details so often in her mind that she almost felt she had witnessed it herself.

After Willie had walked Paloma out, the two of them stood under the guava tree admiring Willie's most recent birdhouses. A Jeep turned off the road and stopped abruptly, parked crosswise in the driveway. Three men wearing fatigues and black masks jumped out of the vehicle, rifles in hand, and charged directly toward them. "Run!" Paloma shouted. Willie started toward the house, but was intercepted before she had taken three steps. One of the men grabbed her around the waist and lifted her off the ground. She screamed. Paloma flew at him, trying to pull him off Willie. She was wrenched roughly away by another of the kidnappers, who swung her by the arm so hard she slammed into the side of her car, denting the passenger door. The man stepped forward and rammed the butt of his rifle into her chest, knocking her to the ground. Barely conscious and overwhelmed by the blow, she couldn't move. Her attacker loomed over her, his gun raised to strike again. The scene swam before her eyes. She heard a man yelling. That was the last thing she remembered until she opened her eyes to see Jaye leaning over her and calling her name. All of that had happened in the space of a minute, maybe a little less.

The doctor had said that Paloma would recover completely. But it made Jaye's heart ache to see her lying here battered by thugs. At least they had spared her life. Her future was still possible. That was more than anybody could say about Willie.

All evening Jaye had felt uneasy and vulnerable, and she hadn't even been touched. What must Willie be going through? She seemed ill-equipped to deal with something like this. She was easily frightened and sometimes childlike in her naiveté. Her life had been privileged and sheltered, and couldn't have prepared her for something this nightmarish.

A television on a swinging arm was mounted on the wall opposite the bed. The volume was turned off, but English closed captioning was on. Otherwise, the only light in the room was a fluorescent tube above Paloma's head, casting a soft glow on her tranquil face. Jaye didn't turn on the room lights. It was so late, she didn't want to wake Paloma. She just wanted to reassure herself that she was safe. Amid the fear generated by today's events, she also wanted to be near someone she knew. She wasn't supposed to be here at all at this time of night, but the station nurse didn't seem to care.

Instead of Willie, the TV displayed a photo of a stranger along with the story of the kidnapping. The young woman on the screen was maybe twenty years old and looked nothing like

Willie. She was edgy-looking with choppy, emphatically blond hair, round, nearly transparent eyes, a small nose and a cunning challenge in her smile. She wore a red leather jacket and several tiny silver rings up the outer edge of her left ear. Her expression was a come-on. Behind her, in the background, was the ridged white roof of a building that looked like Space Mountain in Disneyland. She could have been posing in a magazine ad. There was no denying she was good-looking with her perfect complexion and sensuous mouth. But she had nothing to do with Willie and the kidnapping. How could anybody make a mistake like that, and where the hell had they dug up that photo of the blonde?

The words Jaye had already heard numerous times scrolled along the bottom of the screen. "Megan Willett, an American dentist working for Global Dental Relief on the Caribbean nation of Isla Santuario, was abducted from her clinic in the village of Tocamila today by three men wearing camouflage and armed with assault rifles. Dr. Willett has been in Santuario for the last year providing dental services throughout the region. Her assistant, a local student, was beaten by one of the kidnappers and left behind. She is recovering in a Punta Larga hospital. Isla Santuario has seen a dramatic rise in violent crime in recent months, fueled, it is believed, by the influx of Mexican and South American drug trafficking operations."

The story continued, but said nothing new. They had all the facts correct, no doubt taken from the police report. It was just the photo that was wrong.

Jaye turned away from the TV and regarded her peacefully sleeping friend. As she watched, Paloma's eyes fluttered open. After blinking and focusing on Jaye, her wide mouth stretched into a familiar smile, creating two dimples at either end.

"How do you feel, my little Pal?" Jaye asked.

Paloma made an effort to sit up higher in the bed and winced. "Sore." She let herself sink back to the mattress. "Can you hand me that water?"

Jaye put the glass in her hand.

"What have you heard about Willie?" Paloma asked, her eyes anxious.

"Nothing. No news yet."

"How long ago?" Her eyes darted around the beige walls looking for a clock.

"It's after midnight, so quite a while."

"I'm so sorry I let them take her!" Tears came to her eyes.

Jaye took her hand. "Paloma, it's not your fault. Look at you. You tried to help. That's why you're in the hospital. Thank God you weren't killed. You were very brave, but what could you do against those guns?"

The tears flowed more freely. "What if they kill her?"

Jaye blinked back the stinging in her own eyes. "Why would they do that? They just want money."

"Oh, they do it anyway." She made a fist with her free hand and clenched her teeth. "You know they do. *Hijos de puta!*"

"There's no point letting our imaginations get carried away." Jaye handed a tissue to Paloma, who wiped at her eyes with it.

"This is not my imagination. I know about these men. My brother Eddie runs with men like these. The *narcos* are ruthless. They don't care who they kill. They care about nothing but power and money."

Jaye patted her leg through the blanket, hoping to soothe her.

"What are you doing here?" Paloma asked. "Did you come all this way to see me?"

Jaye nodded.

"If you're here, who's at the clinic? What if Willie calls or escapes and goes there?"

"Don't worry, a couple of police officers are there. They came out this evening to ask questions and look at Willie's files. They're watching the place."

"*La jara!*" Paloma hissed, tightening her fist again. "You left them there alone?" She made a move to sit up, but caught at her chest and eased herself back into bed.

Jaye knew Paloma didn't trust the police. She had complained about police corruption so often, her American friends had also grown extremely wary of police. But Jaye hadn't known what else to do. They said they were there to help find Willie and, obviously, she had to help them. But she had to admit that the officers who had come out earlier to take the report had seemed only mildly interested. It was routine for them. Jaye wasn't convinced that they would even try to find Willie. She wondered if she should have offered them money. Paloma believed the police and local government officials were all bought and paid for by organized crime. Maybe they would file the report in a drawer and never think about it again.

Despite her own concerns, she said, "I'm sure it will be okay. Try not to worry. Focus on healing. Is there anything I can bring you?"

Paloma shook her head, looking morose.

"Call me if you think of something. I'll be staying in town tonight and will come by tomorrow to see you before I go back. I'll let you get back to sleep now." She kissed Paloma on the forehead.

As soon as Jaye left the hospital room, the weight of her weariness settled on her shoulders. It was late, but it wasn't just sleepiness that weighed her down. She was in agony worrying about Willie. For the past six months she had worked side by side with her, getting to know her, becoming her friend, developing trust and affection. Along with Paloma, they'd become a close-knit team, a little family of sorts.

"Family" wasn't a concept Jaye had much experience with. The closest she'd come to having a family of her own was a year ago when Lexie had taken her out to an expensive dinner and gotten down on one knee in the restaurant, offering Jaye a diamond ring. Her face had been full of sincerity and vulnerability. She looked dashing in her white shirt, bow tie and red suspenders. After one glass of champagne, she was still sober. At that point, there was nothing more attractive to Jaye than sobriety.

In a twenty-foot perimeter around their table that night, a handful of other diners and wait staffers came to a standstill, waiting for Jaye's reply. It was touching, unexpected and horribly embarrassing. Their relationship was at an all-time low, the worst possible time for a proposal of marriage. In fact, Jaye was a hairbreadth away from leaving...and Lexie knew it.

The proposal was a desperation move on her part, and she'd done it in public to make it harder for Jaye to turn her down. She also knew that Jaye had wanted to be married for a long time. It was one of her dreams, and she had even suggested it to Lexie early in their relationship when they were happily in love and it looked like forever. But everything had changed since then, for the worse.

Lexie had always been manipulative that way. Jaye had looked around at the people in the restaurant, all of them waiting with tense, expectant faces, strangers inexplicably hopeful that Jaye would say "Yes."

She took the ring, stood up and smiled at everybody, then pulled Lexie to her feet and kissed her on the mouth. There was an explosion of cheers and Lexie looked triumphant. But Jaye didn't put the ring on, nor did she answer the question until later. That led to another ugly fight. But it was the last one. She moved out two weeks later.

Now she had cobbled together a little nucleus of a family in a small village in Isla Santuario. Everything had been going so well. But at the moment, Jaye felt that her family and her world were shattered.

After checking for a room at three hotels, she finally found one at the Fiesta Royale Resort. It was more than she wanted to pay, but it would be morning soon, so unless she was going to walk the streets all night, this place would have to do. All of these hotels were expensive, all of them big, new and luxurious. They were here for tourists and, for this week, students. The only contact the locals had with these resorts was if they were lucky enough to get a job in one of them.

Looking around the cavernous lobby with its gleaming wood, sumptuous furnishings and artwork, she felt a little resentful of the twenty year olds who could afford a week in a place like this. After checking in, she headed back outside to get her overnight bag. She followed a long walkway lined with palm trees that took her past the swimming pool. The gardens were bathed in a soft blue glow from the pool's light. Reaching the edge of the property, she passed under a colorful ceramic arch lit by torches and inscribed with the word "*Bienvenidos*." A breeze blew in from the ocean, carrying its briny aroma. It was so late, the roar of partiers in town had quelled to a low hum.

A group of kids, two girls, two boys, lurched along the sidewalk, coming in her direction amid a chorus of laughter. They were dressed in swimsuits, and there was no mistaking that they were American college students. One of the girls was remarkably tall, and the other was petite, about five-four with short blond hair upswept in front. She walked with a provocative sway, causing her open overshirt to swell around her, covering very little. A handsome, olive-skinned boy wearing a ball cap slung his arm around her. Then he pulled her close, locking her in his arms and pulling her off balance. She fell against him as he planted a kiss on her mouth. She shoved him away, causing him to stumble. "Get off me, you perv!" she shouted, then laughed.

"Oh, baby," he complained, but became docile at her side.

As the four of them neared, the flickering light of the torches revealed the girl's face more clearly. With a start, Jaye recognized her. She was the girl in the news, the girl whose face was being flashed across the world as a kidnapping victim. Jaye stared, trying to be certain it was her. She had the same distinctive hairdo, the same oval face, the pale, round eyes. Her eyebrows were dark in contrast to the unnaturally chalky color of her hair. She wore a skimpy black and white bikini showcasing a flat, tanned stomach and a pair of plump, sassy breasts, nipples clearly outlined by the cloth of her halter top.

She had been cute in the photo on TV, but in person, she was... Jaye gaped, taking in the delicious body of Willie's imposter.

"Hey," the girl challenged, stopping directly in front of her.

Jaye looked up to meet a cynical sneer and listless gray eyes.

"What're you staring at, lady?" She threw her arms back and puffed up her chest. "You want this? Huh? Dream on, Lizzie Lezzie!"

Jaye opened her mouth to respond, but all four kids burst out laughing and abruptly veered under the arch and through the wavy blue light and the palm trees. They stumbled along the path toward the main entrance. She heard the boy in the ball cap say, "Dude, she was totally checkin' you out!"

"I know, right!" The girl shrieked a hysterical laugh before the four of them went inside the building and peace returned to the night.

After a moment collecting herself, Jaye walked toward her parking space, where she got her bag out of the van. Who was that girl, and why was her face all over the news instead of Willie's? Whoever she was, Jaye thought with irritation, she was a jerk!

CHAPTER FOUR

Willie stiffened and went on high alert when the door to the bedroom opened and one of the kidnappers came in, the jumpy one with greasy hair, an awkwardly permanent grin and an overbite. He was about thirty years old and wore khaki pants and a striped tank top revealing bony shoulders and sinewy arms. Despite the leanness of his body, he had a paunch that rested over the waist of his trousers. Willie was dismayed to see that he had a roll of duct tape in his hand. Earlier in the evening, when he had brought in a plate of rice and watery beans, he had cut her hands free so she could eat. It felt wonderful to be able to move her arms again. Now, she feared, they were going to tie her up and leave her that way for the night.

In Spanish, Señor Grinning Overbite ordered her to stand up.

"Do you have to do that?" she asked, also in Spanish. "It hurts. Please don't."

He laughed and grabbed her wrist to pull it behind her. He smelled of beer and sweat.

"Wait," she said. "I have to go to the bathroom."

"*Que?*" he asked.

"*Baño, por favor.*"

He grunted, then jerked her toward the door. As they stepped across the hall, she glanced toward the front room and a nearly straight path to the entrance door, which was closed. She was sure the other two men were in the front of the house, so there was no chance she could make it out if she made a break for it.

Earlier in the day when they'd first arrived here, she had done her best to observe the interior of the house as she'd been pushed through it by the barrel of a rifle. She took note of the layout of the rooms, her imagination groping for an escape route. From what she had so briefly seen, there was a sparsely furnished living room in the front of the house, a kitchen off to the right, a hallway with a bathroom on the right, the bedroom serving as her cell on the left and a door at the end of the hall, perhaps leading to another bedroom. The place didn't look like anyone lived here on a permanent basis. It didn't have the feel of a home, and there was almost no furniture.

She must have hesitated too long in the hallway. Her guard shoved her through the doorway of the bathroom, a tiny, grimy box that smelled like a dead animal. There was no door and no seat on the toilet. She did her best to hover over it and do her business while the man stood just outside the doorway pretending not to be stealing glances. Pervert! she thought.

She heard a phone ring elsewhere in the house. One of the other men yelled from the front room, calling "Miguel" to come to the phone.

He hollered back that he couldn't come unless somebody else watched the woman.

While they were yelling at each other, Miguel leaned away from the doorway, the upper part of his body out of sight. Willie stood at the sink and slid a drawer open. Inside was a comb, a safety razor and a tube of toothpaste. She grabbed the razor just as Miguel filled the doorway and glared suspiciously at her, his smile curled into a snarl. With her empty hand, she held up the toothpaste and said, "I'd like to brush my teeth."

He snatched the tube from her and tossed it in the sink. The older, shaggy-haired man appeared, scowling with obvious anger. He was heavy with a fleshy face and a jagged scar across his left cheek. He was in his early forties, but already had an advanced case of receding gums and periodontitis. It wouldn't be long before he began losing teeth. She wished him the worst.

"*Imbécil!*" he shouted, then slapped Miguel hard across the face. He grabbed Willie roughly by the arm and pulled her back into the bedroom, shoving her inside. "You keep quiet," he said, startling her with his thoroughly American accent. This was the first time he had spoken to her. Up until this moment, she had assumed he was a local or from Latin America like the other two. He slammed the door and plunged her into darkness. In the hallway, the two men argued loudly in Spanish. Willie listened, hoping they would get into a fight and kill each other. Miguel, who was in trouble for letting her out of her cell, called the American by name: Grady. The argument was over quickly and, unfortunately, without injury. From this exchange, Willie got the idea that it was Grady who was calling the shots in this trio.

The room she occupied was empty except for the bare, uncomfortable mattress on the floor. The room was otherwise featureless except for the lone window paned with cloudy glass and covered by a sturdy grid of metal bars. The ceiling light fixture had no bulb. The only light was the moonlight coming through the window and a thin strip of yellow under the door.

Trembling from the excitement of her minor coup, she knelt on the floor, removed the razor blade from the razor and cut a hole in the cloth on the underside of the mattress. She replaced the blade in the razor and pushed it through the hole and out of sight. Then she sat on the mattress in the dark, unhappily considering the prospect of spending the entire night here with nothing to do.

It must be well after midnight, she guessed. For the last several hours, her captors had been in the front room playing cards and, she assumed, drinking. The idea of three drunken criminals controlling her fate frightened her tremendously. She didn't like alcohol. She herself never drank and she preferred not to be around people who did. When people drank, they were unpredictable and uninhibited, and both of those conditions meant trouble.

The air was stagnant and hot, and she still had a headache. She wished she had taken the aspirin when Jaye had offered them. Reminded of Jaye, she thought of how she had last seen her, running from the porch and yelling at the kidnappers, her face distorted by shock and terror. Oh, dear Jaye, how worried she must be!

She was sure Jaye was safe. After they shoved Willie to the floor of the Jeep, she hadn't seen anything, but she also had heard no gunfire. In fact, despite the menacing arsenal of her kidnappers, the entire operation had been carried out without a single bullet being fired.

She was nervous and jumpy, and, sitting in this locked box, was on the verge of a panic attack. She was at her best when focusing on something that required intense concentration, like drilling out a cavity or putting together a birdhouse. Otherwise, her mind flew unfettered in all directions and she became absentminded and disorganized. It had always been that way. Given a book to read, she was calm and focused. On a softball field, she was nearly useless. Too much idle time. Once when she was sixteen she'd been "playing" right field, a position distant from the action, and had become engrossed in the efforts of a caterpillar climbing over blades of grass in the most fascinating process of locomotion. It was slow going because the grass wasn't stiff enough to support the creature, so it would climb and fall, then climb again and fall again, moving ahead, but in the tiniest degrees imaginable. Willie never heard the whack of the bat against the ball or the excited yells of her teammates as they tried to alert her to her moment of potential glory. If she'd heard them, all she would have had to do was hold up her glove. But it wasn't to be. The ball fell beside her, nearly on top of the caterpillar. That was what got her attention, the caterpillar propelled into the air by the ball's impact, reminding her why she was standing in the field.

She'd been a pariah on the team for a while after that. But it didn't bother her much because she had no skill nor interest in sports. And the truth was that if she'd seen the ball coming and tried for it, it would have required a miracle on par with the parting of the Red Sea for that ball to have found its way into her glove.

She'd always been academically gifted and socially awkward, relegated to the odd, geeky class of involuntary loners.

Her left leg was bouncing up and down, she noticed. She tucked her legs under herself and tried to calm her mind by working on the puzzle of where she was.

After the stifling and painful trip on the floor of the Jeep, she was relieved when one of the men had taken the tarp off her and pulled her out into open air. Their trip had ended at an isolated house set back from the road, backed by a tangled wall of jungle vegetation. The house was ordinary, white, single-story, made of wood with an unpainted corrugated tin roof. All of the windows were covered with metal bars and the exterior wall had been spray-painted with graffiti.

The kidnappers had discarded their masks once they arrived at their destination, clearly not caring if she saw them, and that worried her. Grady had been the one who brought her inside, taped her hands behind her back, and locked the door to the room. Miguel had brought her dinner a few hours later. She hadn't seen much of the third man yet.

She had been told before coming to Isla Santuario how to deal with a situation like this. It was part of the standard briefing given by Global Dental Relief, since some of the volunteers were sent to places that resembled war zones. She had never expected Isla Santuario to be one of those. She had been advised on how to conduct herself as a GDR representative, what services to offer, how to sidestep legal traps, and had been given a quiz on how to avoid being a *secuestro* victim. Like making sure your car was in excellent condition so it didn't break down. But there had been nothing in the training that could have prevented this particular kidnapping. They'd come after her at home.

She knew Santuario was becoming more dangerous. But she'd dismissed the danger because of the tremendous sense of achievement gained through helping people who would otherwise have no access to dental care. Many of these people had never seen a dentist before. Their smiles, the gratitude, the rush of joy she felt at helping people, these were everything she had hoped for. Better than she had hoped.

In the space of a month, she had seen more serious problems here than in the course of her year back home in Dr. Carston's office where young people came in for their semiannual checkups with perfect teeth and chatted about how white was "too white."

If you are kidnapped, attempt to visualize the route being taken, make a mental note of turns, street noises, smells, any detail you can pick up. Try to keep track of the amount of time spent between points. When you are rescued or released, this information will be extremely important.

She had tried to make these observations while nearly suffocating under the tarp, but it wasn't easy. She estimated the time they had traveled at only thirty or forty minutes. She believed they had gone south or southwest based on the angle of the sun's heat. At any rate, they had not gone far.

After Grady locked her in this room, she'd watched out the window as Miguel pulled the Jeep behind the house into tree cover. Even knowing it was there, she could barely make out any hint of a vehicle from only fifty feet away. No car on the road or any helicopter overhead could possibly see it. She hadn't heard a helicopter, she realized. Was anybody looking for her?

What about the kidnappers? she asked herself. What do I know about them? If nothing else, she was sure she could commit their teeth to memory. Bodies were often identified by their dental records. Willie wondered if living suspects were ever identified the same way. Would she live to give the police such a description? She didn't know why they had taken her. She didn't know if they were going to kill her. She was terrified.

It was important not to have a panic attack. She'd nearly hyperventilated into a blackout on the drive here. She had to conquer her nerves. She might be here for days. She had heard Miguel say she was "linda," pretty. She wasn't happy to hear that. The thought of any of them touching her made her sick.

On the other side of the wall, in the front room, they had been having a good time all evening with their card game. Their thick, masculine laughter came easily through the wall. But even their joviality frightened her. So far, they had treated her okay. But she knew how serious this situation was. Just because her captors were smiling and joking didn't mean they couldn't cut her throat and have another round of Cerveza on it.

Kidnappers liked to snatch Americans, she had heard, because they assumed any American traveling or working abroad had the means to pay a ransom. She hoped they had no idea about her family's ability to pay, that they thought she was just another poorly paid aid worker whose nonprofit employer would manage, with difficulty, to scrape together a few thousand dollars.

The beans and rice had been tasteless, but she'd eaten everything on the plate. At least she wasn't hungry anymore. Would they have bothered to feed her if they were going to turn around and kill her, she wondered.

You can reduce the danger to yourself, she had been told, by being cooperative and quiet. So far, that had been her strategy. But these men were ruthless, she reminded herself, remembering Miguel's violent attack on Paloma. He might have gone in for a second blow, but his young accomplice had yelled "*Alto!*" at him and pulled him away. Willie had barely registered that at the time, as she was trying to free herself from the brute who was hauling her toward the Jeep.

I hope Paloma's all right, she thought, remembering how she had last seen her, lying motionless on the ground. Willie recalled Paloma's plans for this evening. Was there a young man somewhere who had waited all night for her to show up or call, believing himself to have been stood up? Willie had been surprised to hear that Paloma had a date. In the few months they had known one another, she hadn't heard of a single other instance of her going out. She was studious and serious, far more mature than most girls her age. Apparently someone had broken through to her heart. Willie hoped it would work out for her.

Then there was Jaye, also thoroughly committed to work. Willie had teasingly asked her a while back what sort of woman she was looking for. "I'm not looking," she had said. She had closed herself off from romance. She hoped Jaye would also eventually find someone who could help her find the joy in life. She was such a deserving woman, intelligent and vibrant. It was too bad her last relationship had turned out to be such a disaster. She'd invested so much emotion into it. But the woman had been an alcoholic and Jaye had given her plenty of second chances. She'd been right to leave, though she sometimes seemed like a part of her was missing, like a shell-shocked soldier. She must have really loved that woman. Someday, Willie was certain, she would meet another woman whose eyes would look right inside her and open her up. To see Jaye blooming like that would be something to witness. Willie smiled wistfully.

She realized she was thinking about her friends as if she would never see them again. No, she told herself firmly, I will survive this.

The unexpected silence in the house interrupted her thoughts. There was no more conversation or laughter in the next room. The card game was apparently over. Maybe they were turning in for the night. Maybe...she closed her eyes and tilted her head back with a heartfelt wish...they had forgotten about binding her hands.

But just then the door opened, the light from the hallway silhouetting the youngest of her kidnappers. He wore a Bob Marley T-shirt and black cargo shorts and carried a plastic bucket in one hand. In the other was a roll of duct tape. Willie's heart sank. He stepped inside and the light showed his face more clearly. He was just a boy! His face was smooth except for a few hairs sprouting on either side of his upper lip. A teenager, she thought, with lovely dark eyes and beautiful teeth.

Willie was reminded of Paloma's younger brother Eddie. He too was a teenager, a seventeen-year-old running errands for a drug cartel. Her brother was a *halcon*, she said, "falcon" in English, the lowest rank in the organization, an informant who watched activity on the street and reported anything he heard or saw that might be of interest to those higher up. He wasn't committing crimes, Paloma had assured them. He didn't own a gun and wasn't involved in anything serious like kidnapping and murder. Such crimes were carried out by the *sicarios*.

This boy who came to secure her for the night, as young as he was, had apparently already moved up in the ranks. She wondered if he had ever killed anyone. He approached her and stood behind her, bringing her hands together with a startling gentleness. She obediently clasped them.

"Do you speak English?" she asked him. "Can you tell me where we are? Why am I here?"

He did not reply. She repeated her questions in Spanish with the same result. She had thought that because of his youth, he might be more compliant than the others. He mutely taped her wrists behind her, wrapping the tape precisely in a figure eight, ensuring she would not be able to slip her hands out. Then he put the bucket in a corner and looked at her momentarily, apparently satisfying himself that she understood. Then he left. So, Willie realized, no more jaunty outings to the bathroom.

She sighed and sank to the mattress, her shoulders already aching from being forced back into this unnatural position. She watched a bit of star-filled sky between the bars on the window. There was nothing to do now, she concluded, but try to get some sleep and wait for morning.

CHAPTER FIVE

Megan woke and opened her eyes briefly and begrudgingly to morning sunshine streaming through the open blinds. She fumbled on the nightstand for her phone and opened one eye to check the time. The screen was black. She turned on the phone and waited impatiently for it to come to life. When her eyes quit swimming, she saw it was seven o'clock. Still early, she thought with relief. She could go back to sleep. Her head was throbbing and her tongue was dry and gritty like sandpaper. She could see she had messages, but she wasn't yet up to reading them, so she put the phone on the table and rolled over to go back to sleep.

As she began to drift into unconsciousness, she remembered seeing her face on TV last night. That was funny. *American Megan Willett abducted in Isla Santuario.* It looked like the real thing, a real news story. She'd get the scoop on that later today. Maybe her friends could play the video again so she could hear what that news dude had said about her. Knowing the guys she was with, she was sure it was something totally dope, something like, "The kidnappers had to abandon their plan when, because of the unanticipated weight of Ms. Willett's humongous boobs, their twin engine getaway plane could not get off the ground."

She smiled to herself and listened to Lisa's deep and steady breathing in the next bed. Scenes from the previous day invaded her consciousness, moving past like slides in a PowerPoint show—hundreds of shirtless boys and scantily clad girls, some topless, parading across the white sand beach carrying beer bottles and fruity drinks with umbrellas in them and moving to a beat so loud the bass notes shifted sand. There was nonstop noise, pounding and pulsing through the volleyball court, the taco bar, the outdoor cantina. But as soon as her ears were underwater and she swam through the blue-green domain of tropical fish, coral and sea turtles, it was silent, completely silent, tranquil and serene. Such a contrast, the world of college students and the world of sea creatures. In or out of the water, she was having a great time and looked forward to another day of fun…once she recovered enough from the last one to get her butt in gear.

An hour later she woke to the sound of her phone playing "I'm Not a Kid Anymore," her parents' ringtone.

"Shut that fucking thing off!" Lisa complained, then turned to face the wall. Ah, yes, her partner in misery, she thought, remembering the drinking game from last night. Glancing toward the other bed, she saw that Nicole had already gone out.

Megan answered her phone without raising her head from the pillow.

"Hello." Her mouth was so dry the word came out with a leading croak.

"Megan?" said her mother. "Megan? Is that you?" Her voice sounded frantic. Something was obviously wrong.

"Yes, Mom. What's happened?" The dread in her mother's voice brought her to attention. Had someone died? She swung her legs over the edge of her bed, sending a potent wave of pain sloshing through her head.

"Are you okay?" her mother asked. "Are you safe? Where are you?"

"I'm here in my room at the resort. Everything's fine. What's going on?"

She heard her mother's voice crumble into an audible sob, then her father came on the line and said, "Megan, we're so relieved to hear your voice. So you're really okay? Nothing's happened?"

"No. Why all the drama, Dad? You two are scaring the shit out of me."

"It's all over the news. We've been trying to get hold of you since last night. Your photo is everywhere—the TV, the Internet. Megan Willett kidnapped in Isla Santuario."

Megan remembered the TV spot from the night before. "That was just a prank, Dad. My friends rigged it up." Even as she was speaking, she realized there was something wrong with the story.

"No, honey. It's on all the news stations. A twenty-six-year-old dentist named Megan Willett was kidnapped there yesterday. Haven't you heard this story?"

"I…a dentist?" Megan tried to will her mind out of the fog. "I don't understand."

"I know, I know. A lot of details didn't fit, but it was your picture they were showing so of course we were worried."

Megan ran her tongue over her lips to moisten them. "Dad, whatever it's about, it's not true. At least it's not me. I've been here in Punta Larga the whole time. I'm safe. I'm right here in the hotel room. Lisa's in her bed sleeping not six feet away from me." Lisa opened her eyes long enough to glare. "It's just some kind of mix-up."

"Yes, yes, that's what we hoped. That it was a mistake. That's what the police said last night, that it wasn't you, but we needed to be sure. We needed to hear your voice, to be sure."

"The police?"

"We called the police, of course, when we couldn't get hold of you. They talked to the Santuario authorities and told us about the dentist."

"There's nothing to worry about," she assured her father. "I'm really okay. It's nothing to do with me."

"Okay."

She detected less urgency in his voice as he grasped that the emergency was over. "You don't know how worried we've been.

It's given us such a scare. Look, Megan, we want you to come home."

"What?" She jumped to her feet. A bolt of pain shot out the top of her head. "But, Dad, everything's cool here. There's no reason to come home. We're all having a blast. I'm in Punta Larga. It's totally safe here."

"Megan, I know how much you were looking forward to this trip, but your mother and I have been up all night worried sick about you, especially when you didn't answer your phone."

"I'm sorry about that, Dad, but you're overreacting. Nothing happened to me. Nothing happened to any of my friends. Nothing happened to any of the kids here. Nothing is wrong. It's very safe here. Please don't ask me to come home. At least think about it for a while. Once you calm down, you'll see there's no reason to leave. I'm not in any more danger than Mickey or Nicole. The most dangerous thing here is stinging jellyfish."

She waited through her father's thoughtful pause, holding her breath. "All right, Megan, we'll think about it. Right now I need to call your grandparents and let them know you're okay, so I'll say goodbye. Call us later. Please be safe and don't leave the resort. We love you, sweetheart."

She heard her mother chime in, "Love you!"

"Love you too!" she edged in before they hung up.

Wow, what a wild story, she thought, then went to the bathroom to brush her teeth. Her hair was flattened on top and she looked like a zombie. She lifted her hair with a comb, washed her face, gargled with mouthwash, and felt slightly better, except for the headache. She popped two aspirin.

Returning to the bedroom, she saw Lisa propped on an elbow looking at her, her long legs stretching out from a pink nightshirt with a cartoon owl on it.

"What's going on?" she asked, her hair tangled into frizzy blond cotton candy.

"Some chick was kidnapped yesterday here on the island and the news has got it all mixed up. They're using my Facebook photo, showing my picture with the kidnapping story. You saw it last night."

"I did?"

"Yeah, we all did, at the Blue Parrot."

"I sort of remember that. Why are they using your photo?"

"I think we have the same name. Another Megan Willett, a twenty-six-year-old dentist."

"Why was she kidnapped?"

Megan shrugged. "No idea."

Realizing people were worrying about her, she decided to post a Facebook status to let everybody know she was fine. When she went to Facebook, however, she was stunned to see a hundred and fifty-seven new notifications. Reviewing the notices led her to a public group named "Free Our Megan" where her photo was displayed and dozens of people, most of whom she didn't know, had posted messages clearly intended for the other Megan Willett, the woman who was kidnapped. The group had been created by her friend Sonya who apparently thought, as her parents had feared, that she was the kidnap victim. She opened her email to see another flood of messages.

"Holy shit!" she said quietly.

Lisa jumped off her bed and across to Megan's to sit beside her where she too could see.

"You're a hero, Megan Willett," said one of the Facebook posts. "You're a brave and generous woman and we're praying for your safety."

It was strange to read her name and know they were talking about someone else. Megan stared at her phone and felt overwhelmed. She scrolled through screen after screen of messages all echoing the same sentiments.

"Look at that one," Lisa said, pointing. Then she read it aloud. "'I know Dr. Willett and I want to say she's the most amazing and talented and good-hearted person in the world. She has a tremendous sense of altruism. She's the type of person who could never stand by and do nothing when there was something she could do. I hope we are all prepared to bring the same generosity of spirit to bear in securing her return to safety.'"

"Gee," Megan muttered.

"If he knows her," Lisa pointed out, "why doesn't he know he's posting on *your* page?"

Megan shook her head. "I don't know. Maybe he doesn't know her that well. For all I know, I look like her too."

The phone rang, startling her so much that she dropped it. She picked it up and answered Mickey's call. "Hey, bro," she said.

"Have you heard the news?" His voice was excited.

"If you mean the kidnapping, yes, I've heard about it. I've just seen the Free Our Megan page. It's insane."

"Your email box is full too. I tried to send you a message and couldn't."

"How did these people get my email?"

"It's on your Facebook page." With an unmistakable note of disapproval, he said, "Apparently, you have no privacy settings turned on."

"Yeah, well, it never mattered before."

"Well, you should lock it down," he said more gently.

"I don't understand what's happening. Why are they using my picture?"

"The way things are these days, it might have been a computer that grabbed that. Nobody double-checks anything. Once one network dug up that photo and pinned it on the story, boom, it took on a life of its own."

"What am I going to do?"

"Hey, calm down. We can fix this. As soon as possible, you should post a status that tells the world there's been a mistake, that you aren't the Megan Willett who was kidnapped. Get on Twitter and do the same thing."

Megan took a deep breath. "Okay. That sounds good."

"So are you okay?" Mickey asked.

"Yes. It's just so crazy. Besides, I've got a bitchin' headache."

"No surprise there." He laughed. "Gavin's still in bed and I don't know if we're going to see him at all today. We should try to get this mix-up straightened out. Let's get a pot of coffee in the restaurant and I'll help you. See you in a few."

After posting to her various social media outlets that she was fine and not the Megan Willett who was kidnapped, she put on shorts and a sleeveless shirt, then left her room and walked to the elevator. A woman wearing white capris and a striped boatneck top passed through the open doors into the elevator just as Megan rounded the corner. She sprinted to the elevator and slipped in just before the doors closed. The other woman was inside looking at her phone. She was tall and slender with dark brown hair tucked behind one ear. On her feet she wore a pair of beige canvas flats so klutzy they made Megan grimace.

"Made it!" Megan breathed, checking the panel to see that the lobby button had already been pushed.

Her traveling companion stared at her, revealing gorgeous hazel eyes. In fact, Megan thought, paying more attention, she was gorgeous all over. She had a classically beautiful face with prominent cheekbones, dainty ears, a long, elegant neck and flawless skin the color of buttery caramel. Megan was positive that if she licked it, it would taste like sugar. All of this perfection, however, was marred by the woman's expression of undisguised irritation, as if Megan were grossing her out. *What? Do I have a booger hanging out of my nose?* She ran her hand under her nose, but nothing seemed amiss.

The chick glared at her with those entrancing greenish-brown eyes just a moment longer before they dropped back to her phone. Her hair fell forward, obscuring most of her face. The elevator groaned as it inched downward.

There was something about this woman. She seemed familiar somehow. Somewhere in the deep recesses of Megan's subconscious, she felt she knew this frowning woman, but it was such a dim flash of memory, it might have been from another lifetime. Maybe I knew her in a past life, she thought. Maybe she was a man and she was my husband. Or maybe I was a man and I was her husband. Or maybe…Megan smiled to herself… we were both women and were madly passionate lesbian lovers in a time when it was punishable by death. Maybe they had died together, burned as witches, tied back to back, declaring their love for one another until the flames took their final breaths away. Their love was so intense and their death so horrible, the memory of it transcended space and time. If she looks deeply into my eyes, Megan wondered, will she remember it too?

But Megan could not induce the woman to look at her again, even by trying to talk to her. "These elevators are so slow," she remarked.

The reply was a mumble or growl, no intelligible words anyway, then her elevator chum made a phone call, turning her back on Megan.

"Hi, it's J. How are you feeling today?"

J? Megan said to herself. Was it a name or an initial? Like O, the ultra-sexy O of *The Story of O*. Or perhaps like Q, the mischievous omnipotent being from *Star Trek*. Clearly, she concluded, all single letter names were out of the ordinary. J, she repeated in her mind. How cryptic and erotic. It was interesting, but it didn't ring a bell or churn up any deeply-suppressed past-life scenes of girl-on-girl love action. Megan watched the mysterious J out of the corner of her eye, pretending to stare at a restaurant poster on the back wall of the elevator.

"I don't know," J was saying. "I can't run the place by myself, so I'll have to cancel inoculation day. We'll have to reschedule. I'm on my way to the hospital. See you soon."

By the time J's brief phone conversation was finished, the elevator had reached the ground floor. She swept out as soon as the doors were halfway open, as if she couldn't wait to escape. Megan followed at a more leisurely pace, watching J stride across the hotel lobby to the front desk, where she caught the attention of a young man in a maroon polo shirt and spoke quietly to him, out of Megan's hearing.

Maybe she was a doctor, Megan speculated, based on the bit of overheard conversation. And now she was on her way to the hospital to perform a difficult, life-saving operation, which would explain why she was so serious and aloof. It might have been merely a reaction to being inexplicably snubbed, but Megan found this unpleasant stranger, or former life spouse, fascinating. A few moments later, J had left the hotel.

By the time Mickey arrived in the restaurant, Megan had had time to read several accounts of the abduction of Dr. Megan Willett, jarred time after time by the same Disney photo of herself next to a tale of terror in which a young woman was dragged from her workplace by three armed men and whisked away in a Jeep. It was like something from a book or movie. Totally surreal.

"This is her, the woman who was kidnapped," Megan said, holding her tablet up for Mickey to see. She pointed to a photo of a young woman with a thin face and high forehead, her long hair pulled starkly back into a ponytail and secured with old-school hairpins. She wore a natural smile, as if she were unaware that someone was taking her picture, and her eyes were full of nervous energy. Nobody could possibly have mistaken the two of them based on appearance.

"People are posting all over her Facebook page too. The same kind of thing they put on Sonya's Free Our Megan page. Her family is posting too. Look." There was a post from Nathan Willett, a handsome, well-groomed young man. "Thank you to everyone for your kind words of support and comfort and for your prayers in this time of distress for our family. We're working closely with the American and Santuarian authorities to find Willie. None of us will rest until she is safely home again."

"Willie?" Mickey asked.

"Must be what she goes by. Willett, Willie."

"Do you think they took her for ransom?"

"No idea. This is why they told us not to leave the resort. People are crazy out there. She shouldn't have been out there."

"She was helping people. You have to go where needy people live to do that."

"Maybe, but really, was it worth risking her life for? She didn't have to be here. She could have stayed home in…" She looked at the screen to read the biographical info. "Seattle."

"I hope she's okay," Mickey said, his face somber. "I hope they don't kill her, you know, or…anything."

"It's kind of creepy that she's got my name. Gives me the chills." She turned away from the tablet and leaned back in her chair to look out the window at a swimming pool teeming with half-naked, beautiful tanned young bodies.

Megan's phone rang and she instinctively answered. It was a reporter from Seattle who wanted to talk about what it was like being the "other" Megan Willett.

"Look," she said, "I don't have anything to say about this. I'm just an ordinary college student from USC enjoying my vacation in Isla Santuario. I don't know anything about Megan Willett, the dentist. I never heard of her until last night." Megan glanced at Mickey, rolling her eyes to communicate her exasperation.

"How do you feel about what happened to her?" asked the reporter.

"I don't know her. I don't know anything about her. Her name just happens to be the same as mine. That's all."

"So you don't have any opinion about her work or the fact that she has been violently abducted?"

"Why are you asking me these questions? I have nothing to do with this! Why can't you people understand that?"

"Miss Willett, how has this incident impacted you?"

"It's driving me fucking nuts! Leave me alone!"

She ended the call and threw herself roughly against the back of the chair.

"A reporter, I assume," Mickey said.

She growled. "I'm not answering my phone anymore."

"At least they seem to be getting the idea that there are two of you now. That they showed the wrong photo."

"Some of them do. Lisa's sending emails and making phone calls, trying to get my face removed from the story, but as soon as she gets one of them straightened out, ten more pop up. Not to mention that she's having trouble getting anyone to pay attention. It's like they don't care that they screwed up. Yesterday's news, you know?" Megan shook her head in frustration. "Why did all this shit have to happen to me?"

"Well, actually," Mickey pointed out, "the real shit is happening to someone else, isn't it?"

Megan looked again at the fresh-faced young dentist whose life might already be over. "Yeah," she said softly.

CHAPTER SIX

Jaye delivered a few recent issues of *People* magazine to Paloma, who was overjoyed to get them. She loved her Hollywood gossip, maybe her only guilty pleasure. She also brought her a box of macaroons, which she immediately opened and started devouring. She felt better today, she said. She was sure she would be going home soon.

"I'm worried about the clinic," she told Jaye. "I understand why you're not there, but I'll feel so much better when you're back tonight."

"Me too. You've infected me with your mistrust of the police."

"That's not a bad thing, Jaye." She set the macaroons on her bedside table. "That's just common sense. They shouldn't be left there alone. What if they steal our drug supplies?" She became suddenly angry. "What if…what if they're the ones who took Willie in the first place?"

Jaye caught a movement in the doorway and looked up to see a middle-aged woman in a dark uniform standing against the lighted background of the hallway. Her crisp black shirt was stretched tight across her expansive chest, gaping between the buttons. A gold badge adorned the left side of the shirt above the pocket, and around her thick waist she wore a utility belt complete with holstered handgun. A bale of frizzy black hair floated around the woman's face. Her lips were closed in an expression of suspicion, and her eyes, dark brown and penetrating, were narrowed. She had a heavy chin and solid black eyebrows that nearly met over the bridge of her nose. In one hand she carried a leather portfolio. As she observed Jaye and Paloma, her mouth moved rhythmically, lips remaining closed, and Jaye realized she was chewing gum. Somehow the gum chewing didn't resonate with the scowling cop persona.

"What if who are the ones who took Willie, Señorita Marra?" she asked in a raspy and heavily accented voice. She looked at each of them in turn, waiting for an answer.

Jaye stood and faced the officer. "Paloma is concerned that we've left the clinic with no staff. Normally we sleep there, so it's never left unoccupied. There are valuable drugs and equipment, so, obviously, we're nervous about leaving the place in the hands of strangers."

The officer waved her hand and sputtered, stepping into the room. "*La jara*, eh? You never can tell."

Jaye was surprised to hear her use the street slang for police and implicitly agree with Paloma about their lack of trustworthiness.

"I am Inspector Delgado," she said. She opened the portfolio, removed a pen from it, then peered intently at Jaye. "And you are?"

"Jaye Northrup. I'm the nurse at the clinic."

"Ah. That is good. I would like to speak to you as well." She clenched her teeth and squinted as she wrote Jaye's name, looking up briefly to ask, "Señora?"

"Señorita," Jaye replied. "What's happened to Willie? Did you find her?"

"Not yet. That is why I am here, to see if either of you can help us."

"The first thing you need to do," Jaye offered indignantly, "is get the facts straight. The picture going around in the news is not Willie at all. I can give you a photo of her. She looks nothing like that girl. She's got brown hair, for one thing." Jaye frowned at the thought of the pretty imposter on the news.

Delgado laughed, a startlingly throaty gurgle. "Señorita Northrup, the police have their facts straight. I believe it is the news media you wish to complain to."

She produced a photo of Willie from her file. It was a picture Jaye had never seen, a blown up snapshot of her sitting on a redwood deck with ocean waves in the background. She looked a few years younger, early twenties. Her hair was pulled back in her usual ponytail and, yes, even the bobby pins were there holding her bangs back. Jaye wondered if they'd gotten this photo from her family.

"This is your Megan Willett, no?" Delgado asked.

Jaye nodded, a sharp pain hitting her squarely in the chest at the sight of her friend. "Who is that girl in the news anyway?"

"Her name is Megan Willett also. A case of mistaken identity, that is all." Delgado removed her gum from her mouth and wrapped it in a piece of paper. "Sorry about this," she said. "I am trying to give up cigarettes. One vice for another, yes?" She tossed the paper wad in the wastebasket. "The other Megan Willett, she is a California college student here on spring break. I will question her later today, but it is unlikely there is any connection. Nobody checks their facts anymore, do they?"

"No. It's irresponsible."

"*Sí*, irresponsible. But I, Señorita Northrup," she said, wagging her finger in front of Jaye's face, "I do check my facts." Delgado slid the photo back into the folder. "Let us get down to business. The clock is ticking, as they say. Señorita Marra, what were you doing at the clinic yesterday afternoon?"

Paloma tried to raise herself again. "Delivering supplies." She reached over to press the control that lifted the head of the bed. It whined as it rose up.

"You brought supplies on a Sunday?" Delgado asked. "I thought the clinic was closed on Sunday."

"We weren't seeing patients," Jaye explained. "But we're there all the time."

Delgado gave her a look that said, "I wasn't talking to you," then she turned back to Paloma and asked, "Why were you working on a Sunday?"

"I just wanted to help out."

"So you drove to Punta Larga, picked up the shipment, delivered it to Tocamila, and were preparing to return home to…" Delgado consulted her notes. "San Vicente?"

Paloma glanced at Jaye, who recalled what Paloma had told them about her plans for the evening. She seemed reluctant to answer the question.

"I was going out with a friend," she finally said.

Writing on her pad, Delgado asked, "And then going home to San Vicente?"

"No." Paloma's face was a billboard of embarrassment. "I wasn't planning on going home last night." Though staying overnight with a friend wasn't inherently a criminal act, it was clear from Paloma's demeanor that there had been nothing innocent about her aborted Sunday night plans.

Jaye did her best to avoid registering surprise. Delgado brought the inner edge of her black eyebrows even closer together, then said, "Please give me his name. I will let him know what has happened to you. He must be worried that you did not arrive last night as planned."

"You don't need to," Paloma said. "I've already…it's taken care of."

"But I will need his name so I can question him."

Paloma looked suddenly panicked.

"Why?" Jaye intervened, sensing the need to protect her friend.

"I'm questioning everybody who might have some connection with the clinic."

"I'm sure there's no reason to question Paloma's friend. There's no connection."

"I will determine that, Señorita. You must see that this was not a random crime of opportunity, as we normally see in such cases. This was carefully planned. They came to the clinic with the intention of taking Dr. Willett. They did not want you." She jabbed her pen in Jaye's direction, then did the same in Paloma's. "They did not want Señorita Marra. In other words, they knew who Dr. Willett was and where to find her. They had information. I would like to find out anything I can about anyone who had such information."

"Everybody in Tocamila has that information," Jaye pointed out, beginning to wonder if Delgado could be taken seriously.

"And we are questioning everybody in Tocamila. Now, may we continue?" She held her pen over her notepad, staring intently at Paloma.

Paloma glanced painfully from one to the other of them, then finally said, "Her name is Sofia Mendoza. She lives in Cayucos and works at the Casa Tia Ana."

Delgado wrote the information down without looking up, apparently unfazed. Jaye, on the other hand, was stunned. Paloma had a girlfriend? She stared, meeting Paloma's eyes and noting the apologetic message there. Jaye regarded her with an entirely new perspective. How could I have missed that? she wondered.

Paloma lapsed into panicked Spanish, begging Delgado not to tell anyone about Sofia Mendoza, especially not anyone in her family, as they would not understand and would turn against her.

"I see no reason to tell anybody anything about your personal life," Delgado responded gruffly. "Unless we find out that your friend is involved in the kidnapping."

"She isn't! She doesn't even know Willie."

"Maybe she has not met her, but you have told her about Dr. Willett, have you not? You have talked about her, talked about your work at the clinic?"

"Yes, of course I talk about Dr. Willett to my friends and family. I'm her assistant. We work together. Of course I talk about her."

"I hope your friend is not involved, but we must follow every possible connection, to do everything we can to find Dr. Willett.

You see, we must sift the grains of sand with a fine-toothed comb. When I investigate a kidnapping, I leave no stone unturned." She made a gesture like lifting up a stone to look under it. "You never know which one hides a clue, you see?"

Paloma seemed resigned, but did not look happy.

"I don't understand how this could happen," said Jaye. "Santuario is one of the safe islands."

Delgado raised her languorous eyes. "Safe?" She snorted and shook her head, as if Jaye were an idiot.

"A dozen cruise ships come through every day," Jaye pointed out. "There are no restrictions on travel here. Americans are overrunning the beaches."

"That is true. If you come in on a cruise ship and stay at the resorts, you will probably be safe. And it is true also that this is not Mexico. But there is no place in Santuario these days that is completely safe. There is no place even in the US that is completely safe. We have seen a rise in *turista* kidnappings lately. The drug cartels have unfortunately discovered this island. But it is my intention to make this a very uncomfortable place for them." She tapped her pen against the paper, then turned back to Paloma. "Did you recognize any of the men who took Dr. Willett?"

"No."

"Would you recognize them if you saw them again?"

"No. They were wearing masks. All I could see were their eyes, and only one of them got close to me."

"The one who hit you?"

"Yes. Inspector, I already answered these questions yesterday. The police met me here when the ambulance brought me in."

"*Sí*, and forgive me for putting you through this again. But I have been put in charge of this case and I like to get my information firsthand, you understand? The police you spoke to earlier were the municipal police. The kidnapping of a foreign national is a national matter. I am with the *Policia Nacional*." She tapped the patch on her upper arm proudly with the tip of her pen. "Now, did these men say anything that would help us? Did they call one another by name? Did they say where they were going?"

Paloma shook her head. "They just yelled at me to stay back."

"*En español?*"

Paloma nodded sadly.

"Are you sure it was Spanish? Not Papiamento or some other Caribbean dialect?"

"I'm not sure. There were so few words. The accent, it could have been South American or Mexican." Paloma looked pointedly at the cop. "Like yours, Inspector."

Delgado grinned. "*Sí*, I am from Chihuahua. I was recruited here for the drug trafficking problem because of my experience in Mexico."

Jaye could tell by Paloma's face that she interpreted the word "experience" in a much more negative way than it was intended.

The rest of the interview seemed equally unproductive. When it was her turn, Jaye could add nothing more about the kidnappers. She gave Inspector Delgado some general information about Willie: how long she had been at the clinic, the type of services she provided. Nothing that would help find her or save her.

"What about her personal life?" Delgado asked. "Does she have a boyfriend?" She rolled her eyes sideways in Paloma's direction. "Or a girlfriend, perhaps?"

Jaye shook her head. "No, nothing like that. Willie doesn't date. She works. That's all."

"And she could not have a lover without your knowledge?"

"No, she couldn't," said Jaye flatly.

Delgado seemed satisfied that Jaye knew what she was talking about and went on. "What about enemies? Has she had any problems with anyone? Have there been any threats?"

"No, of course she doesn't have any enemies." Jaye stopped herself, remembering Carlos Baza.

"You have reconsidered?" Delgado asked.

"I'm sure it has nothing to do with this, but there is someone who has made threats against Willie. His name is Carlos Baza. He lives in Tocamila. Just last week he cornered Willie in a market and went off on her."

"What about?"

"We're pretty sure he hits his wife, Maria. She came into the clinic for a flu shot and we noticed some bad bruises on her arm and face. She wouldn't admit it, but I've seen injuries like that before, and her behavior seems typical of battered wife syndrome."

"She had some other explanation?"

"Yes. You know, the usual. A fall. It infuriated Willie. She took Maria Baza aside and talked to her for a long time about her rights and options. She never did get an acknowledgment from her that she'd been hit, but she didn't get a denial either. Somehow her husband must have heard that Willie was asking questions. Maybe his wife tried to scare him by telling him. It was only three days later that Baza met Willie in town and warned her away from his family. His language was pretty ugly."

"What did he threaten to do?" asked Delgado.

"Nothing specific. He just said she'd better get her nose out of his business."

"Were there witnesses?"

"Yes. The shop owner and some customers. It was the Mercado El Barranco."

"*Gracias.*" Delgado made another note. "One more thing. Did Dr. Willett have a smartphone?"

"Yes," Jaye replied.

"Do you know if she had it with her?"

Jaye reached into her bag and took out Willie's phone. "I found it in the refrigerator last night, so, no, she didn't have it with her."

"In the refrigerator?" The cop's eyebrows went up.

"Willie has a habit of leaving things in strange places. She's a little absentminded."

Delgado shrugged. "Well, that was a long shot anyway. But you never know when you will come across a criminal who makes a stupid mistake. We have found a couple that way when they did not get rid of the victim's phone."

"What's your plan to find Willie?" Jaye asked impatiently. "What's next?"

"We have been asking questions, of course, hoping someone knows something. We have set up inspection points on all the roads around the clinic. All the vehicles are being stopped and searched. So far, we have found nothing. Other than you and Señorita Marra, we have no witnesses. Worst of all, we have had no contact with the kidnappers. I am afraid we are stuck in a waiting game."

"Waiting for what?"

"Waiting for the kidnappers to make a move. Or for... something else to turn up." A shadow went across her dark eyes that sent a chill through Jaye. She wasn't about to ask what she meant. "If you think of anything that might help us find these men, please call me. Also, Señorita Northrup, where are you staying here in Punta Larga?"

"The Fiesta Royale Resort, but I'm going back to Tocamila today."

"I see. I've stationed two of my own men at your clinic for the time being."

"Why? Do you think we're in danger?"

Delgado shook her head, sticking out her bottom lip. "No, no. Just a precaution. You and Señorita Marra appear to know nothing about the kidnappers, so you're no threat to them. The report you filed with the local police told us as much, that you cannot tell us their hair color or even for certain if they were all men. I will tell you quite frankly that the kidnappers know this also."

"You mean the kidnappers know what the police know," Jaye concluded bitterly.

"We have to assume that, whether it is true or not. The narcos have eyes and ears everywhere."

Jaye glanced at Paloma, whose expression said, *I told you so.* "Then how do we know we can trust *you*?" she asked.

Delgado looked at them each in turn, then curled her mouth up into what might have been a smile, an expression that did not seem natural to her face. "It is wise to be cautious in Santuario." She took a card from her folder and handed it to Jaye. "That has my personal contact number. You may call me directly if you have any further information."

She then thanked them both and left. When Paloma was sure she was out of hearing, she said, "I don't trust her. Do you think she's really looking for Willie?"

"Oh, my skeptical little Pal." Jaye kissed her cheek. "I do hope so."

Jaye was disheartened by Delgado's report. The expression "no news is good news" didn't apply in a kidnapping case. When a kidnapping went wrong, usually meaning the victim died before the ransom could be collected, there was complete silence. The body was disposed of and the kidnappers went on to their next victim. The family never knew what had happened. Jaye was tense and sick to her stomach, waiting and hoping for that phone call to be made. It had not yet been twenty-four hours, she reminded herself. There was still hope.

CHAPTER SEVEN

Willie lay on her side on the thin, lumpy mattress in a position designed to ease the pressure on her shoulders, but the pain was unrelenting. Between that and the stale hot air in the room, she had been miserably uncomfortable all night. Watching the sky turn from black to gray to golden daylight had been her morning's occupation as she waited impatiently for the moment when her captors cut her hands free for mealtime. Lying awake all night without being able to go anywhere, do anything or talk to anybody was a new and horrible experience. She was no stranger to insomnia, but normally she spent her solitary night hours outside looking at the stars or working on birdhouses while Jaye slept peacefully. Last night had been pure torture. It had taken all her willpower to keep from screaming.

A spider inched unhurriedly from the floor to the ceiling in a direct line, providing a small distraction. Occasionally a car drove by on the road. She tried to imagine who was driving past, where they were going, and fantasized communicating with the driver about her plight. Sometimes she thought she heard a vehicle slow down, as if intending to turn off the road. Each time, she waited in acute anticipation for the sound of some white knight with a bullhorn and tear gas, accompanied by heavily armed and heavily armored American commandos. Or a Santuarian SWAT team, or even a couple of cops with deadly aim coming to rescue her. But it was her imagination that vehicles turned off the road. None had. They just kept going past.

It was still early. So far, she seemed to be the only one awake in the house. She knew that one of the kidnappers was sleeping in the hallway on the other side of the bedroom door. She had heard him snoring off and on throughout the night. They were taking no chances. She didn't know where the other two were, but there was no sign they were awake.

The first sound she heard inside the house was the toilet flushing. Shortly after that, a phone rang right outside her door, startling her. The man who had been sleeping there banged against the door as he roused himself to answer the phone.

"*Bueno*," he said, his voice thick with drowsiness.

Willie got to her feet and walked silently to the door to listen to the conversation, which was in English. She recognized Grady's voice. He told the caller that the dentist was unharmed and cooperative, that everything had gone well. Apparently the caller did not agree because Grady became defensive. "No, they are not a problem. They can't identify us. What did they say to the police?…So, you see, what harm is that? Three men in camo and a military Jeep. So they are looking for a Jeep. There are Jeeps all over Cayucos…Yes, it is hidden, well hidden."

They were talking about Paloma and Jaye. Apparently, the caller thought they should have killed the witnesses. So Grady was the one with the heart in this operation? Or perhaps just lack of brains. Either way, it sounded like Paloma was still alive, and for that, Willie was thankful. The other valuable piece of information revealed by this call was their location. They were in Cayucos. Not exactly GPS coordinates, but it was something. So they had traveled south, as she had suspected, into the neighboring province.

She strained to hear the rest of the conversation.

"Yes, yes, I understand," Grady said. "We will talk to you after we make the call."

"The call," she decided, must be the demand for ransom. Who would they call? Global Dental Relief? Jaye? Her parents? She squeezed her eyes shut and willed herself not to cry. Up until this moment, she had not realized that her family must be going through the same nightmare that Jaye and Paloma were going through. They would have heard about the kidnapping too. Her mother, her father, her entire extended family. How horrible for them all. They had heard nothing from her for nearly two years, not a single phone call, not a greeting card. Then suddenly they hear this! Please don't call them, she silently pleaded. Don't drag them into this.

Ten minutes later, the door opened and Grady stepped inside, again speaking on the phone. "That's right," he said. "Is there any problem with that?"

Willie stood at attention.

Miguel blocked the doorway, his gun at his side.

"Yes, you can say hello," Grady told the caller, stepping over to Willie.

He removed the phone from his cheek and held it against his chest. Then he looked sternly at Willie, his dark eyes cold, his bushy mustache hiding his upper lip. He grabbed her by the arm, pulling her against him and flooding her nostrils with the foul smell of his body.

"Tell him you're okay," he instructed. "Just okay. That's all."

She nodded curtly, trying to keep her body from trembling. Grady held the phone close to her face.

"Meg?" she heard through the speaker. "Meg, are you there?" The sound of her father's voice nearly brought her to her knees. She was surprised at the emotion that swamped her just hearing her name in that wonderful, familiar and worried voice, a voice she hadn't heard for so long.

"It's me, Dad," she said, her voice breaking.

"Oh, darling! Meg, are you okay? Did they hurt you?"

"I'm okay. I'm not hurt." She looked into the emotionless eyes of Grady, who seemed satisfied with her answer.

"We're going to get you out," said her father. "Don't worry, we…"

Grady took the phone away and released her arm, turning his back to her. "You understand what to do?" he said into the phone, walking back through the doorway.

The door closed and was locked after him, and Willie was alone again.

Overcome with emotion, she slid to the floor and curled herself over her knees, remembering the controlled terror in her father's voice. She could imagine him standing in the downstairs sitting room of their stately colonial style three-story house overlooking Palmer Lake. Maybe her mother was standing beside him, listening with barely restrained anxiety, the ostentatious Italian chandelier sparkling over her head. Was her brother Nathan there too? Was her entire family gathered, awaiting news of her fate, perched on the edge of panic and united by their common distress? Imagining the scene, she felt guilty for putting them through this. She also felt angry that they were involved at all. She resented that these criminals had called her parents to ask for money. It was the exact thing she had resolved so long ago never to do. She had sworn never to ask her parents for money. And she never had, even when it would have made so much difference. Everything she had accomplished had been done without anyone's help, and she was proud of that. Having come from a privileged background, she had cut herself free and still been successful. On her own.

When Jaye had first learned that Willie's family was rich, she had hinted that a little money would go a long way to help the clinic. At the very least, she had suggested, they could buy a new X-ray machine. "I don't have any money," she had told Jaye. "If I did, I would happily spend it here." "But your family…" Jaye went on. "I can't ask my parents for money," Willie had explained. "That's not possible." After a while, after Jaye knew and understood Willie better, she no longer asked about money.

Willie easily remembered the last conversation she'd had with her father. It had been an argument, like so often. And like so often, it was over money. She had pointed out his hypocrisy over finding every possible way to avoid paying his fair share of taxes, including, ironically, deducting charitable donations. Her point was that the tax money went in part to fund social programs and infrastructure that benefitted the lower classes.

"You don't understand how it works," he told her.

"I do. The rich get richer and the poor get poorer. You're willing to give money to the poor as long as it's financially beneficial to you."

"You're an idealist, Meg." He had shaken his head. "You won't be satisfied until I give away everything and go live in a drafty shack in a swamp."

"That's an exaggeration."

"Not much of one. If I wrote one big check to the government and said, 'Here you are. Go do good,' what do you think would happen to the money? How much of that would get to the people in need? The only way to effect change is through power. The only way to gain power in this country is with money. If I give it all away, I become powerless. You don't believe me now, but someday you will. See how far you get trying to change the world without money."

When she had left that day, she was full of anger and indignation. And as usual, she had been embarrassed that her family evaded paying taxes through legal manipulation.

She had always been ashamed of the money, of the lavish houses and expensive cars. It had embarrassed her to ride around town in her mother's Jag. It felt like flaunting their good fortune and thumbing their noses at everyone who couldn't afford a car like that, or any car, for that matter.

"Your father worked hard to get where he is," her mother told her on several occasions. "He put himself through college. He started on the bottom rung at Treco Corporation and worked his way up. He did it all through drive and intelligence, which is nothing to be ashamed of. It hurts his feelings that you don't appreciate what you have, what he wants to give you. This is the American Dream, young lady. Everybody wants this. Except you."

It wasn't so much that she didn't want it. She didn't really want to be poor. But the fact that there were poor people living not so far from her American Dream life made her uncomfortable. When she was a young girl, she believed the solution was to give things to people. She tried to give one of her dresses to a friend, but the friend had returned it the next day, saying that her mother wouldn't let her keep it. She had given away other things more successfully, like CDs, toys, a softball glove, but the opportunities for giving things away were less than she would have thought. People didn't like to be given things, it turned out. Most people anyway. They wanted to earn them, just like she did. It embarrassed them to be given something. There were exceptions, she found out. People who were truly needy, like the homeless people in the park, would accept anything. When she was fourteen, she packed her backpack with sandwiches and socks and rode her bike to the park to give them out. The people there were grateful without reserve, and for once Willie felt like she was doing something right.

But when her mother found out, she was horrified.

"What were you thinking?" she demanded in that high-pitched voice on the edge of hysteria. "Half of those people are out of their minds. Most of them are dirty or diseased. You could have been raped, murdered, gotten AIDS or hepatitis or who knows what! This is completely irresponsible. The stupidest thing you've ever done! Here you are, a cute young white girl putting yourself almost literally in the hands of…"

The thought had been left unsaid, but Willie had understood. Her mother was frightened of those people. It was true that they were different in many ways from the people who lived in Laurelhurst. They weren't as clean or as articulate. Some of them talked to themselves and some of them made no sense. Some of them had teeth missing. There was an old woman there with her two front teeth missing, the central and lateral incisors. Willie had asked her what had happened to them.

"Got knocked out, what do you think? Almost twenty years ago now."

In Willie's world, teeth didn't get knocked out. Or if they did, they were soon replaced. She had been confused.

"But how did they get knocked out?" she had asked.

"I got thrown out of a restaurant. I was just asking for a cup of coffee. Thrown out and fell on the sidewalk. Knocked 'em out."

"Why don't you get an implant or a bridge? My grandma had a tooth pulled out and she got a bridge. You can't even tell."

The woman had laughed to the point of nearly crying and so had another fellow who had heard the exchange. Willie hadn't understood what was so funny. Not at the time. But she had always remembered that woman laughing, her mouth open, the wide gap in her upper palate. Eventually, Willie had understood the absurdity of her question.

Another thing she had always remembered was her mother's phrase, "a cute young white girl" putting herself in harm's way.

Her mother wasn't entirely wrong. Willie had been naïve and had no fear of the homeless. But they were desperate people and some of them suffered from mental illness. It was not the smartest thing to do, to be a child alone in their midst. What stood out for her, though, in what her mother said, was the "white" part. Some of the people in the park were black and some were brown, but why should that make them more dangerous? Willie had been taught all her life not to be prejudiced against different races. Her parents were completely appalled by any type of bigotry. She had been told repeatedly that skin color made no difference. And yet, in a moment of distress, her mother had revealed something about herself that had been a small epiphany for Willie. There were the things you said and the things you felt, and they were not necessarily in agreement. It wasn't lying. It was more like a disconnect between the intellect and the emotions. Willie's mother was a champion of civil rights. She belonged to all the right organizations and voted like any card-carrying liberal was expected to do. Nobody would have called her a bigot. But it seemed even Barbara Willett wasn't completely color blind.

No wonder Willie was thinking about this now. In the room next to her sat three brown-skinned men. Here she was, a cute young white girl, completely at their mercy. She wasn't afraid of them because of the color of their skin. She was afraid because they were criminals and obviously capable of violence. They lived outside the law and seemed to her far more menacing than the poor black homeless men in the park back home.

What would happen next? she wondered. They had asked her father for money, she assumed. If she ever got out of this, she would find a way to pay him back. She had always hated the idea of anybody coming to her rescue. However, at the moment, she realized she wanted nothing so much as her father coming to her rescue. Hearing his voice after two years, she had been suddenly struck by how much she missed him. Suddenly it seemed wrong and stupid to her that she had ostracized herself from her family over her angry and stubborn differences of opinion. They didn't have to agree on everything to love one another and protect one another. Clearly, the flood of emotion brought out by the sound of her father's voice on the phone was proof of that.

The long, painful night had left her thinking through her life, sad and happy times, things she'd said or hadn't said. Most of all, actions she regretted. In the end, maybe that's what everybody thinks about, regrets.

More than anything, she regretted her self-imposed alienation from her family. Whenever she'd thought about calling, she just couldn't bring herself to do it because she was still angry, and she knew that none of the facts that made her angry had changed. She'd always been so sure of herself, thoroughly committed to her beliefs, and if somebody disagreed with her, she disapproved of and dismissed them. She was judgmental and self-righteous, she concluded.

Would she ever get the chance to make amends? Her father was a good man and she had treated him like a thief.

CHAPTER EIGHT

All around the hotel, kids were swarming, laughing and screaming. Jaye rapidly scanned the faces of the girls as she walked through the arch and up the walkway, thinking the phony Megan Willett might be among them. She didn't want to run into that girl again. Being stuck in an elevator with her this morning had been uncomfortable, especially since she'd seemed to want to make conversation, as if that rude encounter last night had never taken place.

Inside the lobby, she walked to the desk and asked if she could get a late checkout. It was nearly noon and she hadn't even had breakfast yet. "No problem," said the clerk.

When she turned around, she was startled to see Megan Willett, who had materialized beside her in a sleeveless cotton blouse and Bermuda-length shorts, looking cool and bright, smiling as if she were overjoyed to see her again.

"Hi," Megan greeted her enthusiastically.

Jaye returned a cautious "Hi."

"You're not leaving already, are you?" asked Megan. "I mean, I heard you just now asking for a late checkout. I was hoping you'd be hanging around a while."

"I'm leaving, yes."

"Oh." Megan looked disappointed, but her smile bounced back into place in another heartbeat. "It's J, right? The letter J? Like on *Sesame Street*? Today's episode was brought to you by the letter J." She performed a theatrical hop and laughed at her little joke.

"No," Jaye said flatly. "It's J-a-y-e. It's not an initial."

"Oh, okay. Cool. My name's…"

"I know who you are," Jaye cut her off.

"I knew we knew each other!" Megan said triumphantly. "I thought you looked familiar, but I couldn't remember where I knew you from."

"You don't know me from anywhere. I know who you are because of the news reports, the kidnapping."

"Oh, that!" Megan shook her head. "That's not me. I mean, obviously that's not me because here I am. Like *not* kidnapped. Duh! They're just using my photo. Dumbasses, right? It's just a mix-up. That's some other Megan Willett."

"I know."

"Sucks for her, right? But that doesn't explain where I've seen you before. I mean, before this morning in the elevator. Because that's when it hit me. I'm like, I know this chick. You know how sometimes people look familiar and you don't know why? And you're like, God, it's just on the tip of my brain. It's like that. I know you from somewhere, but I just can't pin it down."

"Maybe from last night?" Jaye suggested derisively.

Megan shook her head. "No, I don't think so."

"You don't remember," Jaye stated. "Figures." She had been through this routine a hundred times before with Lexie. Whatever had happened the night before—a fight, an insult, sex—Lexie didn't remember the next day. For her, it had never happened, which meant it wasn't supposed to matter to Jaye, no matter how hurtful. She didn't want to think about how many times they'd had that particular morning fight. Until Jaye didn't care anymore, until she had given up.

"Were you at the Blue Parrot?" Megan asked, her face appealingly sincere.

Jaye sighed heavily. "I don't have time for this." She took a step around Megan, intent on getting away.

"Wait," Megan said. "Look, you seem kind of pissed off. I'm sorry if I did something to upset you. I don't remember much from last night. I was kind of out of it."

"Oh, really? I had no idea."

"Okay, I know you're being sarcastic."

"Ding, ding, ding, score one for you."

Megan burst out laughing. "I really hope we did know one another in a past life. You're funny."

"Past life? What're you talking about? Look, I haven't had anything to eat today, so I need to get breakfast. Could you please just leave me alone?"

"Hey, let me take you to breakfast. My treat!"

"What is your problem, kid? I said leave me alone!"

Jaye brushed past her and strode across the lobby to the front doors, making a rapid exit. She glanced back, worried that Megan would come running after her, but thankfully the doors remained shut behind her.

* * *

Megan sighed. That had not gone well. She hadn't even managed to raise a smile from Jaye. That was too bad because she just knew Jaye's smile would be spectacular.

Hearing a familiar laugh, she turned to see Lisa coming from the direction of the elevators. She was with that chick from the Blue Parrot, the one she'd been flirting with last night. *Nicely done, Lisa*! They both wore shorts, knit tops and sneakers, Lisa's outfit carefully designed to reveal her midriff and her navel piercing. As they walked, they bumped into one another playfully and laughed. Lisa never took her eyes off that cute coed. If there had been an elephant in her path, she'd have slammed right into it.

"Lisa!" Megan called.

Lisa looked up and acknowledged her with a jerk of her chin. The other girl took hold of Lisa's arm, drawing her attention back, and the two of them left the lobby, their heads close together. Megan watched them until they were out of sight, caught up in her thoughts and feeling a little envious of Lisa until the doors opened again, making way for a conspicuous policewoman. She wore a badge on a too-tight shirt, but she wore no cap, nor could she have without some serious anchoring mechanism to float it over her mane of well-teased black hair. She walked in, scanning the lobby, her jaw working furiously. When her dark eyes met Megan's, she looked suddenly focused.

"Ah! Señorita Willett," she boomed across the room, following rapidly behind her voice to where Megan stood. "It is you, is it not?"

Megan wasn't sure she understood the question. "Uh, I'm Megan Willett, yes."

The woman held out her hand. "Inspector Delgado, National Police. I am in charge of the Willett kidnapping. I would like to speak to you."

"Me?" Megan reluctantly shook the cop's hand. "That's nothing to do with me, you know?"

"*Sí, sí*, I know. But still I would like to ask you some questions. Nothing to worry about. Let us sit over here and talk."

The woman took Megan by the arm and led her to the lounge, which was deserted at this time of day. God, Megan thought, this thing just won't go away.

Delgado was sort of fascinating to watch, Megan decided, as the two of them sat face to face in easy chairs. Her face was expressive, but her expressions all suggested she was struggling to expel an obstinate turd. She was also a hand talker. Almost everything she said was punctuated with a gesture of some kind. Between that and the gum chewing, Megan was transfixed.

It turned out the questioning was pretty easy to take, and the inspector seemed to understand that Megan was an innocent bystander.

Delgado pushed herself up from the chair by the armrests with a grunt. "Try to stay out of this from now on," she advised.

"Oh, believe me, I will! I never wanted to be in it in the first place."

Delgado's phone rang. She unclipped it from her belt and answered, listening in complete seriousness, suspending her gum chewing, and saying, "*Sí*" several times before the call was over. Megan waited in silence, uncertain if she was free to go. The sooner she could be completely out of the Willett kidnapping case, the better.

Putting her phone away, Delgado turned to Megan. "The kidnappers, they have made the ransom call to Dr. Willett's family."

"Oh!" Megan felt a rush of emotion that surprised her.

"Señor Nathan Willett, Dr. Willett's brother, is already on his way to Punta Larga. He left early this morning. He should be here soon. I must meet him at the airport."

"Is Dr. Willett okay?"

"*Sí*. She is alive. She spoke to her father on the phone this morning." Delgado's face brightened. "Tomorrow, who knows? Dr. Willett could be back at the clinic filling cavities." Seeming to be speaking to herself, she said, "I must let her friends know. I believe Jaye Northrup is staying right here, if she has not checked out already." Delgado opened a notebook and ran her finger over the page, squinting at the writing there.

Megan jumped up from her chair. "Did you say Jaye?"

Delgado looked up. "*Sí*. Jaye Northrup, the nurse at the clinic. Dr. Willett's colleague. She will be relieved to hear the news."

Oh, my God! Megan thought. That's my Jaye! "I know her!" she announced too loudly.

"You know Señorita Northrup?"

"Yes. She's staying here. She's gone out for a late breakfast. She'll probably be back soon." Megan was suddenly struck with a plan. "I can tell her the news for you. Oh, sure. We're friends, Jaye and I. I'll just let her know and you won't have to worry about it."

Inspector Delgado regarded Megan with suspicion. "How did you and Señorita Northrup become friends in so short a time? She only arrived here yesterday, is that not so?"

"Yeah, yeah, that's right. I met her last night." Megan laughed. "Well, actually, we didn't get to know each other until this morning. But we really hit it off. She's great, isn't she? So concerned about her...friend. Her friend, right? They're not just colleagues. She really needed somebody to talk to. A shoulder to cry on, you know?" Megan scraped together the details of the kidnapping story from her memory. "I mean, like, the woman was kidnapped right there in front of her. It must have been horrible. And then, the girl, the dental assistant, right? She...I mean, of course Jaye's just a wreck. Understandable. That's why we became friends so quickly. Instantly. Because of the mix-up with my picture and all that. Of course she recognized me. Just like you did a while ago. And then...what can I say?" Megan tossed up her hands. "She needed a friend."

Less is more, Megan reminded herself. Quit babbling!

Inspector Delgado regarded her silently for some moments, then resumed chewing her gum. "Since you and Señorita Northrup have become friends, will you give her the news for me when she returns? That would be very helpful."

"Oh, yes, I will!" Megan felt a tiny bit guilty for misleading the inspector, but it had served her purpose and she wasn't hurting anybody.

"Now I must go," announced Delgado. "Thank you for your time and I hope you enjoy the rest of your vacation here in Punta Larga."

As the policewoman exited the hotel, her hair bobbing side to side in concert with her gait, Megan answered a call from her mother, checking to make sure she was still not kidnapped.

"I'm fine. Everything's quiet around here. So I hope you and Dad aren't freaking out anymore."

"We've reconsidered, Megan. Also, your father spoke with the police this morning and they don't think you're in any danger. Your photo is disappearing from the news and, after all, the criminals, that is, the kidnappers, already have what they want."

"Exactly."

"So if you stay there at the resort, you should be okay. But keep in touch. We want to hear from you every day."

"Thanks! I really appreciate it, Mom. And don't worry, please."

After they said goodbye, Megan took a selfie with the hotel lobby in the background. She sent it to her mother with the message, "Safe and sound in Punta Larga."

Then she ordered a glass of iced tea at the bar and positioned herself in front of the lounge television, her legs tucked underneath her in the chair. From this vantage point, she could see the front entrance of the hotel and a good portion of the lobby. Since the entrance doors made a distinctive whooshing sound when opened, she was certain nobody could go in or out without drawing her attention. She would wait here, she decided, until Jaye returned. She was convinced that Jaye would be so happy to hear the news about her friend that she would soften right up toward Megan, whatever her beef was.

CHAPTER NINE

People came and went and Megan slowly drank her tea and watched the news of the world on CNN. One of the stories cycling through the headlines was the Megan Willett kidnapping. CNN showed the same photo of Dr. Willett that Inspector Delgado carried in her portfolio. It wasn't much different from the photo on Facebook. Dr. Willett was a nerdy type, for sure, Megan concluded. Sort of cute, but plain looking. Somebody could do a bitchin' makeover on her. Give her a hairdo and some makeup. It'd be like night and day.

Willie's father, a handsome man in his late forties wearing a smart gray suit, made a statement to the press, reading from a piece of paper in his hand. "We are working with both the American and Santuarian authorities to bring about a peaceful resolution to this situation. My son Nathan is on his way to Isla Santuario this minute to personally represent the family there. We are doing everything we can to get our daughter back, and are optimistic that she will be returned to us safely. Megan is a remarkable young woman who has done and will continue to do wonderful things for people in need, never giving a thought to herself. She is a great humanitarian and we couldn't be more proud of her. We are humbled by the huge outpouring of love and support we've received since Megan's abduction. Clearly, she has touched many people. Please keep her in your thoughts and prayers during this difficult time." He lifted his gaze from the paper and looked into the camera. "We will bring her home." His voice broke with emotion over the last word.

What a strange, sad situation, Megan thought, on the verge of tears. She sucked up the last of the watered-down liquid in her glass as the elevator doors opened and Mickey emerged in a T-shirt, swim trunks and sandals, his giant souvenir drink cup in hand, empty but ready for the day. His face, legs, feet and forearms were shiny, plastered with sunblock.

"*Qué pasa?*" he called, catching sight of her. "What's this? You started without us?" He nodded toward her drink.

She shook her head. "No. This was just tea."

He raked his fingers through his wavy hair. "What're you doing?"

"Watching CNN."

"Yeah? What's so interesting?"

"The kidnapping story, the other Megan Willett."

"Oh, that." He nodded in understanding. "Have they found her?"

"No. But the kidnappers called this morning and asked for ransom."

"Well, there you go!" said Mickey brightly. "They get their money, let the dentist go, and boom, happy ending."

"I hope so." She put her glass on the table. "Hey, Mickey, do you remember running into a chick last night, tall, beautiful? Not one of the kids. Not a student. She's a nurse. Her name is Jaye. Not the letter J, but, you know, a name. She's a brunette with the most gorgeous hazel eyes."

He shook his head. "Where was this?"

"I don't know. That's what I'm trying to figure out. I ran into her this morning and she's like all stuck-up, and I'm like, what? And she's like, what you did last night!" Megan shook her head.

"But I don't remember whatever it is that's got her ticked off. She's staying here, so maybe it was right here at the hotel, after we came back from the Blue Parrot."

"If it was then, there's no use asking me. I don't remember a thing after Heather took off her shirt."

"Heather didn't take off her shirt."

"Sure she did. You've got to remember that. She got up on the stage, naked from the waist up, wearing one of those frayed straw hats, you know the ones."

"Beachcomber."

"Right, right, and she sang that song, the one where you go, 'Hot, hot hot!'" He punctuated each "hot" with a thrust of his hip.

"That wasn't Heather, you moron. That was Brad." She shook her head. "Obviously, you remember even less than I do."

He shrugged. "Whatever. Now, let's go. We're all going on a catamaran tour. Well, not all of us. Nobody's seen Lisa lately. Nicole tried calling her, but she didn't answer."

"Lisa's busy with something else," Megan said.

"Yeah? You mean she hooked up?"

"Looks that way. I saw them leave together earlier."

"Who is she?"

"I don't know. But she's cute. Great hair, little turned-up nose." Megan recalled Lisa and her girlfriend and how they seemed so happily distracted with one another. "I don't think we'll see much more of Lisa this week."

"Oh, man!" He sounded thoroughly disappointed.

Mickey liked the idea of the gang because of his insecurity about his own coupling prospects. He had confided his fear to Megan that everybody would hook up and leave him out in the cold, the lone and lonely single. But Megan was sure she would still be there for him at the end of the week if his ship didn't come in. She had no intentions of hooking up with anybody. She was here to relax and have fun, period.

"So you've gotta come with us," Mickey pleaded.

"Where to?"

He shrugged. "Who cares? There's free rum punch."

Megan reflected for a moment, then said, "Count me out."

"Why? Don't feel so good? Who does? You just need a couple Bahama Mamas to set you up." He waved his cup. "Hair of the dog, Megan, hair of the dog."

His expression, that of a knowing sage, made her smile. "I don't want to lose touch with this story. I think I'll pass."

He looked concerned. "Why do you care so much about this dentist? A while ago you were just pissed off they were using your picture. Now they're not, so it's all good, right?"

"I don't know. I guess because I've been sucked into the story, it makes it seem more personal to me. I know it's not. I don't know this chick or her family. But even just having her name makes me feel somehow, like, connected, you know? Even if I go on your party boat, my head's gonna be on this."

"Oh, come on, dude. You get out with your mains, have a few laughs and, boom, you'll forget all about this stuff. Don't let it ruin your vacation." He waved his drink cup at her with a mischievous grin.

"Sorry."

He shrugged. "Okay. See you later, then. We'll meet up for dinner."

What she had told Mickey was mostly true. She didn't want to miss out on any developments in the Megan Willett story, but she also didn't want to miss her chance to meet up with Jaye one more time and deliver the good news to her. Maybe she could set things straight with her. And then what? She didn't know. All she knew was that she wanted to see that woman smile at her at least once before she left town.

Fortunately, she didn't have long to wait. The whoosh of the entrance doors drew her attention away from the TV. And there was Jaye Northrup, Jungle Nurse, a straw bag over her arm, gaze steady forward, her long legs carrying her purposefully across the lobby toward the elevators.

Megan leapt from her chair and dashed in the same direction, intercepting Nurse Jaye before she got close enough to press the call button. Her sublime face transformed immediately into irritation.

In spite of the withering look in Jaye's eyes, Megan said, "Hi again" as brightly as she could.

"What do you want?" Jaye asked, reaching up to curl her hair behind her ear.

Now was the moment, Megan told herself. She had to summon her native charm to thaw Jaye's icy demeanor. This was likely her one and only chance to fix whatever it was she had screwed up last night.

"I have some news for you. It's about the other Megan Willett, *your* Megan Willett."

The frown softened. "Willie? Has something happened? What is it?"

"Would you like to join me for a glass of iced tea?"

"No, thank you. Look, just tell me what you know about Willie."

Megan saw that she wasn't making any headway, so she gave up her ace in the hole. "The kidnappers called to ask for ransom. Willie is alive. She talked to her father. She's okay."

Jaye's mouth fell open. "What? She's really okay?"

Megan nodded.

Jaye sucked in a deep breath and let it out slowly. She was clearly overcome with relief.

Don't I get a hug? Megan wondered. A pat on the head at least?

Jaye snapped to attention and said, "I've got to call Paloma." She dug in her bag for her phone. "Wait. How do you know this?"

"Inspector Delgado, the cop on the case, she got the call when she was here talking to me. It's legit."

"Was there anything else?"

"Yes, actually. Dr. Willett's brother should be arriving here in Punta Larga any minute."

Jaye nodded, looking thoughtful. "Thanks." She turned her attention to her phone and turned away from Megan, taking a few steps in the other direction while she called her friend.

Thanks. That was all she was going to get apparently. At least it was better than "Fuck off." Jaye no longer looked or sounded irritated with her. She had been the bearer of good news. Very good news, based on Jaye's reaction. She and mousy Dr. Willie must be close friends, Megan decided, waiting for Jaye to finish her call.

When Jaye turned back toward the elevator, she looked surprised to see Megan still there.

"Can we talk?" Megan asked.

"About what?"

"It's driving me nuts that I did something last night that upset you and I can't remember. I'm really sorry. What can I say to get you to forgive me?"

Jaye looked at her steadily, her face neutral. "I forgive you," she said flatly.

"Oh, come on!" Megan said. "That's not fair. At least tell me what I did. Then I can apologize for the actual thing."

"Now you're making it sound like a big deal. It wasn't. It was just a stupid thing you said. Besides, it doesn't matter. Let's just forget it."

"I'd be glad to forget it, but I can't forget what I can't remember. Just tell me what it was and I'll let you go." Megan put on the sweetest, most sincere look she could muster.

Jaye released an exasperated sigh, then seemed to relent. "I ran into you and your friends outside the hotel last night. It was very late. You were all jollied up with booze. I was minding my own business, standing on the sidewalk, and you said…" Jaye seemed unable to continue.

"What? What did I say?" Megan coaxed anxiously.

"You called me Lizzie Lezzie."

Megan fell back in surprise, stunned into momentary silence. "I don't understand. Why would I say that? I mean, like, I wouldn't say that. Are you sure it was me?"

"Of course I'm sure! I recognized you immediately. Your picture was on TV all night long. You were her, the great imposter!"

"The what? Imposter?"

"Sorry." Jaye shook her head. "But it irritated me that they had the wrong picture. *Your* picture. Especially when I saw you shit-faced and partying it up when my friend was God knows where in deep trouble, maybe even dead."

Megan began to understand that there was more behind Jaye's resentment than a stupid insult. She was about to protest when Jaye held up a hand and said, "I know. It's not your problem. Why shouldn't you be enjoying your vacation, getting drunk, walking around half naked on the streets of Punta Larga with your boobs hanging out, making out with your boyfriend and flinging insults at innocent bystanders if you feel like it?"

Megan glanced instinctively down at her shirt and recalled her costume of the night before—skimpy halter top, open overshirt. Then she remembered. She had nearly collided with a woman on the street whose eyes had been glued to her cleavage.

"Oh, my God!" she said. "That was you! You were staring at my boobs. That's why I said it."

"No, I wasn't." She sounded unconvincing and embarrassed.

"Yes, you were. And I'm like, 'What are you staring at?'" Megan's memory was clearing up. "Oh, dude, I'm sorry I called you Lizzie Lezzie. I would never say that when I was sober. But it wasn't like a gay slur or anything. I'm not prejudiced."

Jaye was no longer facing her. She was looking covetously at the elevators as if willing herself to beam over to them.

Megan felt desperate to fix the damage. "I have gay friends," she blurted.

Jaye frowned, looking offended. "Really?"

"Okay, that was stupid too. Now I'm making it sound like you *are* gay, but that was just me calling you gay."

"In an insulting tone of voice, yes," Jaye agreed. "Like you were disgusted."

Megan shook her head emphatically. "That's not how I think. I'm so pro-gay, you've no idea. My friend Lisa, she's a lesbian. We're all sharing a room, all of the girls, I mean. I'm totally cool with lesbians. More than cool. It would be fine with me if you were a lesbian. Not that you are. But if you were, that wouldn't be a bad thing at all."

Jaye had a hand on her hip, her head tilted to one side and her mouth shut tightly in irritation. She did not seem to be softening up, but Megan felt compelled to keep talking. "But of course you're not a lesbian. Just because I called you that, it doesn't mean anything. Obviously you're not a lesbian. Look at you."

"What!" Jaye looked truly offended now.

"Oh, God!" Megan tossed up her hands, astonished at what she'd just said. "I sound like George Bush, the old dude, you know, when he said Ellen couldn't be a lesbian because…but I didn't mean it that way. Not because you're, like, freaking gorgeous. I meant you aren't obviously…you're not…you don't…except maybe for the shoes." They both glanced down at Jaye's feet and the beige canvas flats in question. Megan groaned and stopped talking, realizing she could say nothing intelligent. She could not count the number of times her mother had warned her against "diarrhea of the mouth." When she got nervous, she let all kinds of inanity escape. She was talking in circles. She tried to mentally slow herself down, noting the incredulous look on Jaye's face.

"I *am* a lesbian," Jaye finally said.

Stunned speechless, Megan looked her over carefully, processing this new information. The expression on Jaye's face was full of indignation.

"Okay," Megan said, trying to speak cautiously. "That's super. I guess that's why it made you so mad when I called you Lizzie Lezzie."

"Because of the way you said it."

"Yeah, because of my tone. I get it." Megan stuck her hands in her pockets and rocked nervously on her heels. "I wish you could have met me under different circumstances, to see what I was really like. I'm really sorry if I hurt your feelings."

"Hurt my feelings? Are you kidding?" Jaye's left fist clenched at her side, letting Megan know she was holding back the bulk of her anger. "I don't give a fuck what some drunk punk kid says to me. The way you acted last night, all that did was show what an ignorant, immature person you are."

"But that's what I mean. I'm not really like that. You got the wrong impression."

"It doesn't matter, does it? It doesn't matter what I think of you. I don't know you. You don't know me. So get out of my face!"

Megan was confused and afraid to say anything because everything she said was wrong. The longer they talked, the angrier Jaye got. While she was trying to formulate a coherent thought, Jaye gave her one last look of contempt before walking past her.

Megan stood looking after her, Jaye's final words replaying in her mind: "It doesn't matter what I think of you."

It matters to me, Megan realized. But why does it matter? She was right. They were strangers. So she thinks I'm a stupid, bigoted slut. So what? She's got her defects too. She's uptight. Jumps to conclusions. Her shoes are ugly.

Making out with my boyfriend? What did she mean by that?

Megan was feeling thoroughly frustrated by the whole encounter until it occurred to her that a totally legit lesbian had been ogling her boobs last night. Well, now, she thought, that was interesting. No matter what babelicious Nurse Jaye said or how much she scowled, there was at least one thing she liked about Megan. She glanced down at her shirt front, realizing that not even a hint of cleavage was showing today. She decided to go up to the room and change.

CHAPTER TEN

Jaye checked the room one last time to make sure she hadn't forgotten anything, stopping at the bathroom mirror to see if she looked as weary as she felt. Her eyes betrayed worry and lack of sleep, but all in all, she didn't look bad. Apparently she didn't look like a lesbian either. She shook her head. That girl was an idiot. She was lucky she had it going on in the looks department because otherwise she'd have a hard time making it in the world. Everybody should have something to fall back on. She was so damned irritating, she'd made Jaye drop an f-bomb. Six months ago, Jaye wouldn't have even noticed she'd said it. It didn't seem to faze Megan, but Willie was so sensitive to cursing that Jaye had radically modified her language in the last six months. She couldn't take the exaggerated wince from Willie whenever she had a lapse. With self-discipline, the lapses had gotten fewer and fewer. Jaye's language was now nearly as clean as Willie's. Usually.

That lapse had felt good, she admitted to herself.

"Fuck," she said tentatively into the mirror. The mirror didn't crack and nobody winced. Encouraged, she let loose with a full head of steam. "Fuck, fuck, fuck!"

She smiled at herself, then tucked her hair behind her ear and rolled her suitcase into the hallway, anxious to get back to the clinic. Paloma's fears about the policemen being there were making her nervous.

Her phone rang just as she let the door shut behind her.

"Is this Jaye Northrup?" a male voice asked.

"Yes."

"Hi. I'm Nathan Willett, Willie's brother."

Jaye stopped short in the hallway. "Willie's brother," she repeated.

"I'm in the lobby of the Fiesta Royale Resort. Inspector Delgado gave me your name. I was wondering if we could talk. Are you still at the hotel, by any chance?"

"Yes, actually, I'm upstairs. I got a late checkout and I was just leaving."

"Leaving town, you mean?"

"Yes."

"Maybe you can stay just a little longer? I would really appreciate it."

"Yes, I think so. I don't actually need to be back to the clinic until this evening. I'll be down in a minute."

Jaye rode the elevator down, anxious to meet Willie's brother, a man she knew almost nothing about. Willie didn't talk much about her family, except to reiterate that she had divorced herself from them all. When the elevator doors opened, Jaye walked into the lobby, looking around quickly. Thankfully, that horrible Megan was nowhere in sight, but there was a young man with sandy brown hair sitting on the arm of a sofa. When their eyes met, he stood and approached, guessing her identity. But Jaye didn't have to guess. Nathan Willett looked remarkably like his sister except for the carefully-trimmed mustache. He was slightly-built like her with the same color eyes, similar facial features and, above all, the same smile. He wore a fawn-colored sport coat over a yellow shirt. An expensive wristwatch emerged as he extended his hand toward her. Overall, he was handsome and graceful. He seemed to have none of Willie's nervous jumpiness.

"So good to meet you, Jaye," he said. "Please sit down."

As Jaye suspected, neither Nathan nor his parents had ever heard of her before. They never heard from Willie, he explained, and only knew she was in Santuario through mutual acquaintances.

"I'm sure she's been happy here," he said. "She's doing what she loves, what she's passionate about."

Jaye nodded. "Yes, I think she's been happy."

"Willie wanted to be a dentist since she was a little girl," he told her. "She turned our old playhouse into a dental office. She painted a sign that said Megan Willett, D.D.S. and hung it above the door. Then she took our cats and dogs inside and tormented them by examining them and brushing their teeth." He laughed. "She used a flashlight to 'X-ray' them."

Jaye laughed, imagining the scene. "Cats?"

He nodded. "Um, yes. There were scratches involved. She said she was going to be a free dentist, that she would help anyone who needed help and wouldn't charge them at all. She would go to the homeless camps and low-rent areas and find her patients there. I was so impressed when she actually did it, came here to do just as she said she would. Especially because my parents thought she was hopelessly naïve. They told her you can't give it all away for free. You have to have capital. You have to charge somebody to buy the supplies and equipment and malpractice insurance. She was naïve, it's true, but she did it, didn't she? She does it all for free."

"Oh, yes, she does it all for free, but your parents were right. Somebody has to provide the capital. And it isn't nearly enough."

"Still, she made it come true for herself." He looked wistful, perhaps remembering that determined girl with her doggie dentist office. That was a nice memory, and Jaye was glad he had shared it.

"What happened between you?" Jaye asked. "Why doesn't Willie speak to anybody in her family?"

"Because she doesn't want to, I guess. Honestly, she's the only one who thinks there's a problem."

"You mean this estrangement, it's all in her mind?"

"Not exactly in her mind, but definitely of her own making. If she showed up at my house or our parents' house, anytime, we'd be overjoyed to see her. She's got a one-sided battle going on."

"So nothing happened between you?"

"Nothing you could put your finger on," said Nathan, crossing his legs. "No big fight or anything. She just started not showing up, you know, to family events. She didn't come around anymore. There was always something else, some excuse. It became clear after a while that she didn't want to see us. Or at least my parents. I was collateral damage, I guess." He pressed his lips together with a look of remorse. "There were so many passionate arguments over the years. Willie and my parents do not see eye to eye. She's not very easy to get along with, really. She's unyielding."

"Unyielding?"

"In her beliefs. Her opinions. Which would be okay except that she feels compelled to express them and insists everyone agree with her." He chuckled. "She's just like my father, actually, and the two of them together are nearly always a bomb on a very short fuse. But don't misunderstand. We love her very much. My parents are so proud of her. They're just sorry she's always rejected their help. They want to help her. Like any parents. And they have the means. But Willie's been adamant about doing everything on her own. They wanted, for instance, to help fund her work with Global Dental Relief, but she wouldn't allow it."

"Yes, she's made it clear she won't take money from her family."

"That seems sort of irrational to me. After all, this nonprofit is getting donations from other rich Americans, aren't they? They have to get funding somewhere, and it seems okay to Willie as long as the money isn't coming from the Willett family. That really hurts my parents, like their money is tainted. But it's not like it's mob money, is it? My father worked very hard to get where he is. He's proud of his accomplishments. I know he wishes Willie was too. I'm pretty sure he's given money to the organization anyway, anonymously." He looked contrite. "Oh, don't tell her that."

Jaye shook her head to reassure him. She had heard Willie's side of this, but her objections to her parents' wealth suddenly sounded less sensible than when she had explained it herself. "She's going to hate this, isn't she? Being saved by your parents' money?"

He nodded with a thin smile. "With a vengeance. I can guarantee you, she'll insist on paying it all back, every last dime, even if it takes her the rest of her life. She simply can't accept help gracefully."

"She's a proud woman."

Nathan sighed, Willie's smile still on his lips.

Jaye remembered the recent incident between Willie and Carlos Baza at the Mercado El Barranco. Although Baza had frightened her, she hadn't backed down.

"She's had a couple of run-ins with the locals," she said, "so I can sort of see what you're getting at. But whenever she gets into it with one of them, she's absolutely in the right and faithfully defends her principles. I mean, you have to admire that."

"I do, absolutely. And so does our father. My sister is an admirable woman. And I'm here to do what I can to make sure we get her back. How has she been? Before this happened, I mean."

"She's been terrific. She's dedicated and loves her work. It's hard to believe anyone would do this to Willie. She's done so much good here. I've been just sick over what's happened."

"I'm glad to know she's made good friends here."

"She has. I'd do anything for her."

He smiled sadly.

"Nathan, if there's any way I can help, I want to."

"There's not much anybody can do right now. Sometime this evening, the hundred thousand dollars should be ready."

"A hundred thousand?" Jaye was dumbstuck.

"Yes. That's what they're demanding. That's an unusually large amount, I've been told, by people who know about these kidnappings. The bank's going to keep it in the vault until we're ready to deliver it. I hope that's tomorrow, but we haven't heard yet. I also don't know how it's going to go down, you know, "the drop," as they say." He sucked in his breath. "This is very cloak-and-daggerish, isn't it?"

Jaye nodded. "So you've talked with Inspector Delgado?"

"Yes, actually, she met me at the airport and took me to the bank."

"Do you think she's…okay?"

He laughed. "Depends on how you mean."

"Paloma…um, Willie's dental hygienist, is rubbing off on me. She doesn't trust anyone, especially not police. They don't have the best reputation here."

"I see what you're asking. I think she's okay. My father checked her out with the FBI as soon as he heard she was on the case. She's been handpicked to work with their kidnapping team, and she has a good track record."

"That's good to know."

"We can't do this alone, can we? We have to trust somebody."

"Yes, that's exactly what I was thinking."

Out of the corner of her eye, Jaye was surprised to see Megan Willett peering at her from across the room. She was half hidden behind a column, so Jaye wasn't immediately sure of what she saw. Nathan was still talking, so Jaye tried to listen while keeping her eyes on the slip of a figure behind the column as it bobbed out and back. Finally, she was sure it was that girl. If nothing else, her distinctive haircut was a definite giveaway.

"What are you looking at?" Nathan finally asked.

"Oh, sorry. It's this college student who's been driving me nuts. She's spying on us."

He turned around to look, but Megan was quicker. She ducked behind the column, which completely concealed her.

"I don't see…"

"She's hiding. I'm beginning to think she's a psychopath."

"Who is she? Is she someone connected with the kidnapping?"

"Oh, no, no, not at all. Well, in a way, I guess you could say so. She's the other one, the other Megan Willett."

His eyebrows came together in confusion for a split second, then full understanding softened his features.

"The USC student? The one on all the newscasts."

"Right."

"She's here in Punta Larga? I didn't realize. Maybe that's why the mix-up." He stood up, peering across the room, but Megan had ducked out of sight. He turned back to Jaye. "You know her?"

"Sort of. Not really. I just met her."

"That was strange, don't you think, that they made a mistake like that?"

"They make mistakes all the time. It just usually isn't your sister, so it doesn't register."

"Well, you're right about that. It was bizarre hearing that story on the news with *her* photo attached to it. I'm glad they got it sorted out finally. But it must have been bizarre for her too."

"I guess." Jaye realized she hadn't considered that.

He looked thoughtful, then said, "I'd like to meet her."

"Nathan, believe me, she's not connected to the case. It was just a mistake. The police are completely sure of that."

"Right. I'm sure of it too. But I'd like to talk to her anyway. After all, the only thing I have to do right now is wait for the next phone call. I'm really thankful to have caught you, to be able to talk to someone who knows Willie, who's a friend of hers. I know you have to get back to the clinic, but I wish you didn't because it feels good to talk. All of this has really brought home how much I miss her, how much we all do." He paused and shook his head. "Such a horrible way to be reminded."

Though Nathan had been composed up to now, his eyes were filled with moisture, revealing the emotional strain he was under. Jaye felt sorry for him. And because of his resemblance to Willie, she also felt a warmth and a sense of trust belying their brief acquaintance.

"I don't have to go just yet," she said. "I don't want to drive back in the dark, that's the only thing."

"How far is it?"

"Almost two hours."

His face lit up. "That's wonderful. Maybe we can have an early dinner then, and you can go back after that. Plenty of time before dark. In the meantime, do you think you could introduce me to the other Megan?"

"Okay," Jaye relented, not really wanting to do it. She had hoped to be finished with that vacuous coed. But she did understand Nathan's need to reach out to anyone with even the smallest connection to his sister's plight. Jaye was sure that after a few minutes with Megan, he would have had enough, so there was no harm in it.

She walked across the lobby on a direct path toward Megan's hiding place. She found the girl leaning against the column, casually talking on the phone, her face as innocent-looking as a baby kitten. She feigned surprise to see Jaye standing beside her, then smiled up at her, her nearly transparent eyes full of delight. She struck a flirty pose, cocking her head sideways and briefly displaying the tip of her tongue at the corner of her mouth. She had changed her shirt, Jaye noticed, and this new number displayed a healthy dose of healthy cleavage. Jaye yanked her gaze up to Megan's face to avoid a rerun of last night's unpleasantness.

"Mickey," Megan said into the phone, "somebody's here. I have to go. Later." Then she ended her phony phone call and batted her eyes at Jaye.

She was still confused about Megan's game. Last night she'd seemed offended that Jaye was looking at her boobs, and now she seemed to be flaunting them at her. *Save it, sister.*

"Megan," she said, "the man over there I've been talking to, that's Nathan Willett, Willie's brother. He wants to meet you."

CHAPTER ELEVEN

How did this happen? Jaye wondered, gazing at her dinner companions. The two of them were engaged in an animated discussion, as they had been throughout the meal. At least Nathan was being entertained. Megan was keeping his mind off his sister, which was more than Jaye could do. This girl liked to talk, and Nathan was the sort of man who knew how to get a woman to talk about herself. So whether she wanted to or not, Jaye was learning a lot about the other Megan.

If Grandma DeeDee were here, Jaye thought, she'd call Megan a "flibbertigibbet." Flighty. Excitable. Young. She *was* very young, young in a way that made Jaye feel old. She thought back six years to when she'd been twenty-one—college, parties, lots of sex, beer and stupidity. Once she'd even been arrested and spent a night in jail after instigating a brawl in a local dive. Maybe Megan wasn't so different from any other college coed. A lot could happen in six years, especially those particular six years, the early twenties. Cynicism could happen, for one thing, and that wasn't necessarily good. But, then, Jaye had been cynical from a much younger age than twenty-one. Not being wanted will do that to a child.

While Megan talked to Nathan about her family in San Diego, her doctor mother, her math teacher father and two older brothers, and what sounded like an idyllic home life, Jaye had her best opportunity so far to observe her without the unnerving distraction of her light, teasing eyes throwing her off-kilter.

Megan wore white shorts and sat with her legs crossed at the knee. Jaye observed the well-defined calf muscle of her perfectly bronzed leg, the wire-thin ankle bracelet below a small dolphin tattoo, the pedicured foot in a white-strapped sandal, and the perfection of her coral-colored toenails. Like her legs, her arms were bare and smooth. Her fingernails were colored in the same hue as her toes. She wore a dainty pinkie ring set with a single amethyst, her birthstone, most likely.

There was something about Southern California girls with their tanned limbs and shimmering golden auras. They seemed to carry sunshine in their pores. Even when they weren't walking on a beach, heat, surf, sand and wind all seemed to be there like a backdrop on a stage, framing them in the scene that set them off so well. Jaye could almost hear an undulating bossa nova beat. She imagined Megan in her bikini and sunglasses, walking with her bare toes in the sand. *Long and tall and tan and lovely...*

She wasn't that tall, Jaye corrected herself, but she was tan and lovely. When a drop of water from her glass fell onto her arm, Jaye realized she'd been holding it for a while without taking a drink. Maybe I haven't been handling celibacy as well as I've been giving myself credit for, she decided. She set the glass down, then heard the music, muddled amid the noise of the restaurant. "The Girl From Ipanema" was playing. Jaye smiled to herself and glanced around at the room. The style of the restaurant was Island—potted palms, rattan furniture, raffia curtains in the doorways, slowly circling overhead fans with leaf-shaped bamboo blades. The fans were mostly for decoration, as the building was comfortably air-conditioned. Despite her troubled mind, Jaye was enjoying this civilized respite from her everyday life. She didn't often come to the coast. With its international mixture of tourists and locals it was a different world from the Isla Santuario of the interior. Within her view, Jaye could see a British pub flying a Union Jack over its door. Next to it was a Bank of America ATM outlet. Beyond that was the marina, crowded with moored boats of every description, including some impressively large yachts. Further out in the sea, three cruise ships dominated the horizon as their tenders motored back and forth to the dock with celebrating vacationers from around the world.

"Mickey and I are both pre-med," Megan was saying. "He wants to specialize in geriatrics."

"You're going to be a doctor?" Jaye was sorry that came out the way it did, sounding like she was in shock.

"That's the plan. I graduate in a couple of months. I'll have my B.S. in chemistry."

"Then medical school?" Nathan asked. "Where'd you apply? Where'd you get in?"

Megan shrugged. "I haven't applied yet. I'm considering Keck, you know, just staying at USC. But there's also Stanford, which would put me just out of reach of my mom and dad, which could be good, if you know what I mean. Or maybe something out of state, just to be somewhere different. New England, maybe. There's always Yale." She laughed. "I'm taking a year off before med school. It's my mother's idea. She thinks I should travel or do something else before I go full force into it. It'll be very intense. I figure she knows."

Jaye wondered if Megan's matter-of-fact optimism about her chances at such prestigious medical schools was warranted, or if she was merely clueless. It did seem that she'd made it through college okay with a degree in chemistry. Not too shabby.

"What kind of doctor will you be?" Nathan asked.

"I haven't decided, but maybe a cosmetic surgeon. My mom knows this cosmetic surgeon in Beverly Hills, Dr. Mooney. He's worked on movie stars, really famous ones. He's sworn to secrecy. He's got vacation homes in Europe and the Bahamas. He works only six months of the year making gorgeous people even more gorgeous. He has a sick Lamborghini and a classic Rolls that sits in a garage in New York except for a couple weeks in the winter when he goes there to visit. He's crazy rich."

She sounds so materialistic, Jaye thought. She's like the anti-Megan Willett or the evil Megan Willett. Jaye drank her lemonade, peering over the glass and amusing herself with her thoughts.

But Nathan seemed to find her charming, the way he smiled and responded cheerfully to her. Maybe they would fall in love and get married. They made a good-looking couple, that's for sure, both of them as pretty as models. Pretty and rich. Nathan was a lawyer, it turned out, and Megan was going to be a doctor with vacation homes in Europe and the Bahamas.

"That would be a very interesting profession," Nathan said. "It's a kind of an art, I'm guessing, to look at someone's face and figure out how to make it more beautiful."

"Exactly," agreed Megan. "You can't just put any old nose on any old face. It will be, like, out of place. A beautiful nose on one person isn't a beautiful nose on another person, necessarily. I think it'd be really fun to change the way somebody looks. Like art, like you said. Like Picasso, rearranging their features."

Jaye snorted a laugh, nearly upsetting her glass. Nathan laughed too.

"Well, okay," Megan said, tilting her head sideways in self-deprecation. "Not like Picasso exactly. I just meant changing it up. You know what I mean." She smiled a fetchingly cute smile. "But I don't know much about plastic surgery. It's just an idea. I might be some other kind of doctor. My mother's a GP. She thinks a year traveling will help me figure it all out."

Megan took a bite of her jerk chicken, smiling at each of them in turn while she chewed. Her eyes held Jaye's for just a second, but delivered a wallop of mischief in that brief span of time. Then she turned to Nathan and asked, "Are you married?"

Jaye stiffened, wondering at this girl's moxie. Making a move on this man while his sister was being held captive by murderous criminals? She's a player, Jaye decided, flirting with both of us at the same time, hoping somebody will succumb to her golden glow. Or maybe she's just a flirt with no follow-through. It doesn't matter, Jaye reminded herself. I'll soon be rid of her.

"No," Nathan replied. "I'm divorced. We were only married five months, so no kids. What about you, Jaye? Married? Kids?"

Jaye shook her head, noting in her peripheral vision that Nathan's question seemed to amuse Megan. "Neither."

"Where are you from?" he asked.

"I'm from nowhere in particular. I was living in Idaho for a few years before coming here. Before that, I went to nursing school in Lincoln, Nebraska. And before that, I lived with my grandmother for a couple of years in South Dakota. Before that, it gets hazy. Too many places to remember."

"Were you an orphan?" Megan asked.

"In a manner of speaking. My mother was a drug addict, and when the system didn't separate us, she usually did. I was in foster homes growing up and lived with different relatives. I lived in a car once with my mother for about three months. That was in New Mexico." Jaye leaned back in her chair. "Good times." She laughed involuntarily.

Megan watched her, quiet and serious for a change. Jaye didn't like talking about her childhood for this very reason. Despite her attempt at humor, it almost always brought the mood down.

"Sounds rough," Nathan remarked. "That's something to be proud of that you went from that kind of childhood to becoming a registered nurse."

"I never wanted to live in a car again."

He nodded thoughtfully, poking through his salad until he found a chunk of bleu cheese, which he stabbed with his fork and brought to his mouth. Jaye glanced at Megan, who grinned and batted her eyes.

"How long are you here for?" Nathan asked Jaye.

"I haven't decided for sure. When I signed up for this, it was for a year. I figured that would be long enough to…" She stopped herself, not wanting to get into her personal story. "A year seemed like the right amount of time to be out of the country. So I've got six months left. After that…" She shrugged.

By the time their plates were taken and coffee was served, the subject of conversation had returned to Willie.

"If she were at work tomorrow," Nathan asked, "what would she be doing?"

"I can tell you exactly what she'd be doing tomorrow because we had plans. It was to be a special all-day event. We've had posters out for a month. We were going to give MMR vaccines to all the kids."

"MMR?" he asked.

"Sorry. Measles, mumps and rubella."

"Isn't Willie doing dentistry?"

"Yes, she is. But the staff is so small, we help each other out, and since she's a doctor, her skills come in very handy. We vaccinate all year round as people come in, but this was a big drive to make sure they come in. Not just the locals, but some of the outlying families too. Some of the people who live up in the mountains hardly ever see a doctor. They don't have cars or health insurance or much money. Most of them have never seen a dentist, so you can imagine what Willie's been dealing with. But they do understand the value of vaccinations and we were anticipating a good turnout."

"But now you aren't going to do it?"

Jaye shook her head. "I can't do it alone. Paloma's in the hospital. She may be going home tomorrow, but she won't be ready to come back to work. There's no way I can handle a big deal like this by myself."

"That's too bad," Nathan commented. He tasted his coffee, then added some cream and swirled it with a spoon.

"Yes, it's very bad," Jaye agreed. "Arranging this wasn't easy, to have the vaccine on hand and all the supplies." She was about to try her coffee, but stopped with the cup halfway to her mouth, noticing Megan looking at her with her face full of taut excitement.

When she saw Jaye had noticed, she said, "I can help!"

Jaye put her cup back in the saucer and eyed Megan wordlessly. Her eyes were wide and expectant. She waited for a reply.

Jaye shook her head. "That's ridiculous."

"Why?"

"Because being a pre-med student does not make you a doctor. You're not qualified. You wouldn't know what to do."

"But you said you could do it with Paloma, right? She's not a doctor either."

"But I barely know you. This is serious. I need someone I can rely on. It would be a long, hard day. Not much fun, in other words."

Megan looked genuinely hurt. "You're right, you don't know me. You don't know that I can work hard and be relied on. I'm not a flake."

Jaye backpedaled, realizing she was being needlessly rude. "Sorry. I appreciate the offer, but I need somebody with experience."

"I'm sure I could help," Megan insisted. "I'm good with kids."

Nathan looked from one to the other of them with mild curiosity. Jaye was well aware of his presence. It had the effect of tempering her ill will toward Megan because she knew that if she let her true feelings show, she would look like a royal bitch. But, she realized, her feelings had actually softened in the last hour. She remembered Megan saying that if they had met under different circumstances, Jaye's opinion wouldn't be so low. Maybe she wasn't as empty-headed as Jaye had imagined. Seeing her sober helped a lot.

"Would you be able to go forward with Megan on board?" Nathan asked, taking on the role of self-appointed arbiter.

Jaye considered the question for a moment, evaluating Megan, who sat straight up in her chair with a solemn look on her face, as if she were auditioning. "Possibly," she admitted.

He gazed at her over his coffee cup, his eyes conveying a very Willie-like expression that Jaye normally interpreted as, "Well? What's the problem?"

She turned to Megan and asked, "What about spring break? Your vacation?"

"Screw it!" Megan said without hesitation.

"I don't understand why you want to do this. You won't get paid."

"I know that. It would be good experience for me. Hands-on stuff. Maybe I can even get credit for it. We have these volunteer projects we have to do. It's pretty flexible." She must have been able to tell the pendulum had swung just a bit in her direction, because she was getting cocky. "I figure, like, you can put all those kids at risk of disease or you can let me help. I'm all you've got."

She did have two hands and, one had to assume, a reasonably competent brain, although Jaye wasn't yet convinced that she was sane. But Nathan, the current equivalent of Willie and her good judgment, apparently wasn't hearing any alarm bells going off. Good with kids, she claimed. Jaye *was* in a real bind. Ultimately, all that mattered was that the job got done.

She glanced at Nathan, who looked encouraging. Afraid she would bring disaster upon the entire town of Tocamila, Jaye reluctantly said, "Okay. Pack your bag. We'll leave in half an hour. And you'd better be serious about doing this job."

Megan's triumphant smile was infectious, and Jaye had to give in to her own impulse to smile. Damn, she's cute! she thought, biting her lower lip.

CHAPTER TWELVE

"Your engine runs crappy," Megan remarked as they drove out of Punta Larga, leaving the beaches and partiers behind.

"Yeah," Jaye replied. "Thanks for the bulletin, kid."

"I'm just sayin'." Megan shrugged and looked out the window.

"Okay. I know it runs crappy. That's one of the reasons I didn't want to wait until dark to go back. We'll get it fixed eventually, but there's no money in the budget for car repair. Besides, this just started getting really bad a couple days ago."

"Acts like a misfiring cylinder."

Jaye glanced at Megan. "Do you know something about cars?"

"Old ones like this. Sure. My brother Rick loves old cars. He buys junkers and restores them. He used to let me help back in the day. They're actually pretty easy to fix if you can get parts. Not like the rolling computers they make now. It's all mechanical. Nuts and bolts." Megan smiled easily. "I'll look at it if you want."

"That would be awesome. Thanks."

On the drive to the clinic, Jaye had many chances to observe Megan out of the corner of her eye as she watched the scenery. They drove past impenetrable foliage, scattered residences and the occasional cluster of stores and gas stations. It must have looked to Megan like they'd traveled much further than thirty miles from Punta Larga and its dozen glitzy resorts. This was where the people lived, the native people, not the diverse mix along the coast. They were descendants of the Taino and the Spanish colonists who had come here in the sixteenth century.

"There're a lot of old cars here, aren't there?" Megan asked.

"Yes. Not many people here can afford new cars."

The further they traveled into the interior of the island, the worse living conditions became. Some of the houses were rusted tin shacks, some had thatched roofs and everywhere there were goats and chickens. They passed a grammar school, Our Lady of Fatima. Then a grocery store with a huge battered *Mercado* sign on the roof. There were three men sitting on old car seats turned into sofas in front of a barber shop. Then a fruit stand built of scrap lumber selling bananas, papayas and coconuts.

Megan read the sign on a bright green building. "*Panaderia.* That's a bakery, right?"

"Yes. You don't know Spanish, do you?"

"*Poquito.* Just a few words I picked up. We have a lot of Mexican stores in San Diego. And I have some Spanish-speaking friends, of course. So I know a few swear words."

Jaye laughed. "My high school Spanish was pretty rusty when I got here, but it's getting better."

"I never took Spanish. People were speaking Spanish all around me, so it didn't seem that interesting. Our maid Inez used to watch the telenovelas while she worked, so Spanish was just there in the house. When it came time to study a language, I dismissed it, which seems dumb now because I had a head start, right? I could have aced it no problem. Instead, I chose something from a completely different linguistic family." She shook her head in a self-deprecating way. "My languages are Mandarin Chinese and Russian."

Jaye turned to look at Megan, who was watching the scenery. Okay, she thought, maybe not an idiot after all.

After crossing a bridge over a ravine, they passed a makeshift camp with a couple of "teepees" made out of overlapping sheets of corrugated tin roofing and plastic tarps. A boy of about five stood in front of one of them, his round brown eyes trained on their vehicle, his expression indifferent. He was barefoot and wore only a pair of red shorts.

"Wow," said Megan in a quietly stunned voice.

Jaye saw no reason to comment. The scene spoke for itself.

As they followed the road, it rose up to cross over the mountains, giving them a sudden and breathtaking view of the coastline. "Look," said Jaye, bringing it to Megan's attention.

A strip of white sand was bounded on one side by deep green vegetation with palms dominating the upper region, and on the other by aquamarine water that grew deeper and deeper in color as it extended further from land. From this vantage point, there was no sign of the resort hotels or even the marinas with their rows and rows of boats. There were no cruise ships in sight. One lone sailboat was visible on the sea, and the beach itself was empty.

"Oh my God!" Megan said. "That's beautiful."

In a moment, they had dipped back into dense foliage and the view was lost. The next time they emerged from the jungle, they were faced with undulating hills planted with even rows of coffee trees.

"What is this?" Megan asked.

"Coffee plantation. This is the brand we use at the clinic, actually, so you'll get to taste it. And the family who owns this place is sending a bus up to the clinic tomorrow so the children of their employees can get their vaccinations."

"That's cool." Megan reached toward the controls to adjust the air conditioner vent. "Thank God for the A/C," she said with a short laugh.

Jaye nodded. "Wish you were back at the pool?"

Megan shook her head. "No. I'm excited to see more of the country. Something other than the tourist areas. This is really interesting. I don't think I've ever seen coffee growing before. Do you like living here?"

"Yes. I love it."

"Why did you come? Why are you doing this kind of work?"

"Everybody always asks that like there must be some complicated story. Why *not* do this kind of work? It's rewarding. And I get to live on a beautiful tropical island."

Jaye observed Megan's expression to see if that answer satisfied her. It did not, but that was all she was going to get, at least for now. Jaye recalled her initial meeting with Willie, when both of them had wanted to know the answer to that question. It was natural to be curious. Why had Willie left her lovely home and the guarantee of comfort and luxury in a private practice in Seattle to work in this remote village where half the homes had dirt floors, where resources, tools and medicine were limited, and where almost nobody spoke English? In fact, in Tocamila, not all of them spoke Spanish, and that was where Paloma became essential. She could speak the native dialect, a Spanish-derived Creole language that defied even Willie.

Willie's answer had been typically humble. She wanted to go where the need was. She had come here for no other reason than to do good. As soon as she had been fully licensed, she'd needed a mission. She had been planning all along to go somewhere outside the United States. She wanted to travel the world and devote her life to helping people in need. This opportunity came up with Global Dental Relief. She thought highly of their organization, so she seized it.

Willie, of course, had asked Jaye the same question. Why was she here?

Jaye's reason had little to do with altruism and everything to do with escape. A failed love affair had sent her fleeing. She wanted to get away and start a new life, and it seemed easier to do that in a place that bore no resemblance to the old one. Also, she needed to be needed again. Her ego was wounded and her heart was mangled. She had always heard that a nurse can go anywhere and find work. That was true. Everywhere you went, people were suffering. Here in Santuario, the people in the island's interior had little access to modern medicine. The Santuarian government had set up a few free clinics in the remote regions, but it was hard to staff and fund them, and that's where the international nonprofits came in.

On this island, Jaye had found a place remote and foreign with no reminders of Lexie. At least none that were visible. There were still the ones in her memory, but they tormented her less and less. She was recovering.

Jaye had been in Santuario six months. Here in an alien country, she felt at home. There was no one in the US who missed her in any way that mattered. She was not on good terms with her mother over the whole lesbian thing. But that was really just an excuse. They had never been on good terms, not from the day she was conceived. Jaye's father was just some tweaker her mother had hooked up with at a party. When pressed for details, she said, "He had light-colored eyes like yours." She couldn't even remember his name. It might have started with J, she guessed. John, Javier, Jared. With her usual bitter humor, she had wanted to name her daughter J after him. Just the letter J. Jaye glanced at Megan, thinking, yes, you were almost right. Grandma DeeDee had intervened and insisted on a real name, so a compromise was found.

Grandma DeeDee's real name was Dierdre. When Jaye was small, it was natural to call her DeeDee, and the nickname had stuck. As a child, Jaye had devised a story to create a false cachet for her name. "Letter names are a family tradition," she told her friends. Her grandmother was DeeDee. She had an aunt whose name was Tee. And her cousin, Tee's son, was named Z, but because her family was descended from British royalty, everybody called him Zed.

She did not, in fact, have any such relatives, and she had given up this affectation by the time she had started high school.

There were the stories she made up about her father too, not just for her friends, but for herself. The ideal of "father" fueled her young imagination. She wished she could find him because she was sure he would adore her and want her with him, if only he knew she existed. She imagined him as incredibly handsome and rich, a race car driver or an actor. She watched for him in movies, a tall, swarthy man with hazel eyes. But those stories had lost their magic by the time she was sixteen or so. She had given up a lot of fantasies by that age.

She and her mother had never reconciled, but during the few years Jaye had lived with her Grandma DeeDee, she did occasionally see her. They didn't even pretend they loved one another on those occasions. She resented and disapproved of her mother, and her mother felt the same toward her. Jaye's presence reminded her that she had been a lousy mother. Her daughter's lesbianism was just another ironic dagger in her side, she believed, proof, if any more was needed, that she was a failure. It was less painful to keep away from each other. Her mother had problems, and Jaye had been just another one. The time Jaye had lived with her grandmother, her high school years, had been the most stable of her life. But Grandma DeeDee had passed on a couple of years ago, and Lexie had been the last thread holding Jaye to anyone or any place.

Though it had been terrifying to launch herself into the unknown, she had learned that she could make a good life anywhere, that there was no reason to stay in a painful and destructive situation. She had come here by chance when Willie had sent out feelers to bring in doctors and nurses. As a dentist, she was not equipped to deal with the overwhelming medical need she saw on the island. She'd arranged for the funding, put the program in place, and then recruited a staff. She got Jaye and Paloma.

What Jaye had found in Tocamila was a well-disciplined, effective organization designed by Willie. She had escaped the chaos and uncertainty that had characterized most of her life. Life here was rewarding, calm, purposeful and orderly. Her days were just as she wanted them. This was her home, the home she had chosen and made for herself. Maybe she would stay here forever, she sometimes thought.

She had no intention of explaining all of this to Megan Willett. There were very few people she could comfortably talk to about her personal life. Willie was one. Maybe the only one. Many evenings at the clinic were spent talking. There was almost nothing Jaye felt she couldn't say to Willie, and she was pretty sure that feeling went both directions.

Inoculation day was Willie's idea. She had made it happen. What would she think about Jaye's plan to go ahead with it? Out of the corner of her eye, she observed Megan. Can I trust this disaster? she thought.

Megan's arms were folded over her chest and she was staring glumly out the window. She had grown surly, no doubt because Jaye was unwilling to make conversation. She decided to try to draw her out again.

"What did your boyfriend say when you told him you were doing this?"

Megan looked surprised and unfolded herself. "My boyfriend?"

"Yeah, the guy kissing you last night."

"Nobody kissed me last night."

"I saw him. Dude in a baseball cap. Dark features, nice looking."

"Gavin?"

Jaye shrugged.

"He's not my boyfriend. It's freaking me out, hearing about these things I did last night that I can't remember."

"That's the drawback to partying. Lots of fun that you don't remember."

Jaye's thoughts drifted again to Lexie and too many nights of binge drinking. Jaye would have a couple of drinks to be companionable and set the pace, but her example never worked. Lexie drank almost every night until she passed out. And far too many times, she got horny before she did.

"The worst has got to be blackout sex," Jaye said.

"Blackout sex?" Megan looked startled. "You mean where you drink so much you don't remember having sex?"

Jaye nodded.

"Have you done that?"

"No. I never have."

But I've been on the other end of it, she thought. Frantic, impersonal fucking during which she could have been a lamppost. Lexie with no memory of it the next morning. After a while, Jaye didn't even bother to mention it to her. She also learned to say no when Lexie had had too much to drink. Sex was just one more thing that had died in their relationship because of booze.

"Have *you* ever had blackout sex?" Jaye looked pointedly at Megan.

"Not that I remember." Megan laughed at her joke.

Jaye couldn't help smiling. She could see that Megan was delighted she'd pulled a smile out of her solemn traveling companion.

"If Gavin kissed me last night," Megan said, "I'm gonna kick him in the balls."

"He probably doesn't remember. It wasn't much of a kiss."

Megan chuckled to herself.

"So Gavin's not your boyfriend. Somebody else?"

"I don't have a boyfriend."

Jaye turned a corner leading off the main road toward Tocamila.

"Why don't you ask me if I have a girlfriend?" Megan challenged.

Jaye glanced at her to catch the look on her face, which was defiant. "Why would I ask you that?"

Megan swiveled on the seat to face her. "Why do you assume I'm straight?"

"I don't know. Maybe something you said last night. I don't think a lesbian would have said that."

Megan let out an exasperated sigh, but seemed to have no comeback.

"Okay," Jaye relented, "do you have a girlfriend?"

"No."

Jaye laughed. "Have you ever had a girlfriend?"

"No," Megan said quietly.

"Then what was that all about?"

"Just because I haven't doesn't mean I wouldn't."

"Okay," Jaye said, taking the dare. "Would you *like* to have a girlfriend?"

Megan sat up brightly. "Are you offering?"

Jaye laughed again. "No! I'm just trying to get a straight answer out of you. Men? Women? Both?"

Megan sat back in her seat and grew surprisingly thoughtful before she answered. "I'm not sure. I've had thoughts about women, certain women." She glanced quickly at Jaye before looking away again. "But I've never been with a woman, you know what I mean?"

Megan sounded suddenly so serious, Jaye wasn't sure what to think. "Yes, I know what you mean," she answered.

"I figure I'm not going to know for sure without more experience. I mean, how do I know if I'll like it? How do I know unless I've tried it?"

Jaye decided to treat that as a rhetorical question. Megan stopped talking while they passed a yard with three goats grazing.

"It's like cantaloupe," Megan said when the goats were out of sight. "When I was little, I was afraid of that stuff. It was supposed to be a melon, but it was the color of salmon, and I hated salmon. People would try to make me taste it and I'm like, no way, José. Melons are supposed to be red. And salmon is fish, so… Anyway, I was thirteen before I tasted it by mistake. It was a sorbet, you know, those fancy ice cream things. I thought it was peach ice cream, which is one of my favorites, by the way. So I took a spoonful and I'm like, wow, what is this? And my brother's like, 'it's cantaloupe sorbet.'" Megan shook her head. "That blew my mind. Now it's one of my favorite things. My brother carved a cantaloupe into the shape of a salmon once and I'm like, 'Dude, that's so freaking cool!'"

Megan grinned and didn't seem inclined to return to her original subject. Maybe she had forgotten. That was fine with Jaye. She wasn't comfortable with Megan chatting about lesbian sex. Did she really think it was like cantaloupe?

A moment passed before she said, "Oh, so, anyway, I'd like to try it sometime, you know, with a woman. I'd like to find out what it's like. It's something I've wondered about for a long time."

Oh, God! Jaye thought, suddenly catching on. She wants to be initiated!

Suddenly seeing an animal in the road, Jaye swerved to avoid it, reaching over instinctively to hold Megan in her seat. After averting the collision, she glanced over to see her right hand clamped over Megan's left breast and Megan calmly looking down at it. Jaye quickly pulled her hand away.

"Oh, shit," she muttered. "Sorry. It was just...reflex, you know."

"No problem," Megan smiled suggestively. "What was that thing anyway?"

"Agouti. The island version of squirrels."

Megan nodded, then the lusty smile returned to her face.

"Just so you know," Jaye said, feeling unnerved, "I've already got a toaster oven and I'm not in the market for another."

By the look on Megan's face, Jaye could see that the reference went right over her head. That truly was an inside joke, apparently. She decided to give Megan a more mature response.

"Look, Megan, if you're serious, if you think you might be a lesbian, there's plenty of time to find out. No reason to rush it. If you're meant to love a woman, someday you'll meet her and fall in love and everything will be perfectly clear."

Megan held Jaye's eyes for a moment, then she grinned. "I think it's clearing up already."

CHAPTER THIRTEEN

The door opened and Miguel, wearing khaki shorts and a sweat-stained blue shirt, brought in Willie's dinner. He smiled in a way that made her nervous. The smile became more of a leer when he straightened up from setting down her plate. She caught a whiff of an astringent, artificial scent, and hoped he hadn't gussied himself up for her sake. He pulled out a knife and stepped toward her. He took hold of her arm and turned her around so he could cut the tape on her wrists. She flexed her sore shoulders gently. Miguel's demeanor frightened her, so she shrank against the wall and didn't approach the food, waiting anxiously for him to leave.

"Frijoles," he said, pointing at the plate.

I can see that, Willie thought. "*Gracias*," she said, hoping he would be satisfied with that.

But she could tell by the nervousness of his wiry body that he wasn't ready to leave. He stood twitching for a moment, his eyes unblinking, then he leapt at her like a panther, clamping his arms around her and trying to kiss her. She struggled ineffectually, held securely against his chest. She managed to stomp on his foot, but it didn't faze him. His arms were like iron bands. When he touched her mouth with his, she wrenched her head away and screamed. She continued to struggle, jerking him this way and that until his feet hit the edge of the mattress and he fell, taking her with him. He rolled on top of her and laughed into her face because he knew she was now helpless under his body.

The door burst open and Grady rushed in, yelling at Miguel to get off her. Grady pulled him to his feet, shaking him and scolding him in Spanish. "Later, do you understand me! I told you later. You'll have your chance after we get the money. Now get out!"

He shoved the young man through the open door, then turned back to Willie, gazing at her with cold, hard eyes. "Bitch!" he hissed, slamming the door behind him.

Suddenly, Willie had no doubt how this story would play out. They were going to kill her, no matter what. Ransom paid, not paid, it didn't matter. Panic rose in her throat and she ran to the door, pounding on it with her fists and screaming, "Let me out! Let me out!" Total silence answered. She slid down the smooth surface of the door, landing in a crumpled heap on the floor, and started to cry. She hit the door once more with her fist, then let her head fall against it.

Now she knew her fate. They had intended to treat her well as long as she might be needed for negotiations. But once they got their money, once she was of no more use, they would have their horrible way with her and kill her. But, why? she wondered. Why did they have to kill her?

After a while, her tears dried up and she crawled to the mattress, letting herself fall limply onto it. She could still smell Miguel's scent, a cheap, revolting aftershave. The odor and the thought of him touching her made her sick to her stomach. Even death was better than… Maybe she could think of a way to get herself killed, she thought. If she tried to escape, they might shoot her. That would be an easy way to go. She remembered the razor blade hidden in the mattress. There was that. Could she do it? she wondered. She'd never given a thought to killing herself before. But if it meant spoiling the fun for these three monsters, she might be able to summon the nerve.

She laughed out loud, a bitter, wild laugh that made her wonder if she were losing her mind. Irony, that's what this was. She'd held on stubbornly to her virginity all these years, waiting for something truly special. Apparently, this was it.

She had turned away all the boys in high school, even Matt, whom she had truly liked. He had gotten as far as fondling her breasts. When boys realized that's as far as they were ever going to get, they usually quit going out with her. Matt hung around longer than the others. As a teenager, Willie had some strict ideals about love and sex. It had been nothing to do with morality for her. It was more to do with ego. She had liked Matt, but she hadn't loved him enough to marry him. She wanted sex to be beautiful and meaningful, an act of true love. She had been a romantic back then. Maybe all teenagers were romantics, but their ideals took them in different directions. Hers had kept her virginity intact.

In college, things were different. She barely dated at all. The peer pressure wasn't there like it had been in high school. Her interest in marriage had diminished in favor of her career. She did nothing special to attract men, wore no makeup, wore loose, comfortable clothes that hid her unexceptional curves, let her hair fall straight and natural, usually tied back in a ponytail. Young men didn't see her as a potential date and she didn't care. She had other plans for her life. She saw men only as friends and colleagues, not lovers. Maybe she had always seen them that way. Maybe that's why she didn't sleep with them. She didn't desire them. She didn't desire women either, though there had been a few passes from women during college, no doubt encouraged by her androgynous clothing and comfortable shoes. She didn't know why she had no interest in sex. It seemed like so much fussing for so little reward. She chalked her case up to diluted libido and considered herself lucky because, unlike so many of her classmates, she wasn't distracted from intellectual pursuits by lust. And so she had managed to reach the advanced age of twenty-six with maidenhood intact, as they say in historical romance novels.

Now she would go to her death like a sacrificial virgin… or nearly. Would it just be jittery Miguel, or would all three of them take her? Yes, it was very funny, funny in a way that made her want to cry. She pictured Matt's lovely, eager smile. Poor frustrated boy. Maybe he had loved her. He had stayed with her for a long time. Maybe she had loved him. What do I know about love? she thought bitterly. Maybe there was no such thing. Maybe that kind of love was as much a myth as the Easter Bunny. Even if she hadn't been about to die, there wasn't much chance that true love would ever have come her way anyway. She had known that for quite a while. There are some people who are meant for other things. She had told herself that years ago when men were not asking her out, that she was meant for grander things than love and marriage. There was a higher calling for her. Like Joan of Arc and Mother Teresa.

She laughed out loud. Oh, poor little lonely Willie with your delusions of grandeur!

Now she would have neither love nor a body of work to distinguish her life. She would be one more statistic in the drug wars, and her family would be out whatever they were being asked to pay. In return for their money, they would get only grief.

She summoned Matt's smooth young face to mind. *I should have let him have me. What the hell was I saving myself for?*

CHAPTER FOURTEEN

Working under the hood of the van, Megan took out another spark plug and held it up to the light hanging above the engine. While she'd been working, the sun had gone down, and the clinic's whitewashed walls now reflected an orange glow from the sunset. She didn't know what she had expected from this place, but the idea of a medical clinic had obviously influenced her expectations. The reality of the "clinic" was something else. The building was a modest single-story stucco home painted white with a red tile roof. The porch was framed by a wide arch, and on it sat two chaise lounges. The house was set amid a clearing of less than a quarter acre at the end of a gravel driveway where a makeshift lean-to of palm fronds sheltered the van. Town, Jaye had told her, was just around the next bend. In front of the house was a guava tree shading most of the open space between the house and the edge of the clearing. On the wall beside the door clung a huge iguana named Chuck that had scared the shit out of Megan earlier when she'd first stepped onto the porch. She'd thought it was a wall decoration, like the omnipresent geckos back home, until it blinked its eyes.

"It's freaking huge!" she had remarked after leaping backward and almost falling off the bottom step.

"It won't hurt you," said Jaye. "Actually, this one lives here. We see him all the time. You can give him a snack later."

"Forget that! I'm not going anywhere near that dinosaur's mouth."

Jaye had laughed at her, the first laugh Megan had heard from her. Like the first smile at the restaurant that afternoon, the first laugh had been spectacular, as expected. God, she was so beautiful, Megan thought, remembering the sparkle in Jaye's eyes and the self-conscious smile that followed her laughter.

Both of the cops stationed here, Santos and Perez, seemed to be amused watching Megan working on the van. They spoke to each other in Spanish, laughing a lot, and Megan assumed they were making fun of her, but as she progressed, they laughed less and nodded more. Santos was affable and handsome with thick black hair and heavy eyebrows, one of them cut in two by a pale scar, a feature that continually drew one's eyes. Perez, a thin-faced young man with a long, narrow nose, was quietly observant. Santos was clearly the more outgoing of the two, or maybe he was just the one comfortable with English.

When Jaye and Megan had arrived, Perez remained quiet while Santos reported on the day's activities. They had spent the day questioning the locals, trying to find someone who knew something. Everything was in order and there had been no mishaps, no sign of trouble since the kidnapping. "There is nothing to worry about," Santos had assured them. "We are here to protect you." Megan didn't feel like she was in danger, but if she had, she wasn't sure these two would make her feel any safer. They seemed very easygoing and nonthreatening, like having a golden retriever for a guard dog.

Megan liked tinkering with car engines. She liked the way the tools felt so solid in her hands and the way nuts and bolts went together with such precision. They were simple devices, but so effective. She also liked the sense of calm that came with working on something with her hands. As she removed the rest of the sparkplugs, her mind wandered over what she had seen so far of Jaye's living quarters. All in all, the house gave the impression of a painfully spartan lifestyle. Except for one small bedroom that they shared, a bathroom and the kitchen, all of it was devoted to the business of caring for patients. Everything was utilitarian, as if there were some kind of rule against color and personality. Except Willie's birdhouses. The birdhouses were awesome and completely unexpected because Megan had already formed an image of the dentist that precluded something so playful.

"It's Willie's hobby," Jaye had explained. "She makes them. It keeps her busy."

Megan had picked one up to examine its details. It was designed to look like a gingerbread house and was brilliantly whimsical with candy cane stripes painted on its walls and tiny green gumdrop-like fixtures on the front ledge to simulate shrubbery. "These are wonderful!"

"She's gotten better and better at it. She can spend hours on the tiniest detail. Those gumdrops, for example. She may have gotten those a little too real looking. She gives these to the local kids, part of her plan to encourage them to be kind to the planet and all of its creatures. In this case, I'm afraid they're going to eat the birdhouse instead of hang it outside."

"It's really darling." Megan touched the bead of white "frosting" that outlined the brown panels of the miniature house. "She could sell these!"

"Why would she sell them?" Jaye had asked, her voice tinged with disapproval. "She does this for fun and the children love them."

"I just meant they're good enough that people would buy them. I didn't mean she *should* sell them."

Jaye still thought she was a flake, she realized. Maybe by tomorrow she could change that.

She unclamped the distributor cap and held it close to the light to examine the contacts. They were a little worn, but not too bad. As she expected, the main culprit seemed to be the fouled spark plugs.

"Do you know where I can get parts for this thing?" she asked the cops.

"Not so late at night," Santos replied, leaning over the fender to get a look at the cap himself. "*Mañana*." He held up the blackened air filter and shook his head.

"Tomorrow's going to be a busy day. I don't know if I'll have time for this. I'd better put it back together just in case we need a vehicle."

When she had finished with the van, Megan wiped the grease off her hands and went inside. She found Jaye unpacking a box and putting supplies into drawers.

"How did it go?" she asked.

"It just needs a tune-up. New points, plugs, air filter. The plugs had quite a bit of carbon on them, so I cleaned them off. That actually helped a lot. It's running better now, but they should be replaced."

"How much is all that going to cost?"

"Not that much, as long as you don't have to pay for labor."

"Thanks for doing that." Jaye smiled. "You've got grease on your face. Come into the kitchen."

Megan followed her into the next room where a simple wooden table with three chairs resided against one wall. The kitchen, like the rest of the house, was old, cramped and shabby. It had stainless steel counters and worn linoleum. The pattern was completely worn off in some places, leaving a grayish-brown surface underfoot. Some of the cupboards had doors and others were open, their doors lost to time. The white appliances were old, older, she was sure, than she was. The plumbing groaned when Jaye turned on the water and the handles were encrusted with rust where the connections were made.

Megan always complained that the apartment she shared with Nicole back home was too small and hopelessly uninspired. But compared to this, it was living high.

Holding Megan's chin with one hand, Jaye wiped at her cheek with the other with a wet paper towel. With Jaye standing so close, her fingers touching skin, Megan's pulse quickened. But Jaye remained very nurse-like, completing her task with efficiency, then stepping away.

"What do you do for fun around here at night?" Megan asked. "You can't be working all the time."

"No, of course not. We're free most evenings."

"Do you have cable? I'd be seriously bummed if I couldn't get my *Dancing with the Stars*, you know?"

"We have Internet, so we get TV and movies that way, but it's spotty. We play board games. Willie's a champ at Scrabble. And chess. She taught me how to play, but it's very rare for me to win." Jaye paused, looking doubtful. "Probably none of that sounds like fun to you."

"Sure, I guess," Megan said noncommittally. She rubbed her left temple, assailed again by the persistent hangover headache.

"Are you okay?" Jaye asked.

"Yeah. Just a headache."

"Do you want some aspirin?"

"That would be awesome…if it's okay. I know you have to keep track of all your meds."

"Yes, but aspirin is one thing we can get easily enough, and it's not controlled. Besides, Willie has a bottle in her desk. She gets a lot of headaches." Jaye led the way to the exam room, a converted bedroom that contained a wall of cabinets, a dentist's chair and a doctor's examination table. Jaye pulled open a drawer and produced a bottle of generic aspirin.

As Megan tapped out two tablets, she noticed the lab coat hanging on a hook behind the desk. Stitched in red on the white cloth was the name "M. Willett." She laughed spontaneously. "Hey, I could wear this tomorrow instead of that paper nametag you made for me." The nametag, which she was to pin to her shirt, said simply, "Megan."

Turning to look at Jaye, she saw her scowling.

"I would prefer you didn't," she said.

Megan handed the aspirin bottle back, irritated at Jaye's tone.

"The patients might get confused," Jaye explained. "They might think you're Willie."

"Well, we can't have that!" Megan replied.

"No, I mean, they might think you're a doctor. It wouldn't be ethical. It would be a kind of fraud, like you're pretending to be the real Dr. Willett. And you're not her." Jaye's voice became strained as she said, "You're nothing like her."

"I know I'm not her." Megan felt her own anger surfacing. "She's some kind of superhero and I'm...hell, I don't know what you think I am. What is it with you, anyway? Why do you hate me?"

Jaye looked stunned. "I don't hate you."

"Really? Because it sure feels like you do. I know we got off on the wrong foot, but give me a freaking chance. I was drunk. I was stupid. Okay, so being drunk doesn't absolve me of my crimes, but who did I kill, anyway? Who the fuck did I kill? All I did was fling a little insult at a stranger. And I've apologized for it."

Megan abruptly stopped her monologue as Jaye lowered herself slowly to the desk chair, looking contrite, her head down. It was so quiet then that Megan could hear the wall clock ticking. When Jaye looked up at last, her eyes shone with a film of liquid.

"It wasn't just that," she said quietly. "It's hard to explain. Last night when I saw you having fun with your friends, so carefree, so *free*, after what had happened to Willie and Paloma, I was really angry at you...even before you said a word. I know it doesn't make sense. I know you have nothing to do with Willie or what happened to her. You never heard of her before last night. But somehow the way the media merged the two of you together made me feel like you had some responsibility. If not responsibility, at least awareness, and you should be more respectful. And because of that, I thought, 'how dare you act so blatantly unconcerned,' as if everything were wonderful when Willie...who knows what she's going through." The tears brimming in her eyes fell in unison to her cheeks. She wiped them away with the back of her hand.

Megan felt nearly bad enough to cry herself. She sat on the corner of the desk as Jaye reached for a tissue.

"I do understand," Megan said softly. "I had that feeling myself today. The gang wanted to go out on a catamaran tour, but I just couldn't tear myself away from the television. I watched the story of the kidnapping over and over, waiting to find out if there were any new developments. And worrying about your

Willie. Like you say, there's something about the way the media mixed us up that made me feel involved, made me care about her. Not like you, of course, but not like a stranger either." Megan reached over and touched Jaye's hand. "I hope she's okay."

Jaye looked up and attempted a smile. "I've been really hard on you, haven't I?"

Megan shrugged.

"It's been rough, dealing with this, and I've been taking it out on you."

"It's okay. Of course you're upset. She's a close friend." Megan wondered for the first time if there was more than friendship between Jaye and her dentist.

Jaye was no longer crying. She tossed the tissue in the wastebasket. Megan felt like a jerk for making her cry. She should have realized Jaye couldn't forget for a moment the terrifying ordeal her friend was going through. And all Megan had been thinking of was how to arouse Jaye's libido. Yep, I'm a jerk, she thought.

"Tell me about her," she asked gently. "What's she like?"

Jaye smiled. "She's great. She's very dedicated. She'll travel hours away to fill a cavity if no other dentist can be found. And she always follows up because you can't count on people to come back, necessarily, if there's a problem. They don't feel like they can complain when it's all for free. She loves these people."

"She's all about work," noted Megan.

"She's mostly about work. She's a giver. But she finds it hard to give anything to herself, like time…or money. So, yes, she works hard. But she's funny and very clever. We laugh a lot." A fond smile appeared on Jaye's face as she spoke of Willie. "You can see that side of her in the birdhouses, can't you?"

"You really admire her, don't you?"

"Yes, I do. She's passionate, principled, honest and self-sacrificing. She's everything you would ever want in a doctor."

Or a lover? Megan wondered.

"Those creeps who took her," Jaye went on, "don't have any idea how valuable she is. Whatever they're asking, she's worth so much more to the hundreds of people she's helped here."

She hit the table with her fist. "Bastards! Every time I think of them, I could scream. I just hate sitting here doing nothing." Her shoulders slumped in defeat and she went silent.

"Hey," said Megan, rubbing Jaye's shoulder, "let's get something to eat. Then maybe later we can throw some eggs at that police van and get those cops going."

Jaye smiled and gave Megan a look that told her she wouldn't half mind doing it. Oh, yeah, Megan thought, there's a bad girl in there just screaming to get out.

CHAPTER FIFTEEN

After dinner, Megan and Jaye sat in the yard, far enough away from the back door to escape most of the light from inside the kitchen. Jaye had opened a package of addictive coffee-flavored candy that sat on the table between them. Megan couldn't get over how many stars she could see. A distinctively river-like swath of the Milky Way was brilliantly on display. You forget why it's called the Milky Way, she thought, until a view like this shows up. Her eyes were continuously drawn upward. Living in the urban sprawl of Southern California, her experience of night was completely different.

It was a nice night, not too hot, and definitely cooler outside than inside. Thirty feet from the house, everything was inky black, so much so that Megan couldn't make out any individual plants.

"Are there wild animals out there?" she asked. "I keep expecting a pair of red eyes to appear out of the dark."

"Yes, of course there are animals." Jaye unwrapped another candy. "At night we sometimes see bats. But there aren't big predators like cats. Once people came to the islands, most of the larger mammals became extinct. That agouti we saw earlier is one of the biggest animals we have. And monkeys."

"Are there poisonous snakes?"

"No, no poisonous ones. But Willie's terrified of snakes, so whenever one shows up, it turns into an all-day drama." Jaye laughed. "Are you afraid of snakes?"

"No."

"Are you afraid of anything?" Jaye asked.

Megan laughed shortly. "Nothing like that. Nothing that would make me scream and take off running."

"Willie's afraid of everything."

"Then it's amazing she manages to get anything done."

"I know! I used to wonder about that myself. Somehow she just does. She fights through her fears because she's so determined. But she's still afraid. I can't imagine how she's coping right now." Jaye sucked on the candy and leaned her head back on the chair, her eyes skyward.

Megan listened to the sounds of the jungle. An occasional strange animal call, insects chirping. Somewhere in the village a dog was barking. Every once in a while the faint sound of a crying baby would reach them, reminding Megan that she was not utterly alone in the world with Jaye. While she was looking at the sky, a bright streak of light zipped by almost directly overhead, then disappeared.

"Did you see that?" she asked.

"Yes. That was a nice one. We see them all the time here because it's so dark. There are no streetlights anywhere around here. Not for eighty miles."

"Back home, we can't even see a major meteor shower."

"No, I know. It's really beautiful, isn't it?"

"Uh-huh." Megan leaned in Jaye's direction. "And very romantic."

Jaye lifted her head to look at Megan, then shot her a discouraging frown, but said nothing. A moment later, Megan asked, "Jaye, when did you know you were a lesbian?"

Jaye remained silent some moments before saying, "I didn't know for sure until I was twenty years old. Before that, there were plenty of times I wondered. I had crushes on women when I was young and I fell in love with a girl in high school. But nothing happened because I kept it to myself. It was a small high school in rural South Dakota, and the only time anybody mentioned gays was as an insult or a reason for burning in hell, so unless you were incredibly brazen, it seemed smart to keep quiet. It occurred to me over time that everybody who interested me was of the female variety. I liked boys, but not in that way. I actually never dated boys."

"You've never slept with a man?" Megan was incredulous.

"No. The idea of it creeped me out. I did end up kissing a couple of them, but I didn't like that either. Scratchy chins. And they aren't really into kissing. It's just a way to distract you while they unzip their flies. I always knew I wanted to kiss girls, but I never got the chance until college. There were lesbians all over the place there. I dated women seriously then. It was incredible. I had the time of my life, honestly. But I wasn't completely sure, still."

"You were kinda dense, weren't you?"

Jaye laughed. "Maybe so. But sexual orientation isn't just about sex. At least not for me, and I would guess not for most women. It's about love. Finally, when I was twenty, I fell in love, really fell in love and fell hard."

"What was her name?"

"Lexie. Sexy Lexie. She was a dream to me, beautiful and smart. I met her in my microbiology class."

"And?" prompted Megan.

"We got together. It was unbelievable. It was blissful. And finally I knew for sure. No more wondering. No more pretending. The internal struggle ended."

"The internal struggle ended," Megan repeated to herself. Wow, she thought, what a gift that would be! "What went wrong between you and Lexie?" she asked.

"That's a long story."

"Can't you give me the Cliff's Notes version?"

There was a long pause before Jaye said, "Addiction. Mainly alcohol. She barely drank at all when we met, but it gradually became more and more a part of our lives until she was drunk all the time. I didn't see her in the morning because I left for work early. When I got home, she was already buzzed. After a few years, I almost never saw her sober. She just wasn't the woman I fell in love with."

Hearing this, Megan thought back to the first time Jaye had seen her, drunk out of her mind. They had met at the worst possible moment, considering Lexie. No wonder she had wanted nothing to do with Megan after seeing her like that.

"That's sad," Megan said.

"It was sad, yes, because she used to be so clever and funny and loving. But she changed so much. She was inconsiderate and, frankly, stupid, most of the time. I quit drinking entirely for a while, thinking it might shame her into sobriety. That was pointless. She didn't even notice. I tried to get her into rehab, but she didn't think she needed it. I threatened to leave her if she didn't stop drinking. Maybe she didn't believe me. I don't know. What it boiled down to was that she chose alcohol over me. That really hurt. But I don't know why I was so naïve. It's not like it hadn't happened before, that I came second to drugs and alcohol."

"What do you mean? It happened before?"

"Oh, look, we don't want to get into that. Another long story."

Megan wanted to know everything she could about Jaye, but understood that couldn't happen in one night. That was such a sad story about Lexie. What a stupid woman! Jaye loved her. She could have had the world in Jaye's arms.

Megan observed Jaye in the faint light. Jaye was looking at the sky, her head tilted back, her neck arched and exposed. Megan imagined herself leaning down to kiss that neck, brushing it teasingly with her lips, and Jaye closing her eyes and arching her neck even more, coaxing Megan's lips to touch her skin, her soft, velvety skin. What would she do, Megan wondered, if I actually did it? Maybe she would like it. Maybe she would turn her head and offer her lips, and Megan would kiss her. Her kisses would be so incredibly awesome that Jaye wouldn't be able to tear herself away. She would be wild with desire for

Megan, would tear her clothes off and lay her on the table right here and… No, she thought. The table was too splintery. No, Jaye would be so aroused that she would lift Megan off the ground, carry her into the bedroom, and ravage her like a lion eats her prey, ravenously and ruthlessly. No, no, no! Megan said to herself, gazing at Jaye's tender neck. She would be gentle and patient. She would move slowly and bring out all kinds of sex toys like feathers and lotions and whipped cream and turn every nerve in Megan's body on, one at a time, until Megan thought she would die if she had to go another nanosecond…

Megan swallowed hard, then took another piece of candy. Jaye turned her head and smiled casually.

An indistinct light flashing through the trees drew their attention. It flashed by again, then they heard the sound of crunching gravel. Megan realized the light was a flashlight moving in their direction from the road. Jaye stood up.

"*Hola*," she said in the direction of the flashlight.

"*Hola*," called a soft female voice. "It is Maria Baza."

Jaye approached the woman and walked her up to the house.

"*Buenos noches*," she said to Megan. The woman was in her thirties and roundish, wearing a loose dress and a burnt-orange shawl over her head and shoulders. She looked worried and hugged the shawl close around her face. Jaye asked her in, and the three of them went through the back door into the kitchen.

Before they had closed the door, Officer Santos leapt into the room with his gun drawn, his ebony eyes flashing, his odd split eyebrow arched. Where had he come from? Megan wondered.

Their plump visitor let out a cry of alarm and started to flee toward the hallway. Jaye caught her by the wrist while addressing Santos sharply. "Put that away!"

He lowered his gun, and Jaye spoke reassuringly to the woman, finally coaxing her to sit at the kitchen table.

Once Maria Baza was seated, she slipped the shawl off her head and they were able to get a look at the problem. She had a bloody gash along the top of her right cheekbone.

"Maria," Jaye said, gesturing toward Megan, "this is Megan. She's helping me here." She turned to the cop and said, "Santos, make yourself useful and ask her how this happened."

While Santos questioned Maria, Jaye cleaned the wound with warm water, then disinfected it.

"She says she tripped and fell on a sharp rock," Santos explained.

The look on Jaye's face told Megan she didn't believe the story. "It's not very deep," she said. "I think we can use Steri-strips."

Jaye taped the wound together while Megan watched. Jaye was gentle, precise, efficient, and while she worked, she spoke to her patient, asking her if she wanted to spend the night. She said she couldn't, that she had to get home to take care of the children. Then Jaye offered to take in the children too, but Maria turned down the offer repeatedly. She said "*Gracias*" over and over, her manner becoming more and more agitated. All of this was in a confusing mixture of English and Spanish, but Megan got the gist of the conversation with the help of expressions and gestures.

When the wound was shut, Jaye left the room with Santos, telling Megan to keep Maria there until she got back. She could hear Jaye arguing with the policeman in the front room, but couldn't hear what they were saying. Their guest waited nervously, like a rabbit about to bolt. Her melancholy eyes darted away every time Megan met them.

When Jaye returned, she looked frustrated. "Worthless son-of-a-bitch," she muttered.

"What's going on?" Megan asked.

Jaye sighed. "Her husband did this. It's not the first time. Santos says there's nothing he can do."

"You mean the police here don't arrest wife beaters?"

"No, they do, but it's the same problem we have in the States. She won't talk. So Santos can't charge him with anything."

"He is very angry," Maria said in English. Then she launched into an explanation in Spanish, after which Jaye summarized for Megan.

"Apparently," she said, "after the police questioned him this afternoon about the kidnapping, Señor Baza went off on Maria here. He blames her for getting him into trouble because if it wasn't for her coming to the clinic to have her wounds treated, Willie and I would never have interfered in their lives in the first place."

"That's ridiculous! If he wouldn't have hit her…"

"Yes, I know. But that's the sort of logic you get from this guy. He feels like he's being unfairly ganged up on. And now he feels like somebody is trying to pin the kidnapping on him." Jaye placed her hand on Maria's shoulder.

"You don't think he did it, do you?" Megan asked.

Jaye shook her head. "I think he hates Willie enough to do it. But I don't think he has the connections or resources to do something like this. But it's possible. In the beginning, I thought this kidnapping was just about money, but I don't know anymore. The police seem to think there could be something else going on, the way Willie was targeted very specifically."

"Sure, but she was targeted because her family's rich. That's enough of a reason."

Jaye nodded, but didn't look satisfied.

All three women flinched at a thud against the back door. A moment later someone banged impatiently at the door and a man's voice boomed through it, a stream of enraged Spanish alerting them to his angry state of mind.

Jaye turned to Maria and asked, "Señor Baza?"

Maria nodded, her look both apologetic and frightened. "*Está borracho!*"

"What did she say?" Megan asked.

"She's telling us he's been drinking, so he's not his usual sweet self."

"Santos!" Megan called toward the hallway.

Santos rushed into the room. The man on the other side of the door continued pounding and making demands until Santos opened the door. Megan didn't need a translator to know what was going on. Baza, a slender man with straight, thin hair and a hooked nose, caught sight of his wife beyond Santos and lurched toward her. Santos caught him and attempted to hold him back, but he was clearly *muy borracho*. He was a small man, but emboldened by rage. He broke free of Santos and lunged into the room, grabbing his wife by the arm and hollering at her. Between his curses, her screams and both Santos and Jaye barking at him, the cramped kitchen was pandemonium.

Santos grabbed Baza's free arm, but Baza ripped it loose and swung around to throw a jab at the officer. He missed, but threw himself off-balance and crashed into Santos. Santos went down, bouncing off the stove before hitting the floor. Jaye knelt beside him. Baza turned his attention back to his wife, grabbing her arm again. It looked to Megan like he was going to slap her. Megan lunged for him, hitting him like a linebacker and running him hard against the far wall. When he slammed into it, the shelves above his head rattled. A couple of water glasses fell to the floor and shattered. Before he could take a breath, Megan kneed him hard in the groin. He groaned, doubled over and dropped to the floor. Santos knelt beside him, pulled his arms behind his back and handcuffed him. Baza mumbled unintelligibly, then made himself fully understood when he trained his blazing red eyes on Megan and spat, "*Pinche puta!*" No translation needed, she decided.

Megan saw that Maria Baza was looking at her with wonder. Megan smiled at her, eliciting a nearly imperceptible answering smile.

"What are you going to do with him?" Jaye asked Santos.

"I will turn him over to the local police and tell them to put him in jail tonight."

"Then what?"

"They will let him go tomorrow. This one will not press charges." He flipped his thumb toward Maria.

Santos led Baza out, and Jaye spoke to Maria for a while, no doubt trying to counsel her on her rights and let her know that there was a support system if she wanted to get away from her husband. Was there a support system here? Or was it just Jaye and, of course, her partner in missions of mercy, Willie? Would they personally provide and fund Maria's safekeeping if she agreed to take their help?

Megan left them talking in the kitchen and went to the only bedroom, a small, rectangular space containing two parallel twin beds separated by a bookcase and covered with hand-woven wool blankets. Considering their dorm-like sleeping arrangements, it didn't seem like Jaye and Willie could be lovers, though that might just be for appearance's sake. They could certainly push the beds together whenever it suited them.

The room contained one small window, a stand-up chest of drawers, and a tiny closet that they shared. There were few personal belongings—shoes, books, toiletries. An electric fan near the door oscillated from one bed to the other.

Above the head of Willie's bed were several framed prints of nature scenes—a Yosemite waterfall, sunset on the Serengeti, a flock of geese rising from a misty lake, a tropical beach with coconut palms and one red canoe on the sand. They were pretty, but impersonal. Beside the bed was a table with a lamp, a clock and a shelf containing magazines, *National Geographic* on top. Megan thumbed through them to see if there was anything more risqué in the stack. *Dentistry Today*, *Time*, *Scientific American*. The most salacious of the bunch was the *National Geographic* after all.

Jaye's bed was against the wall six feet away from Willie's. There were no photos or artwork on her wall, but there was a cork bulletin board with cards and notes pinned to it, as well as a small calendar, the kind where you rip off the month when it's done. Next to that was a hook holding a rain jacket. Megan checked the shelf next to Jaye's bed to find a *People* magazine and a paperback mystery novel. There were no photos of people here, she noticed. No relatives or friends. Looking at Jaye's few possessions, she just couldn't get a sense of who Jaye was. These two lived like hermits. Maybe they were happy that way. When she had met Jaye in town, she'd had a different impression of her, as someone more spirited and fun-loving. Seeing the way she lived, Megan was reassessing her earlier opinion.

The more she saw of Jaye's lifestyle, the bleaker it appeared. She might be living on a gorgeous tropical island, but her house lacked comfort and beauty, and she was nowhere near a beach. It was a life of self-sacrifice and self-denial, and although Jaye seemed like a giving person, there was something about this situation that just didn't seem right. Jaye seemed out of place. Scrabble and chess? Was that really Jaye's idea of fun?

Megan shook her head ruefully. After changing the sheets on Willie's bed, she put on her nightshirt and folded her clothes, placing them in her overnight bag. She fished her phone out of her bag, then flung herself on the bed, anxious to see what everybody else had been up to today.

CHAPTER SIXTEEN

Megan scanned through the messages posted on Willie's Facebook page. "Megan," read one, "you are a true American hero, and we are praying for your safe return." Another said, "We're heartbroken to hear of your abduction, Dr. Willett. We know how hard you work to give a better life to those less fortunate, and all of us who have known you, however briefly, are in mourning today. Please, please, come home safely. All of us in Seattle love you and are so proud of you." There were messages from people in Santuario too, some in English, some in Spanish. Though Megan couldn't understand most of those in Spanish, she was sure they were just as laudatory as the others.

Maybe I should nominate her for sainthood, Megan thought resentfully, then scolded herself for being catty.

She had already sent texts to her friends in Punta Larga, catching them up, by the time she heard Jaye in the bathroom. A few minutes later she came in wearing a bathrobe over a pale green, unrevealing nightgown that fell just above her knees.

"Did you get anywhere with Mrs. Baza?" Megan asked.

Jaye shook her head. "I doubt it. But you never know if your words might someday take root in a person's mind and move her to action. It happens. At least she and the kids won't have to deal with him tonight."

"How many kids do they have?"

"Two. A little boy named Carlos after his father and a six-month-old baby. Maria doesn't work, and you can see how she must feel stuck. How could she support herself with two little ones to take care of?"

"Relatives?"

"She doesn't want to burden them. Nobody in her family is that well off."

"It's a tough situation. It always comes down to money, doesn't it?"

Jaye nodded and sat on the edge of her bed facing Megan.

"I have to say," Megan said, "it's more exciting around here than I thought it would be."

"We don't have that every day." Jaye smiled, then brightened further. "You were a ninja in there earlier."

Megan laughed. "A ninja?"

"Awesome, anyway, for such a small thing."

"Thanks. I was a wrestler when I was a kid for about three years. Taught me how to use my body as a weapon."

"A wrestler? Interesting. What made you want to do that?"

"Watching it on TV." Megan turned on her side facing Jaye and dropped her phone on the bed beside her. "My older brother loved to watch the WWE. It was on all the time, so I got hooked. We'd watch *Smackdown!* together and holler at the TV, you know. I loved it. Especially the women. Divas, they call them. I can still remember some of them: Jazz, Ivory, Sable. But my favorite was Trish Indigo. Have you heard of her?"

Jaye shook her head.

"No, you wouldn't. Not unless you'd been a fan. These women wrestlers, even the champions, aren't well known, not like football stars. Anyway, Indigo was one of the champs. She was rocking hot, you know? Long blond hair, buns of steel, a flat stomach with a six-pack any dude would envy. The matches might be phony, but the conditioning, the athleticism, it's real.

She had muscles everywhere, like even in her forehead, I swear, and she was badass. Indigo, she was the reason I begged my mom to get me into wrestling. She was amazing. I had posters of her in my room. I even wrote her a fan letter."

Remembering a photo of Indigo in a wet T-shirt, Megan went silent, feeling a little light-headed, until she saw Jaye's highly amused smile.

"How old were you when this was going on?"

"I was twelve when I started wrestling."

"That's about how old I was when I had my first crush on a woman."

"Crush? It wasn't a crush. I didn't want to do her. I wanted to *be* her."

"Sure. That's how it is at that age. That's what I thought too…about Miss Ingalls. She was the school nurse."

"No kidding? Is that why you became one?"

"It might have started there. Miss Ingalls was nothing like your Indigo. Physically, I mean. She was middle-aged, a little dumpy, and wore the ugliest shoes you ever saw."

Megan laughed, glancing at Jaye's shoes.

"Those clodhoppers were big too," Jaye added, tucking her hair behind her ear. "Her feet must have been at least size ten. She had brown wavy hair and thick, unplucked eyebrows. No makeup, no jewelry. Very plain and always dressed in pastel polyester pants and a floral print top. Scrubs, basically. I used to beg to go to see the nurse for the smallest paper cut. Once I even faked an injury to get sent to her. I just loved that woman. I loved her efficiency and the way she spoke soothingly to distract you from what she was doing. She was so gentle and compassionate. She made me feel cared for, cared about in a way I wasn't used to."

"You weren't used to being cared about? What about your grandmother?"

"I didn't live with her then, not until high school. When I knew Miss Ingalls, I lived with my aunt and uncle. They had a nice place and I liked it there, but they had kids of their own, so I was sort of the ugly stepsister."

"Ugly stepsister? I'm sure you were more like the beautiful and tragic Cinderella." Megan laughed. "Except for the shoes. Cinderella was all about the shoes." They both glanced at Jaye's feet nestled in their canvas slip-ons.

"They're comfortable." Jaye smiled a naturally self-deprecating smile that warmed Megan all the way through. "Yes, well, let's just say that as a kid I was a sucker for any woman who acted concerned about my welfare, and Miss Ingalls was such a woman."

"Did you ever tell her how you felt?"

"No. But I'm sure she knew because of how often I ran into her when she got off work, how I just happened to be leaving school the same time she was, having stayed late for one reason or another, so we could walk together to her car. I thought I was stealthy, but how could she not have known?"

"What happened?"

"Nothing. I went to high school and got over it. But I never forgot her." Jaye reached down to remove her ugly shoes. "It's late and I'm exhausted. Unless you need something, I'm ready to pack it in." She tucked her shoes under her bed.

"Sure you don't want to push the beds together?" Megan asked mischievously.

Jaye laughed dryly. "Dream on, Lizzie Lezzie!"

Megan chuckled, then turned off the light and got into bed. By the nightlight, she could see Jaye remove her bathrobe, hang it on the wall hook over the raincoat, then lie down in her bed. That was kind of a funny story about Miss Ingalls, she thought, stalked by a dreamy twelve-year-old girl with her phony illnesses.

Megan observed the shape of Jaye's figure as she turned on her side to face the wall. "Thank you for telling me about Lexie and Miss Ingalls and all that," she said.

"Sure," said Jaye sleepily. "Now I'm going to fall asleep, Megan, whether you're done talking or not."

"Okay. I hope Willie comes back tomorrow. And nothing bad happened to her."

"Me too. Good night."

Megan lay on her back, listening to the sounds of insects outside. There were so many things whirling around in her mind, she couldn't sleep. She knew she was attracted to Jaye and had been since their morning encounter in the elevator. That was why she was here. That was why she had been watching her, asking for absolution from her, wheedling a way to stay with her. She recalled how Jaye had asked her, obviously confused, why she would want to come work in the clinic when she could be out partying with her friends. She had come to the island paradise of Santuario to party, after all. She'd said the first thing she could think of that might make sense to Jaye, that she could earn some college credit. Even if she had wanted to answer truthfully, she would not have been able to articulate her feelings, not at that moment, and certainly not with Nathan Willett listening.

Because I want to be with you. Because I think you're wonderful and beautiful and I can't quit thinking about you.

If she had said these things to Jaye this afternoon, Megan was sure, she would not be lying six feet away from her this evening. Jaye was too wary of her.

Megan wasn't surprised to have these feelings for a woman. The question of her sexual orientation had plagued her for years, ever since she was fifteen when she and her best friend Kate ended up rolling around on her bed one evening, kissing and fondling one another.

If Megan's mother hadn't come in and caught her with Kate's tit in her mouth, who knows where that would have led. As it happened, Megan was sent to counseling to discuss what had led to this interesting behavior and why it would never be repeated. The counselor, Ken, as he wanted to be called, had been an easygoing, handsome young man who relied on a gentle version of scaring Megan straight. It was gentle enough, in fact, that she wasn't even aware at the time that it was his intention to turn her away from lesbianism. They had insightful, adult conversations about human sexuality and about Megan's goals in life, her aspirations for career, family, ultimate happiness. It seemed she had come to the conclusion all by herself that a homosexual lifestyle would not result in happiness, not for her and not for anybody she cared about. It made so much more sense to be straight. And so she had tucked her desires for women away somewhere inside, anxious to avoid all of the pitfalls and heartbreak of a deviant lifestyle. Ken had done his job well.

Her mother took down the Trish Indigo poster from her bedroom wall, apparently concluding that Indigo's oily, muscled thighs might have been about something other than sports. She also took Megan out of wrestling. Tussling with girls...maybe not, her parents concluded. She knew they watched her closely after that, looking for any evidence that she was turning lesbian. Her mother even forbade her from wearing plaid. She hadn't wanted to disappoint her parents and plunge them into suicidal despair, which was what she would be doing, Ken seemed to be saying, if she chose the wrong path. Through their quick and decisive action, her parents had helped her through that dangerous phase. They didn't want her to be gay, they said, because they wanted her to be happy. Being gay is a tough life. It's so much easier to be happy as a heterosexual. That had made sense to Megan back then. But the older she got, the less it made sense. How could you be happy living a lie? And how can you choose to be something you're not?

In the intervening years, she had found herself occasionally looking at a woman and remembering Kate, remembering how silky her lips were and how good it had felt to touch her. She wondered more and more if she was meant to be with women. She had spent the last six years wondering. Sometimes she was sure she was gay, sometimes just the opposite.

How did you know for sure? Some people were sure from birth, apparently. And others... Even Jaye, who had never slept with a man and had never wanted to, hadn't been convinced until she met Lexie.

One thing for sure, it was Jaye who was bringing up all these questions. There was no doubt Jaye was in her head...and rapidly advancing into her heart.

CHAPTER SEVENTEEN

"Make sure you eat a lot," Jaye cautioned, scooping up a forkful of scrambled eggs. "We probably won't have time to take a lunch break."

Megan sat down across from her with her own plate. "Thanks for letting me help out today."

"You might not be saying that by tonight. Besides, I should be thanking you." Jaye smiled at Megan, then took a sip of her coffee.

Wearing a plain blue smock with her paper name tag pinned to the front of it, Megan looked almost sedate today. That was probably going too far, Jaye mused. With that hairdo, multiple sets of earrings and those mischievous eyes, she still looked like trouble.

"How did you sleep?" Jaye asked.

"Not so great. Strange bed. A lot on my mind."

"What's on your mind?"

"The stuff we talked about last night." Megan put her fork down. "About your Miss Ingalls and how you finally figured it all out." She paused and watched Jaye eating her toast until Jaye became self-conscious and stopped.

"What about it?" she asked.

"I feel like that sometimes," Megan admitted. "I've mostly dated guys, you know. Well, only guys, actually. But, like, there was a girl when I was in high school. We sort of messed around a little bit one night."

"Did you like it?"

"Yeah, sure. It felt good."

"But nothing came of it."

"My mom caught us. My parents freaked out and sent me to counseling. You know the routine. Scared straight. Besides, I was just a stupid kid. I didn't know what I was doing or what I wanted. I wasn't ready then."

Jaye took another sip of coffee, giving herself a moment to consider Megan's angle. "But you think you might be ready now?"

"It might be fun," she said casually, her tone suddenly lighthearted. "A woman's gotta be good at it, right? She knows what buttons to push." Megan laughed.

Jaye regarded her without comment, then went back to her breakfast. She just couldn't figure Megan out, but she suspected she was being played somehow.

"I'm actually serious," Megan said. "I could be a lesbian. I've thought about it a lot."

"Anything's possible," Jaye said noncommittally. "Now hurry up and finish your breakfast. We've got ten minutes." She finished her eggs in one big bite, then took her plate to the sink.

Jaye wasn't sure what the breakfast true confessions was all about, or even if they were true. What was Megan up to? Was she trying to seduce Jaye, having sensed her attraction, for the challenge of it, or for the exotic pleasure? She wouldn't be the first straight woman to go that route. Or was it possible she was being sincere, that she was ambivalent about her sexuality and searching for answers? Had Jaye awakened some suppressed lesbian desires in her? She didn't know Megan well enough to answer any of these questions, but she had heard enough to be on guard.

She hadn't slept that well herself between worrying about Willie and being hyperaware of Megan in the other bed. Sleeping beside Megan was entirely different from sleeping beside Willie. Even in the beginning, before she knew Willie well, there had been no sexual tension between them. Willie didn't give off that kind of vibe. Besides, Jaye had buried her libido in a sad, dark place deep inside her. The first day, Willie had asked her if the sleeping arrangements would be uncomfortable for her. She had barely understood the question because her mind had been so far removed from all things sexual. She liked sharing a room with Willie. It was comfortable and comforting. In a small way, it was a fulfillment of one of her childhood fantasies—to have a sister. But having Megan so near during the night had felt completely different. It wasn't comforting. It was disturbing because it played havoc with her thoughts and invaded her dreams. Clearly, her libido was no longer buried in that sad, dark place. It had awakened and was rattling the cage.

She didn't want to think about Megan anymore. She was thankful for the havoc about to descend upon them. It would take her mind off both Willie and her seductive namesake.

Even before they had opened the doors, villagers had lined up to get their vaccinations. Jaye had dressed Officer Santos in light blue scrubs to assist as an orderly. He seemed pleased with his role. He would take care of logging everybody in on the computer with his two-finger typing. He could also assume Paloma's usual role of translator when Jaye's adequate but limited Spanish came up short. They had two electric fans going at full speed, one on either side of the room. Their supplies were neatly arranged for easy access. It looked like they were ready.

Jaye smiled reassuringly at Megan, then nodded at Santos and said, "Let's go."

He pulled open the door, greeting the bustling group of mothers with children with a hearty *"Buenos días!"*

Jaye didn't know how long the line was. She couldn't see out the door. But with their little assembly line, they went through patients at record speed. There was an endless swarm of fussy children, some of them crying, some of them screaming, and some of them pouting in big-eyed, silent distress. There were those who smiled and laughed as well, not the least bit troubled by the needle. And there were those who were so fascinated by all the noise and people and the unfamiliar surroundings that they never knew they'd been touched. Megan distracted the scared ones by making faces, giving them balloons and talking to them while she swabbed them with alcohol. Then Jaye delivered the shot. Megan covered the wound with a tiny bandage and handed out flyers with post-inoculation instructions in both Spanish and one of the more common Creole dialects.

While they stood in line, the mothers and the occasional grandmother or father, talked to one another or on their phones, balancing the littlest ones on a hip with one arm while they rapid-fired Spanish at some unseen listener. Some of them had enough kids in tow for a basketball squad. With the fussing, yelling and crying of the children and the loud talking and sharp-tongued reprimands of the parents, the room was bedlam.

But somehow, one by one, the kids got their shots, then filed back out, each of them sucking on a lollipop awarded them by Megan.

Jaye kept an eye on her, watching her cheering up children and wordlessly charming mothers. She seemed to be enjoying herself and Jaye could find nothing to fault her for. There was no grousing, no eye rolling and no smart aleck behavior. She worked like a professional. Jaye was both surprised and relieved.

About ten o'clock, Father Guerrero and one of the nuns from the orphanage filed in with a group of frightened kids. Before they left, Jaye got Santos and Perez to load their van with boxes of clothes they had collected. And so the day proceeded, getting hotter and more uncomfortable, but the job was getting done.

As she attended to another child, Jaye saw the Gallegos family at the head of the line. Juanita Gallegos, wearing a shapeless floral print dress, held her four-year-old, Luna, in her arms. Carmen Gallegos, seven, stood at her mother's side, waiting impatiently for her turn. Who knows how long they had been standing in line, Jaye thought. It seemed the entire village had already come through the clinic today, and it was clear from the records being generated that they had succeeded in bringing in children from miles away. Jaye was grateful she had not had to cancel, especially for the sake of those who had traveled to be here.

Carmen was tipping side to side, banging into her mother's hip every time she leaned to the left. Luna had her face buried in her mother's neck, so all Jaye could see of her was her thick brown hair and her cotton knit shirt, white with tiny black and red rocking horses all over it. As soon as they were done with the boy in the chair, Jaye thought, she would warn Megan about Luna's scars to prevent her from showing surprise. Luna was self-conscious enough as it was. She didn't need to be reminded by a startled young woman.

But just as Jaye was about to speak to Megan, Santos hollered at her from his station by the door. He seemed to be having an argument with an old woman.

"Señorita Northrup," he called, gesturing impatiently for her to come to his aid. "Can you explain this document to this lady, *por favor*? She does not believe what I am telling her."

"Just a moment, please," Jaye hollered back.

When she turned back to Megan, she saw that Mrs. Gallegos had already handed Luna off to her. Megan smiled into Luna's face and lifted her onto the stool, giving no indication that she was alarmed at what she saw. Luna's wounds had healed long ago, but they had left one side of her face permanently disfigured. Her mouth was crooked, downturned on the right side, and her right eye was nearly shut due to scar tissue.

"There you go, sweetheart," Megan said. "I like your shirt."

Megan knew that many of the kids didn't understand English, but she thought they would be cheered and calmed by the sound of her voice anyway. For the most part, she was right, but Luna never lifted her gaze, never looked at either of them while she submitted passively and silently to her injection. She didn't even look at Megan when she handed her a sucker. She simply curled her small fingers around it and reached for her mother, who smiled gratefully and said a quiet "*Gracias*." Then it was Carmen's turn. She was talkative and outgoing. She spoke

English well and kept up a conversation with Megan about the books she was reading in school. When the Gallegos family had gone, Megan turned to Jaye and asked, "What happened to the little one?"

"A house fire. She's got scars on her arm too. Her vision is perfectly okay, but she can barely see out of the right eye because of the scarring. That happened before I was here. Sad, isn't it? We've tried to draw her out, but she's already so self-conscious about her appearance."

"It's not that bad. It's not hideous."

"It is to her."

Jaye went over to Santos to resolve his problem. When she returned, Megan had a little boy ready for his shot. It was Carlos Baza, Junior. Mrs. Baza stood beside him, the bandage on her face covering her wound, her eyes nervously darting toward the door every few seconds. Her behavior suggested she expected her husband to burst in and tear the place apart, which put Jaye on edge. They definitely didn't need any more drama today. When she asked Carlos to be still and he did not instantly obey, his mother spoke sharply to him, bringing him to attention. He immediately quit fidgeting and submitted to his shot.

Jaye asked Maria how she felt, then removed the bandage to take a look. There was no sign of a problem. After getting a new bandage, Maria Baza and her son moved on.

"Why was she so nervous?" Megan asked quietly.

Jaye extracted a new needle from its plastic sheath. "My guess would be that her husband doesn't know she's here, and if he did, he wouldn't be happy about it."

"So he's out of jail already?"

"Probably."

"He may be an asshole, but why wouldn't he want his kid vaccinated?"

"It's not so much that. He just has a grudge against us. He thinks we're butting in where we don't belong and he wants nothing to do with us. He's not the only one. A handful of the villagers don't want us here. They resent outsiders. The men especially. Some of them feel threatened and emasculated by

American women who might give their wives ideas. And I've got to admit they might have a point. After all, I spent a half hour last night trying to persuade Maria Baza to have her husband arrested. I'm just glad Willie wasn't there when he muscled his way in. Given the grudge between those two, somebody might have ended up dead. But I loved the way you handled Baza last night."

"I think his wife did too. At least she had the guts to bring her son in today. That's pretty defiant, don't you think?"

Jaye nodded in agreement.

Megan didn't look anywhere near ready to stop talking, but they were suddenly hip-deep in a new family of kids.

* * *

The afternoon, like the morning, was horribly busy. There was no time to rest, only quick trips to the bathroom, and Megan began to wonder how and when they would close the doors. Her head was spinning with the events of the day, with so many kids and so many mothers, many of them younger than herself. Then there were the orphans with their matching hand-me-down shoes and poor little Luna whose face kept returning to Megan's thoughts. There was the busload from the coffee plantation, who seemed to trail the aroma of fresh-roasted coffee into the clinic with them. Most of all, there was Jaye. Megan could tell by the sweat on her brow and the way she shifted from one foot to the other that she was tired and hot and achy, but she smiled at every child and every mother and was always patient and kind.

At six o'clock, Jaye called over to Santos, "How many more out there?"

He left his desk to look outside. "*Viente*," he called back.

"Twenty," Jaye repeated for Megan's benefit. "Thank God."

They made it through the last of them in record time and even managed not to run out of suckers. When everyone was gone and the doors were locked, it was six forty.

Jaye put a hand on Megan's shoulder and gave it a squeeze. "Good work! Thank you."

Jaye's praise filled Megan with warmth. Not a flake anymore, she thought. She had won Jaye over, at least regarding her work ethic. As for the rest, Megan wasn't sure. She followed her into the kitchen where Jaye filled two glasses with ice water and handed one to her. Jaye swallowed a deep gulp.

Megan sat in a chair and pulled off her sandal, rubbing her sore foot.

"Now you understand about the shoes," Jaye remarked.

They exchanged a smile. "I had a good time today."

"Did you?" Jaye leaned against the counter. "It's a far cry from plastic surgery, though, isn't it? This is grunt work. I can understand why you'd choose something more glamorous, like making gorgeous people even more gorgeous."

"Well," Megan grinned, "if *you* ever walked into my office and asked me to make you more gorgeous, I'd say that was impossible."

Jaye looked askance at her, took another drink, then set down her glass.

Megan put her shoe back on and stood up. "You always look suspicious when I compliment you. But I mean it. I think you're hot. And I never thought I'd say this to anybody, but you're rockin' those scrubs."

Jaye looked unimpressed and unmoved, then she rolled her eyes and took another drink of water. Rolling her eyes maybe wasn't the most encouraging sign, but it could be worse. Megan willed up the courage to make a move. She stepped up to Jaye, who stiffened as her space was invaded. Megan took Jaye's cheek in her hand, then drew closer and kissed her on the lips, tenderly and briefly. Jaye's lips were cool from the water, soft and completely unresponsive. Not exactly the reaction Megan had hoped for, but at least she hadn't slapped her. Megan stepped back, feeling self-conscious. Jaye's eyes, with their amber and green sparks, looked almost angry.

"Why are you doing this?" she asked.

"Doing what?"

"Flirting with me. Coming onto me."

Megan laughed nervously. "Why do you think? I like you. You're gorgeous and smart and sexy. There's, like, some kind of chemistry between us. I felt it right away the first time we met. Actually, the second time, yesterday morning in the elevator. The first time, you know, I don't remember that much. I'm just really into you, which is weird for me, you know, because I've never felt this way about a particular woman before. I've fantasized about sex with women, in general. I mean, I've read *The Joy of Lesbian Sex* like twenty times all the way through." Jaye looked alarmed, but Megan couldn't stop herself. "But there's never been a particular woman I wanted to…I have these feelings, you know, in the pit of my stomach. You know what I'm talking about, right? It's like this crawling, gnawing…it makes you want to…" She held up both hands like claws, gritting her teeth, and noted the look of alarm growing on Jaye's face.

Damn, Megan thought, women are hard! All you've got to do to get a man to kiss you is smile once.

Jaye regarded her sternly, then shook her head. "This…" she gestured first at Megan, then at herself, "isn't happening. You gotta believe that."

"Why not? Is it because of Willie?"

"Willie?"

"Are you and Willie a couple?"

Jaye looked stunned. "No! Where'd you get that idea?"

"You two seem to be tight. I thought maybe that's why you haven't tried anything with me."

"Willie and I are just friends. That's nothing to do with it."

"Then why not?"

"Do you think lesbians are all sex maniacs who jump on any woman who wiggles her tail?"

"No. I don't think that. But I can tell you like me. I mean, you like my killer bod anyway." Megan posed with her chin over her shoulder in a way she had practiced in front of a mirror many times. She knew it was totally disarming. "I know you think I'm cute."

Jaye laughed bitterly. "Oh, yeah, you're cute, but it takes more than that to get me going. You've got the wrong woman. I know what you're after and I'm not interested."

"What am I after?"

"Fun. Sex. A walk on the wild side. I'm not going to be your spring fling." Jaye's eyes flashed with ominous intent. "So just forget it, baby dyke."

She breezed out of the kitchen and back to the front room with Megan following. Santos sat with his feet up on the desk, leaning dangerously far back in the desk chair, the stick of a sucker protruding from his mouth.

"Have you heard from Delgado?" Jaye asked him, her tone tinged with annoyance.

He pulled his feet off the desk, and the chair abruptly returned to its upright position, nearly flinging him out of it.

"*Sí*," he said, hopping to his feet. "She says nothing has been heard since yesterday. Nathan Willett is waiting for instructions from the kidnappers, but they have not called."

"God, I hate this waiting!" Jaye said. "Are the police out looking for her at all?"

"*Sí, por supuesto*. Yes, yes!" Understandably, Santos sounded defensive. He couldn't know that Jaye's annoyance was with Megan, not with him. "They are looking for the Jeep. They are showing her photo, asking everyone if they have seen her, if anyone knows anything. But many people do not want to get involved in police business."

Jaye looked disgusted, then must have realized she was taking her frustration out on the wrong person. "Thank you for all your help today, Officer Santos. It was very generous of you to volunteer."

"No problem. I like to keep busy. And now, if you do not need me, I will go into town for a little while. There is a fiesta tonight. You are both invited also. Do not worry. Perez will stay here, so the clinic will not be left unprotected. I will not be gone long."

"A fiesta?" Megan asked.

"*Sí*, everybody comes out and has a good time. They will have food and music and dancing. You should go."

"Oh, yes, I want to! Let's go, Jaye."

Jaye looked skeptical. "I don't know."

"It'll be fun. Come on."

"I don't really feel very festive."

"You mean because of Willie?"

Jaye nodded.

"I can understand how you feel," Megan said, "but it doesn't help Willie for you to sit around here worrying. We did a long day's work. We deserve a night out."

"Okay," Jaye relented. "But I don't want to stay out too late."

Megan changed her clothes, putting on a sleeveless top and sky-blue shorts, then touching up her hair. She unbuttoned another button on her blouse, still hoping that Jaye could be swayed. Though she said she wasn't interested, Megan didn't believe the heat between them was flowing in only one direction. The fact that she'd gotten upset after Megan kissed her was proof she was emotionally invested.

She examined herself closely in the bathroom mirror and involuntarily smiled. "How can she resist me?" she asked, giving the top of her head a quick fluff. "I'm adorbs."

CHAPTER EIGHTEEN

From what she'd overheard, Willie believed the ransom would be paid tomorrow. Then one of two things would happen. Either she would be released to return to her life, or she would be killed. She was sure it was the latter. A list of things she would now never do rushed nonstop through her mind. *I'll never jump out of a plane. I'll never go to Africa. I'll never see my mother again.* The idea that she might have less than twenty-four hours to live had put her emotions into a tailspin.

When the teenager brought in her dinner, she tried again to get him to talk to her. "Once you get the money from my father," she asked, "will you let me go?"

Characteristically, he did not reply, but she felt he understood her, so she didn't repeat her question in Spanish.

She knew she wasn't supposed to provoke her captors, but she was on the verge of panic. She also remembered that this young man, Eduardo, had stopped Miguel's attack on Paloma. Maybe he had done it out of compassion. Maybe there was some good in him.

"Why are you going to kill me?" she asked. "My family will pay the ransom. You'll get your money. There's no reason to kill me. I don't know who you are. I won't tell anybody anything. I couldn't if I wanted to."

He simply stared at her with his cold brown eyes. How could such a young man be so hard? she thought.

When he turned to leave her, she reached for his arm. He jerked away and spun around, scowling.

"Please don't let them kill me, Eduardo," she begged, keeping her voice low. "I can get you the entire ransom amount if you help me escape. Just for you. You won't have to share it with anybody. Get me out of here and you'll have more money than you've ever seen before. Believe me, I can get the money."

He regarded her silently and expressionlessly. "I know you can," he finally said, his voice soft, even pleasant. His eyes darted toward the door, reassuring himself that they were alone. "I told them to ask for a million, but they were afraid."

She caught her breath. "A million?" She gathered herself together, anxious to take advantage of the boy's willingness to talk. "Then you know I can make you rich."

"Yes, I know. But I don't want your money."

Willie heard the ghost of her own voice in his words. "I don't want your money." She had said that to her father more than once. Oh, God, she thought, I'm such a hypocrite! Just like my mother and her "cute white girl" sentiment.

When push comes to shove, she thought, noble principles get set aside. *I don't want his money…until I really need it.* She had always thought of herself as more ethical than her parents and a lot of other people just like them. Now she realized that she would use any amount of her family's money to save her own life. Yet there were people who came into the clinic, people who could be saved by a few thousand dollars, money she could have easily obtained. And she had let them go away without hope.

Willie thought of Jaye. She was sure she had thought about the Willett fortune, about how much good it could do. When Jaye had explained to Mrs. Alvaro that she had breast cancer and it could kill her if she didn't get treatment, Jaye knew, and

Mrs. Alvaro must have known too, that she couldn't possibly get treatment without help. Jaye put her on a waiting list for the hospital in San Vicente where a few doctors did pro bono work, but the longer she had to wait, the less likely she would survive. Willie wondered if Jaye blamed her for these people's suffering. But she couldn't save the whole world, even with her entire family fortune. There were too many people who needed help.

She stared into the chillingly accusing eyes of Eduardo. *I can't save everybody! I can't even save myself.*

She knew why she had turned down her father's money, for some high-minded ideals that had no more claim on reality than her earlier ideals about true love. But why would this boy turn it down? He was a criminal, already happy to take her father's money. It didn't make sense.

"Why?" she asked. "Why don't you want my money?"

He thrust out his chin and gazed at her with stony eyes. "Because I would not help you for any amount of money," he said in a near whisper. "Because of what you did to my sister. You deserve to die for that."

"What? Your sister? Do I know your sister? Was she a patient of mine? If there was a mistake, I can…"

His face turned ugly, so ugly it stopped her cold, then he strode out of the room. She sank to her knees on the floor. She tried to make sense of the boy's words, trying to remember anyone she might have harmed. But in the time she'd been here on the island, nothing had gone wrong, at least nothing she knew about, nothing serious enough to provoke such hatred. She'd treated a lot of teenaged girls. There could have been an infection that she didn't know about. But surely that didn't warrant kidnapping and killing her!

She had no appetite and didn't touch her dinner. Grady came in an hour later and taped her wrists together and took her plate away, but he said nothing, nor did she attempt to speak to him. She didn't even look at him. She felt despair, and as the evening wore on, she moved through a range of emotions from self-loathing to terror, sometimes concluding that she couldn't wait for them to kill her.

But as the night deepened, she was gradually able to overcome the depths of emotion and focus on her problem in a more lucid way. Even if there was a chance they wouldn't kill her, she decided, leaving it up to them seemed like a stupidly passive thing to do. Cooperation seemed more and more like the foolish choice with these men. She could sit here and let them kill her or she could take matters into her own hands. She thought through her options: suicide or escape. The former was not very appealing. The latter, not very likely.

There was one other way out, she realized. She might be rescued. At any moment, a SWAT team might bust through the doors of this building and whisk her to freedom. Were the police looking for her? Was the FBI on the case? She was sure Nate, Jaye and her parents would do anything they could to find her, but what could they do? Nobody knew where she was. They might have no idea who had taken her. She couldn't count on the police. If half of the horror stories Paloma told about the Santuarian police were true, looking to them for help would be the most loco thing of all.

She could count on only one person right now—herself. Even if escape was unlikely, it was worth a try. It was better than doing nothing. If she was ever going to make a move, it had to be tonight, because tomorrow was the end of this nightmare, one way or another.

CHAPTER NINETEEN

The festival was a casual, informal affair, neighbors out on the streets with musical instruments, singing and dancing. Jaye was used to these festivals. They were frequent occurrences here. She had heard that before the Spanish conquerors arrived, the Santuarians had a festival every twenty-three days. Their descendants in Tocamila might have had them beat.

Normally, Jaye came to fiestas with Willie, and that was one reason she'd been reluctant to come here with Megan. She was hesitant about letting Megan occupy any territory that belonged to Willie. It wasn't logical, she knew, just a gut feeling that Megan and Willie should remain in mutually exclusive worlds. That was most likely the reason she had reacted so strongly when Megan had suggested wearing Willie's lab coat. And tonight it was the reason she would steer Megan away from Willie's hands-down favorite treat at these celebrations— coconut rice pudding. Willie always ran right for it, even before the main course. Jaye knew it would have no bearing on Willie's enjoyment of the pudding if Megan sampled it, but out of some stubborn sense of loyalty, she didn't want to share Willie or her pudding with Megan.

The other reason she'd resisted going out tonight was that Megan was getting to her. After working with her all day and after that moment in the kitchen when Megan had kissed her… it had been touch and go. It had taken everything she had to keep from sweeping Megan into her arms and taking her right there. Jaye was wound up and on edge. Part of her wanted to run for her life. But a lot of her wanted to stay right there and keep looking into Megan's lively and seductive eyes.

They were well past hunger when they arrived at the chaotic town center where an ancient stone fountain poured water into a concrete pool. At the bottom of the pool, scattered on the blue and white tiles, were numerous small-denomination coins. Strung overhead were cords of naked lightbulbs illuminating the night. A man was cooking chicken on a barrel grill and a group of women sitting on a mat on the ground made tortillas.

"That looks good," Megan said, pointing to the grilled chicken.

"I want you to try a traditional dish," Jaye said. "Come on. It's the Santuarian version of pit-roasted pig, cooked in banana leaves with tamarind and cumin and chilis. I'm sure you'll like it."

The pork was served with tortillas, onions, roasted chilis and a side of fried yucca fritters. "Cerveza," Jaye instructed the woman handing over the food. She turned to Megan. "Two?"

Megan looked startled, then nodded. "I thought you didn't drink."

"Now and then," said Jaye, holding up two fingers to the server. "There's nothing better than a cold beer with spicy food. Besides, alcohol was Lexie's problem, not mine."

Jaye felt a little daring ordering beer. The truth was that she hadn't had a beer since coming to Santuario. Willie didn't drink, so alcohol wasn't a part of life at the clinic. That had suited Jaye just fine after all the battles over alcohol with Lexie. But tonight was different. She felt like having a beer.

They took their meals and found a low wall where they could sit, eat and watch children dancing to the music of a guitar.

Another young man accompanied the guitarist with a tinkling set of bells in one hand and a rattle in the other. Ear-jarring pops went off frequently as people set off firecrackers.

Emilio Sanchez, a local store owner, caught sight of them and snaked his way through the crowd. Emilio was easily recognizable with his striking head of white hair and characteristic limp, not to mention Cisco, the blue and gold macaw that traveled on his shoulder wherever he went. He took Jaye's hand in both of his and said how sorry he was to hear about Willie. If there was anything he could do, he offered, he was there to help. He loved them both, he said, like daughters. Jaye thanked him and introduced him and Cisco to Megan. Emilio spoke to her in Spanish until Jaye intervened. "She doesn't speak Spanish."

"Oh, I am sorry," he said good-naturedly. "Nice to meet you, Megan. I'm glad you came out this evening to enjoy our little fiesta. My grandson, he was one of the children you took care of today. He said a very pretty lady gave him candy. That must have been you."

"Yes, that was me. Nice to meet you too, Mr. Sanchez. You have a beautiful bird."

Emilio smiled and made a slight bow before leaving. Cisco spread his wings and squawked loudly as they moved on.

"He's a good guy," Jaye said. "One of the ones who's glad to have us here." She picked up her tortilla and took a sizable bite.

The pork was juicy, messy and delicious. Jaye glanced at Megan, whose leg was jumping to the music. A line of juice ran from one side of her mouth as she bit into her meat-filled tortilla. Jaye reached over with her napkin to wipe it off. With her mouth full, Megan laughed with her eyes and nodded a mute thank-you, then set her plate down on top of the wall. She hopped off to pick something up from the ground. "Look," she said, holding up a firecracker.

"Go ahead and set it off."

"Do you have a match?"

Jaye shook her head. "We'll find one."

Megan shoved the firecracker into her shorts pocket.

Finished with her food, Jaye tipped up her beer bottle and drank the last of it just as two little girls came by, the older one dragging the younger behind as she skipped. Jaye recognized Luna and her sister Carmen. Luna, as usual, was holding back, uncomfortable with the crowd. Jaye elbowed Megan to get her attention, jerking her head toward the girls.

Megan wiped her mouth rapidly with the back of her hand. "Luna! Carmen! Hola!" She waved at the girls, then beckoned toward them. Carmen skipped over, dragging her sister behind. "Are you having fun?" Megan asked them.

"Yes, we're dancing," Carmen replied. Luna half hid behind her and peeked out with one eye. Only the undamaged side of her face was visible, and Jaye noted how truly beautiful she was.

Megan slipped her phone from her pocket. "Let me take your picture."

"Why?" Carmen asked.

"Because you're beautiful girls and I want to remember you. Come, Luna, stand out here beside your sister so we can see you."

Carmen pulled Luna to her side. Luna stood stiffly with her arms at her side, a squinting frown on her face.

"Will you smile for me?" Megan urged. To illustrate, she grinned widely. Carmen did the same directly in front of her sister's face, demonstrating how to do it.

Seeing that Luna was determined not to smile, Megan transformed her face into something like a monkey, her head cocked to one side, her mouth spread wide, her eyes crossed, nose crinkled up. Not only did this make Luna smile, but it made Jaye break into spontaneous laughter. Megan snapped the photo. "*Gracias, bonita muchachas!*"

When the girls had gone, Megan looked at the photo, zooming in on Luna's face, her demeanor serious.

"What're you going to do with that?" Jaye asked.

"Send it to my mother. See if she knows somebody who'd be willing to help. She knows people. Like the cosmetic surgeon I told you about. She could probably talk somebody into doing it for free."

"That's thoughtful of you, Megan, but it takes a lot of effort to arrange for something like this. Chances are Luna would need multiple surgeries, and even if the surgeon's fee was waived, there would still be expenses."

"I know. But I can ask. Maybe they can find a doctor here in Santuario. If there's a doctor who's willing to do it, I could make it happen. I'm actually pretty good at making things happen."

Jaye recalled how Megan had earlier said she was good with kids. That had turned out to be true. Jaye was beginning to think Megan was good at a lot of things. She observed her earnest face and believed her, believed at least that she wanted to help. But she didn't know how complicated something like this would be. The actual surgeries might turn out to be the easy part. This was the first time Jaye believed Megan wasn't thinking of herself at all. Maybe she was redeemable.

Megan held the phone up and snapped a picture of Jaye. "*Gracias, bonita muchacha*," she said.

She's a charmer, Jaye thought, feeling lucky that she had managed to resist those charms. Megan was just toying with her. She wanted a lesbian, that's all, any lesbian. She didn't care about Jaye. She barely knew her. All she cared about was that Jaye was attractive and exciting, a woman who could help her learn about her own desires. Megan wanted to use her. There was nothing evil about that, Jaye decided, not if they were both willing and both knew the score. She didn't blame her for being curious and wanting the experience, but there was nothing in it for her. One night of passion?

She glanced at Megan beside her, at the soft curve of her cheek and the row of hardware decorating her ear. She too was attractive and exciting. Am I being an idiot? she asked herself. It would be so easy to give her what she wants. And nobody would be hurt, would they? Would I? After the heartbreak of Lexie, she was afraid of what her heart would want. She could already feel herself softening toward Megan. She was already feeling more than physical desire. She couldn't let that develop into something deeper. This young woman, brought into her life in such an odd way, would be out of her life forever in a day or two. It would be so much better if she walked away as nearly a stranger.

"What do we do for dessert?" Megan asked, putting her phone away. "I think I saw some pastries."

"Have you had the hot chocolate they make here?"

Megan shook her head.

"You have to try it!"

Jaye led the way to a station where steaming mugs of dark liquid were being handed out. She took two and walked them back to Megan, noticing Carlos Baza, Senior, leaning against a wall and staring in Megan's direction, his expression full of contempt. Jaye was sure Megan hadn't seen him. Just as well. Baza must have felt her looking at him because he shifted his gaze to meet Jaye's eyes with the same glare of contempt. Feeling a momentary chill, she rethought the possibility that he had something to do with Willie's disappearance. She tore her eyes away from him and stepped over to Megan, handing her the mug.

"Be careful. It's hot."

"Ummm," said Megan after tasting it. "This is so good. So rich and...oh, it changes after you swallow. Is there something spicy in there?"

"Yes." Jaye tasted the brew. "Good, isn't it?"

"It's awesome. Hardly sweet at all."

"Nothing like the kids' stuff back home."

After drinking their chocolate, they walked a little further in the direction of the music. A firecracker suddenly went off right beside Megan and she jumped sideways, crashing into Jaye. Jaye grabbed her by the shoulders and they found themselves in a loose embrace. Having Megan in her arms felt really nice. She had to order herself to let go. Megan smiled meaningfully before stepping away.

When they reached the source of the music, they found a circle of people watching a group of women dancing. They wore vividly colorful cotton dresses and flowers in their hair. They followed a stepping routine that reminded Jaye vaguely of line dancing. Outside of the dancing area, two men provided music, one with a wooden flute and one with a drum. The young man on the drum also sang sporadically, as if narrating the dance, but the song was in one of the native dialects and Jaye didn't understand it. Four of the women raised their arms to form a pair of arches, stepping in place, and a fifth passed under the arches.

Emilio Sanchez, Cisco still on his shoulder, was watching the dance. Jaye edged up next to him and asked, "What is the meaning?"

"It's a traditional folk song," he said. "A wedding dance. The bride celebrates her nuptials."

After an orderly routine in which the "bride" went through the "arches" and raised her arms in joy and thankfulness, the drum grew louder and the flute played faster, and one by one, some of the bystanders joined the dance, whereupon it became more disorderly. Cisco seemed a little nervous, or perhaps he was dancing, as he stepped first one way, then the other, moving back and forth over Emilio's shoulder.

"Now it is the reception, more or less," explained Emilio. "Everybody can dance."

"Can I dance?" Megan asked eagerly.

"Of course. Anybody."

"Come on, Jaye."

"You go ahead," Jaye urged with a brush of her hand. She and Willie never joined in. They just watched.

"You're coming too," Megan said, grabbing Jaye's wrist and yanking her into the circle.

Megan let herself go, doing her own version of the dance. She looked ridiculous, but happy. She nodded encouragement at Jaye, a wide grin on her face.

Jaye did her best to imitate the basic steps of the dancers. She felt awkward, but she could tell that Megan was delighted to see her dancing. It was soon apparent that a lot of other people were too. They weren't used to foreigners joining their festivities in this off-the-tourist-charts town. Jaye saw and heard the giggles of the girls in the wings. Old men were clapping and grinning, watching the young women with pleasure. Jaye hoped Megan's gyrations, which resulted in a pronounced bounce of her bosom, wouldn't throw any of them into cardiac arrest.

When the music finally stopped, Jaye was winded. The crowd dispersed and Megan came up and took her arm, squeezing it and leaning into her. Jaye relaxed, enjoying the pressure of Megan's body against her.

"That was fun," Megan said.

"It was."

Megan picked up an abandoned plumeria blossom from the wall of the fountain. She sniffed it, looked up at Jaye and smiled. Then she reached up and tucked the flower behind Jaye's ear. Megan had been really fun to be with tonight, Jaye thought. She didn't seem to be actively flirting anymore, not in the affected way she had earlier. She was no longer the self-aware seductress. Now she seemed more natural and more sincere, more like a woman out for a fun evening, and Jaye found herself responding warmly to the change.

"It's time we went back," Jaye said, "don't you think?"

Megan nodded, then remembered something. "Oh, but not before I make a wish." She opened a change purse and extracted a fifty-centavo coin, closed her eyes for a moment, then tossed it into the fountain. She smiled brazenly at Jaye. "Want to know what I wished for?"

"I think I can guess."

They walked back in the dark, saying good night to everyone they encountered, until they were walking alone, the noise of the revelers subsiding behind them. Except for the stars and the moon, the road was dark. Megan still clung to Jaye's arm, and they walked side by side, bumping against one another playfully. Jaye was aroused, the tension mounting in her body. She no longer cared to resist, and now that she had changed her mind, her thoughts were racing well ahead of them along the road.

When they passed an ancient rock wall that marked the last bend in the road before the clinic, she grabbed Megan and pulled her behind the wall into the cover of trees and vines. She brought her up close to her body and tasted her mouth tentatively. Her lips were soft and sweet. Jaye savored Megan's mouth, kissing her more hungrily. Megan held on and pressed close against Jaye's body, her mouth, like the rest of her, eager and willing, offered up with an endearing responsiveness. Jaye placed her hand on the small of Megan's back and brought their hips tightly together, sending a surge of desire rocketing through her limbs.

"Is this what you wished for?" Jaye whispered close to her ear.

"Yes!"

Jaye cradled Megan's face in her hands. Her eyes sparkled like the night sky. She kissed her again, thinking that Megan had wasted her wish, wishing for something that was destined to happen anyway.

Kissing Jaye was a dream come true, but it wasn't exactly what Megan had wished for at the fountain. She didn't want to tell Jaye what she had really wished for—not that Jaye would kiss her, but that Jaye would fall in love with her. She'd never met anybody like Jaye and had never felt so close to someone so quickly. And now that their lips were burning against one another's, she was completely convinced that Jaye was the answer to every question she'd ever had about love.

Jaye planted a series of kisses down Megan's neck, sending her soaring, then returned to her mouth where she made it clear that she was excited and impatient. Just the thought of Jaye's hands on her bare skin lit Megan's body on fire. She couldn't wait to be naked in her arms.

"Let's go home," Jaye whispered, her breath hot against Megan's ear.

CHAPTER TWENTY

Willie had been sitting in the same spot for hours, lost in her thoughts and mostly unaware of what was happening in the house. Now that she'd made up her mind to escape, she remained where she was for fifteen, twenty minutes, listening. There was no sound. Maybe everyone was asleep already. After drinking beer all day, her captors might have gone down for an early night. She didn't know what time it was, she realized. It might be midnight or two in the morning or nearly dawn.

With her wrists taped together, she maneuvered her body with difficulty to the spot where she had hidden the razor. She blindly searched for it, then extracted it from its hiding place. She carefully removed the blade, holding it between her thumb and forefinger. Working behind her back, she began the process of cutting the tape. It was an awkward position and she could get no good angle, but she felt the blade connect with the tape a few times, and she gradually found a hand position that led to small successes. On one swipe of the blade, she felt a sharp pain across her wrist. She'd cut herself. Maybe I'll end up slicing my wrists open by accident, she thought ironically. She felt the sticky wetness of blood on her hand, but it didn't seem to be a gusher. She continued making minute cuts through the tape until she was finally able to pull hard enough to rip it through the rest of the way. With her hands free, she was able to quickly remove the tape completely. She got up and stood by the window to examine the cut on her wrist by moonlight. It wasn't serious. The bleeding from the smooth-edged wound had already stopped. She stood and stretched her arms gently, popping her sore shoulders.

So far, so good, she thought, stepping silently to the closed door. She listened, her palm pressed against the wood. There was a man breathing deeply on the other side of the door, low to the floor. She thought she could feel vibrations each time he exhaled. She decided he must be lying against the door. That was a complication. She didn't know where the other two men were or if they were as gone to the world as this guy, but she hoped they had all enjoyed their party with equal enthusiasm and were all in a deep beery slumber. If one of them was on watch, she would have no chance.

She took two bobby pins from her hair and spread them both fully open. If she were methodical, patient and quiet, she believed she might be able to unlock the door. When she was a kid, she and her brother had played private eye on many occasions, and they had become surprisingly good at picking locks like this one. It was a skill she had not used in a long time, but one she had never forgotten.

She removed the plastic from the ends of each pin. After bending the end of one to a ninety-degree angle, she began to work. With one tool in the top of the lock, she wiggled the other one in the bottom, working the lock pins one by one. The job was made more difficult by her far-sightedness. Without her glasses, close-up work like this was rendered imprecise by the blur factor.

Each click or scrape made by her actions caused Willie to hold her breath, listening for any response. She knew the noises she was making seemed much louder than they actually were.

The process seemed to take an excruciatingly long time, but she was finally able to turn the top pin, smoothly drawing in the latch bolt and freeing the door.

She bit her bottom lip, then gripped the doorknob solidly. There was nothing holding the door shut except the toe of her shoe pressed against the bottom. On the other side of the door, a heavy solid object pressed inward. She could feel the opposing force on her foot. She moved her toe a quarter inch to allow the door to open just a sliver, pushed by the man sleeping against it. The hallway was lit only by filtered light coming through a small window in the bathroom opposite. She could see the man through the narrow slit, huddled on his side on a mat with his back against the door, snoring peacefully. His bulk identified him as Grady. He had apparently trusted no one else with guarding her. Under his head was a case-less pillow. From the angle of his body, she didn't think he would pitch backward when she opened the door further, but to be sure, she moved the door cautiously inward. Grady moved with the door about an inch, and then the door moved free of him. He remained on his side, sputtering a couple of times before resuming his snore.

Pulling the door open further, she listened to the house. There was no light on and no sound of movement. Outside she heard the familiar cadence of insects, familiar but seeming much louder than normal. Her hearing was on high alert. A rifle stock was visible under Grady's right knee. He was sleeping on top of his gun. No chance of taking that without moving him, she decided.

She planned her step over the sleeping man with precision, first rolling up the legs of her pants to minimize the chance of brushing against him. Her heart pounded almost audibly as she took the step, aided by a firm grasp on the doorframe. She cleared him cleanly, then stood in the hallway, suspended by fear and the thrill of having gotten this far.

When at last she got the courage to take another step, the floorboard creaked under her weight. She froze again, wondering how smart it would be to make a mad dash for the front door and hope to outrun them. But if the door was locked, she'd be delayed in the front room where the other two would have her cornered.

As tempting as it was to bolt, she opted for stealth and edged along the wall of the hallway, finding the floorboards less noisy closer to the wall. When she had nearly reached the front room, she thought she heard a voice and froze, backed up against the wall like a plank. The sound of wheezing reached her. At least one of the others was sleeping in the front room. The house was dark, but there was enough moonlight through windows to see doorways, and she cautiously passed through one into the main room. Now she could hear the wheezing more distinctly, but nothing else. She couldn't see anyone, only large shapes and shadows. It was still possible there was a third man awake and on guard somewhere. He might even be sitting across the room right now, watching her. A chill ran up her spine, then crawled across the top of her skull.

With her next step, she imagined, she would hear the strike of a match and see it flare into a flickering flame that revealed the self-satisfied face of Miguel looking directly at her. Though she was not far from the front door, this image drove her to choose the kitchen as her flight route. It was a few paces to the left. She again resisted the urge to run and took a tentative step. There was no flare of a match, no indication that anybody was aware of her.

She took another step, then reached for the doorframe and stepped lightly into the kitchen, glancing quickly into its interior to make sure she was alone. The room smelled of onions, the remnants of dinner.

This room had more light than the living room because of an uncovered window in the door. Standing just eight feet from that door, Willie felt incredibly excited to think that freedom lurked on the other side. Still, that eight feet seemed like an extraordinarily difficult distance.

When at last she was able to make her move, she quickly and lightly crossed the width of the room, relieved that her progress was silent. Through the window in the door, she could see the bare dirt of the yard and the blackness of the jungle behind it.

She saw nothing else, nobody sitting on the back stoop with a rifle across his knees. She took hold of the handle of the door, then rotated the dead bolt slowly with her thumb and forefinger until she felt it pull free. Then she turned the knob and made one swift motion to put herself on the other side of the door. She stood in the balmy night air with nothing overhead but the vast open blackness of space and its billions of twinkling lights. She was free. She could breathe!

Like a rabbit released from a trap, she waited for a second on the steps, her heart pounding fast, before she could make herself move. In the moonlight, she saw a glint of metal in the tangle of vegetation, reminding her that the Jeep was parked there. She ran to it, knowing that her best chance of reaching safety was with a vehicle. She checked the ignition, which was empty. She opened the glove compartment, but found no key. Maybe she should have looked around in the kitchen for the key before she came out here. Without a key, what use was a vehicle? Her dubious private eye skills did not include hot-wiring a car. She opened the passenger side door and slid into the seat, checking above each of the visors, knowing that there was almost no chance the key was anywhere in the vehicle. She had been in such a hurry to get out of the house, she hadn't formed a logical plan. She hadn't stopped to think things through. It was just like her to do that. Now what?

She glanced at the house, at the door she had just escaped through. The key might be hanging on a hook in the kitchen. Or tossed on the counter. Everybody tossed their keys on the counter, didn't they? She hadn't even thought to look. Now she was certain the keys were right there inside the door. She could go back, just to the kitchen, and grab the keys. It would take only a couple of minutes. The thought made her almost sick to her stomach, but that key could easily make the difference. No matter what they did after she left, with a vehicle she would have a huge head start. By the time they got organized, she'd be back in Tocamila with Jaye.

She sat on the seat with her feet on the ground outside, imagining arriving at the clinic where Jaye would grasp her thankfully in her arms and she would be safe. It seemed so long ago that she had been wrenched from her home. She was reminded of poor Paloma, shouting bravely at them and leaping at Grady like a puma. But she had been nothing to him and Miguel had easily overpowered her, pulling her free of Grady, then felling her with one blow. Willie had seen her go down and strike her head against her car before she lay still on the ground. She didn't know how badly she'd been hurt.

Money, she thought bitterly. All of this was for money. Willie sat with her head hung down, momentarily brought to despair at the thought of how greed ruled the world. A part of her—not a small part—pulsed impatiently to walk back into the house, take a gun off one of those sleeping bastards, and blow them all to hell.

She was roused from her fantasy by a frantic male voice yelling inside the house. A light came on and she knew her escape had been discovered. She leapt from the Jeep into the jungle foliage and ran, stumbling, palm fronds whacking her face, running blindly, fleeing in a wild panic.

CHAPTER TWENTY-ONE

Jaye was flooded with heat, pulling Megan closer and deepening their kiss. With her eyes closed and her arms full of this sensuous woman, she forgot that her best friend was missing and that a police officer was sitting outside in the dark smoking a cigarette. The only thing she was aware of was the sublime sensation of Megan's skin against hers. She kissed Megan's neck, her face, her eyes, and tongued the rings along the edge of her ear.

They crowded close together in Jaye's narrow bed, exploring one another's bodies with their mouths and hands, caressing, kissing, arousing one another into a haze of heated desire.

"What do you like?" Jaye asked.

"I don't know. Everything…anything you want to do. I trust you."

Making love to Megan was so satisfying. Her body came alive wherever Jaye's fingers touched. It had been so long since she had felt like this, engulfed by desire. She wanted to touch Megan everywhere, to reach her depths, to show her what loving a woman was all about.

When Jaye's hand reached for the moist center of her, Megan let out a small cry, then threw her head back on the pillow. Jaye watched her face, how she tensed up, bit her lip, then relaxed and became one with the rhythm of her touch. When Jaye slipped inside the warm depths of her, she moaned low and pushed her deeper, wanting more.

"Ummm," Jaye murmured, feeling her own body tingling in response.

Megan bucked against her, her arms locked like a vise around her shoulders, while Jaye focused her touch on the pleasure point. Megan was slippery and anxious. She too had been more than ready for this. She was nearly whimpering. Then, quite suddenly, she curled up and muffled her scream against Jaye's shoulder. Jaye collected her and lay beside her, embracing her tenderly.

Megan turned on her side and snuggled close into Jaye's body while Jaye stroked her hair.

"That was incredible," Megan whispered. "Oh, God, that was the best ever, I swear."

Jaye kissed her lightly. "You might want to hold off on the ratings for a while."

"What do you mean?"

"I'm not done with you by a long shot."

Megan giggled and pressed her face into Jaye's chest. Jaye held her closer. She closed her eyes and breathed deeply, feeling incredibly satisfied just lying next to this woman, savoring the moment and anticipating what was coming next.

CHAPTER TWENTY-TWO

Megan woke sometime in the middle of the night, her body pressed against Jaye's back. She put her cheek on Jaye's shoulder, enjoying the gentle sound of her breathing and thinking about the delicious night in her arms. Wow! Just wow! All of that coolness Jaye exhibited to the world, it meant nothing. Jaye was a passionate lover. Megan's body vibrated with the memory of her touch.

The only light in the room was from the nightlight near the door and the sliver of moonlight in the gap between the curtain panels covering the lone window. Except for the sound of nocturnal animals, everything was silent. She fell asleep again and slept soundly for several hours until she woke to sunshine coming through the window and the sound of movement in the kitchen. Jaye was gone. Megan stretched luxuriously, then pulled on sweats and a T-shirt and went to the kitchen where Jaye stood at the counter in capris and a sleeveless blouse. Megan went up to her and encircled her in her arms. They kissed, causing an immediate blaze of desire to spark in Megan. She couldn't even look at Jaye without a physical reaction in her gut.

Smiling mischievously, Jaye handed her a coffee mug. "Haven't you had enough?"

"You'd think." Megan sat down with her coffee. She glanced at the wall clock, noting that it was already after nine. "Have you been up long?"

"No. This is my first cup."

A knock on the back door startled them both.

"Señoritas, it is me, Santos."

Jaye unlocked and opened the door. Santos stuck his head in.

"*Buenos días*," he said. "You slept in this morning, *sí*?"

"It was a rough night," Jaye said, her lip curling up on one side in an aborted smile.

"Oh, *sí*, your mind, it is full of worry." He shook his head sympathetically.

"Do you and Perez want coffee or something to eat?" Jaye offered.

"No, no. We have been already to breakfast. *Gracias*. I am here to tell you Inspector Delgado is on her way here. She will be arriving in about an hour."

He ducked back out and Jaye shut the door.

"Do you think he and Perez were in their van last night doing what we were doing in here?" Megan grinned.

"My guess would be no." Jaye sat across from Megan and drank her coffee.

"This coffee's great." At a tone from her phone, Megan looked at it. "Text from my mother," she said. "She's put out some feelers about Luna. She says there's a plastic surgeon in Cancún she might be able to lean on. That's close, right?"

"Yes. Not far at all. If a person had a boat." Jaye sounded skeptical.

"I know, I know. Logistics and all that."

Jaye nodded.

"Don't sweat it. First we get a doctor. We'll figure the rest out later."

"I hear you're good at making things happen."

"Exactly!" Megan chuckled. "Look what I made happen last night."

Jaye smiled self-consciously.

Megan read the rest of the message from her mother and laughed. "Look out for jellyfish, she says."

"Jellyfish?"

"She thinks I'm still in Punta Larga." Megan shrugged. "I sort of promised I'd stay at the resort." She typed a message back to her mother.

"What are you telling her?" asked Jaye.

"That I haven't seen a single jellyfish so far today."

Jaye pressed her lips together in an expression of disapproval, but it melted almost immediately into an amused smile.

"I wish Delgado wasn't coming," Megan said. "Then you and I could spend the whole day in bed together."

"Seriously? You may be on vacation, but I'm not."

"Oh, Jaye, loosen up. Nobody punches a clock in the tropics. If the fish are biting, you close up shop."

"That's so true…if you're a local. But that isn't how this place operates. We're open every day, all day, except Sunday, and we're open Sunday when needed. We'd probably be open Sunday regularly except Willie thinks it's good public relations to follow the local customs." Jaye turned thoughtful, staring into her coffee cup as if she had left the premises.

"What're you thinking about?" Megan asked.

Jaye looked up, a distant smile on her lips. "I was just thinking about Willie, wondering if she's scared or hurt or…alive."

Megan reached over and covered her hand with her own, squeezing it reassuringly. Then she put down her cup, moved behind Jaye and leaned over her shoulder. She kissed her softly behind the ear. Then she kissed her neck. Jaye leaned her head to the side in response. Megan kissed her collarbone. Jaye reached up and pulled Megan to her side, drawing her down for a kiss on the mouth. They kissed hungrily, then Jaye rose from the chair and the two of them stood close together in one another's arms, kissing with increasing passion.

"Sure you don't want to go back to bed?" Megan murmured. She ran her index finger around the waistband of Jaye's pants, stopping at the button, which she pushed open with her thumb and forefinger. She covered Jaye's mouth with her own again, kissing her anxiously, then sucking her tongue while she unzipped her pants. She slipped her hand between them, her fingers passing over Jaye's soft fur. Jaye kissed her deeply, gripping her shoulders, and Megan opened her up and felt for her wetness. Jaye released her mouth and moaned.

"I want to go down on you again," Megan said, gently stroking with her fingers.

Jaye leaned her head back. "You like that, don't you?"

"Uh-huh." Megan ran her tongue along Jaye's neck while her hand moved further into her depths.

Jaye leaned back against the counter, looking beautifully submissive with her eyes half closed, her mouth open. Megan knelt before her and was about to yank her pants down when the sound of a vehicle out front captured her attention. Car doors shut and voices reached them faintly.

Both of them bolted to attention.

Jaye zipped her pants. "Delgado already?" she asked, buttoning the top button. "Didn't Santos say an hour?" She dashed into the front room.

It turned out it wasn't Delgado after all. Two young women dressed similarly in light-colored pants and blouses were standing on the front porch, one of them arguing heatedly with Officer Santos, shaking her fist at him and cursing him in Spanish. His features were drawn into a resentful scowl, knitting together his eyebrows so the scar completely disappeared. As soon as the woman saw Jaye, she stopped cursing, her features softened and she turned to embrace her. The other woman stood placidly to the side. She was lanky with an oval face, large sable eyes and a short, pixyish haircut.

"Ah, Señorita Northrup," Santos said. "These ladies have come to visit you, but they will not show me their identification."

"It's okay," Jaye said. "This is Paloma Marra and this, I believe, is Sofia Mendoza."

Sofia nodded and Paloma grinned with self-conscious pleasure.

"They're my friends, but thank you for being so vigilant."

Santos said something under his breath as he withdrew. Jaye invited the women inside, then said, "Are you okay, Paloma? Are you in pain?"

"I'm fine," she said. "It only hurts when I breathe." She chuckled, then winced. "Or laugh."

Sofia winced in sympathy.

"Oh, look!" said Paloma, her eyes connecting with Megan's. "It's the girl on TV! Look, Sofia."

"You're right," Jaye said. "This is Megan."

"The other Megan," Paloma acknowledged. "What's she doing here?"

"That's a long story," Jaye said light-heartedly. "But she's been here since Monday night. She helped me with the vaccinations. Megan, this is Paloma and her girlfriend Sofia."

Megan waved.

"How did it go yesterday?" Paloma asked.

"Awesome."

Paloma turned to Megan. "Thank you for helping Jaye. This was an important day and I was so sorry I couldn't be here."

"No problem," Megan said. "It was a blast. Sorry about what happened to you."

"Oh, it's nothing," Paloma said. "I'm much better already."

"Come on in," Jaye said. "We were just having coffee." She glanced toward Megan, who grinned, thinking about what they had been doing moments ago.

"No, thank you, Jaye," said Paloma, looking troubled. "I must speak to you right away."

"Sure. Let's sit down."

Paloma pointedly shut the front door, then she regarded Megan thoughtfully. "I would like to speak to you alone. It's about Willie."

Jaye reached over and put her arm around Megan. "You can trust Megan, Paloma." Jaye kissed Megan's cheek.

A flicker of understanding appeared in Paloma's eyes, then she smiled. The four of them sat at a table furthest from the front door. Paloma seemed nervous and uncertain. Sofia nudged her with a nod of encouragement.

"What is it?" Jaye asked.

"It may be nothing. But ever since that day, I've been hearing his voice and thinking about it."

"Whose voice?"

"The man, the kidnapper who stopped the other one from hitting me. He said only a few words and then I blacked out. I wasn't sure I heard what I thought I heard. I didn't know if it was a dream. His voice…"

Sofia wrapped herself around Paloma's arm comfortably.

"Did you recognize his voice?" Jaye asked.

Paloma nodded and lowered her gaze. "He sounded like my brother."

Jaye drew back. "Your brother Eddie?"

"I could be wrong," Paloma added quickly. "I pray to God I'm wrong. But I've been thinking about it ever since. And nobody's seen him for almost a week. I texted him and left voice mail, but he doesn't answer." She placed her phone on the table, looking at it with disappointment. "At first, I tried to call him because I thought he might be able to help us find Willie. He might know something because it's his job to know what's going on. But then when he didn't answer me at all, I started to worry."

"Does he usually answer?"

"Yes. He always answers texts. Our phone plan has unlimited texting." She laughed shortly. "I gave him my old phone and he's on my account. It's cheaper for us both that way."

Jaye placed a hand on Paloma's arm to keep her focused. "Paloma, you said you and Eddie are close, despite the trouble he's gotten into. You said he's protective of you."

"Yes, he is. I know he's done some bad things, but he always treats me well. And Mama too."

"Then why would he put you in such danger? Why would he be a part of something where you might be hurt or killed?"

"Don't you see? I wasn't supposed to be here. It was Sunday. I don't work on Sunday. He thought I was home with the family." Her lip quivered. "I can't believe he would do something like this. It wasn't him. It couldn't have been. If only he would answer my texts."

"Paloma, does your brother know about Willie's family, that they're rich?"

She shrugged. "I talk about you and Willie sometimes, but I don't think I ever said anything about her family. You know she doesn't talk about them herself."

"No. But it's the sort of thing that would be easy to find out."

"If he's involved," Paloma said firmly, "then she is safe. He would never hurt someone I care about. He wouldn't do anything like that."

Jaye glanced at Megan, communicating her troubled thoughts silently.

Megan stepped forward. "You said he has your old phone?" she asked. "Is it a smartphone?"

"Yes, it's the one before this." She held up her phone. "I'm one of those tech nerds, you know, that has to have the latest." She laughed self-consciously.

"Do you have an online account where you register your phones?"

Paloma looked confused. "I…maybe. Yeah, I think I know what you mean."

Megan smiled at Jaye. "Maybe there's a way to find Eddie… if his phone is on."

She asked Paloma to log in to her account on the computer. As she did so, the three of them crowded behind her to watch the screen. When she displayed her devices, there were two phones and a tablet computer listed.

"Choose Eddie's phone," Megan instructed.

Paloma selected it.

"Now click the button that says 'Find My Phone.'"

"What is this?" Jaye asked.

"It's a tracking app for a lost phone. If you register your phone like this, then you lose it or somebody steals it, you can locate it through this software. It uses the GPS receiver in the phone, as long as the phone isn't turned off."

They waited impatiently until a map finally appeared on screen. A blinking blue dot also appeared to the southwest of Tocamila.

"It worked!" Megan said.

"That's got to be less than an hour from here," Jaye pointed out.

"That's where Eddie is," Megan said. "Or at least that's where his phone is."

"Maybe Willie's there too," Jaye said hopefully.

"What are we going to do?" Paloma asked.

Jay placed both hands on Paloma's shoulders. "There's only one thing we can do with this information."

Paloma turned to stare at Jaye momentarily before saying, "Oh, no, no, no!" She got up from the chair. "You can't give it to the police. They'll go in there and kill everybody. They'll kill Eddie."

"What do you think we should do?" Jaye asked her. "This information could save Willie's life."

"Jaye, Eddie wouldn't hurt her. He knows how important she is to me. He knows we're good friends. He was telling my father a couple of weeks ago how much I admire Willie and how working for her has meant so much to me." She chuckled nervously. "I think he was a little jealous even. He told our father that his sister was trying to be like these American women. He was worried about me."

"Worried how?" asked Jaye.

"Oh, it was nothing. What could it be? That I read too much *People* magazine? That Willie has got me hooked on Arizona iced tea? It's nothing. Just little things. Nothing anybody would take seriously. My father wasn't concerned at all."

Jaye and Megan both looked from Paloma to her girlfriend at the same time, no doubt arriving at the same thought simultaneously, that there was one lifestyle change Paloma had picked up recently that might trouble her family. Sofia stood up straighter, seeming to read their minds. "Nobody knows," she said quietly.

Paloma looked alarmed. She clamped her hand over her mouth, her eyes wide.

"You said he was a *halcon*," Jaye remarked. "His job is to see and hear everything. Maybe he doesn't just watch the police and the rival gangs."

Paloma sank back into the chair. Sofia moved closer and put her arms around her shoulders.

"I'm very sorry, Paloma," said Jaye. "But Willie's life is in danger. We have to use this information."

The sound of crunching gravel told them a vehicle had arrived outside.

"That must be the inspector," said Jaye. "Paloma?"

Paloma looked up, tears forming in her eyes, and nodded fatalistically.

CHAPTER TWENTY-THREE

Santos drove, Delgado beside him in the passenger seat. All that was visible of her from the backseat was her hair, frizzed out to a glorious, shimmery black disk that obscured most of Jaye's view through the windshield. Megan had volunteered to stay at the clinic to work on the van. She was unhappy with Delgado anyway because the inspector had told her she had to come back to Punta Larga with her this afternoon.

"I'm not going back," Megan had argued. "I'm staying here. I want to stay with Jaye."

"The FBI has instructed me to take you back. It seems your parents did not know you had left Punta Larga. They are most upset and are blaming the police for putting you in danger."

"I'm not a child. My parents don't have any right to tell me where I can and can't go."

Megan did not make any progress with her objections. Delgado had her orders from the FBI and she wasn't about to disobey. "You cannot wander around like a lure on a fishing string," she had told Megan. "You will pack and be ready to go back when we return."

Jaye had tried to soothe her with some sweet goodbye kisses, but it had done little good.

"I'm not in any danger here," Megan had objected. "Nobody cares about me. I don't understand why I have to leave. I want to stay with you, Jaye."

"Let's see how this morning goes," Jaye had told her. "If we find the kidnappers and bring Willie home, maybe the inspector will change her mind."

By the time Jaye left, Megan was somewhat placated. She was sitting on the front porch, Chuck the iguana perched on the railing beside her, drinking the last of her coffee. She had waved cheerfully as they pulled away.

Jaye was having a lot of complicated feelings about Megan this morning. She worried about what would happen next and was even a little glad that Delgado was taking her away. Jaye's mind and body were in turmoil. She couldn't think straight, and every time she closed her eyes, she was drawn back into the passion that had engulfed her overnight. Sex makes you crazy, she concluded.

She remembered the first time she had slept with Lexie. It had been an all-nighter, an out-of-body experience. All the next day she'd been high, almost like she'd smoked crack. It was sort of like how she felt now, but back then, she'd put no barriers on her feelings. It was all good. Now she most definitely had barriers. She hoped Megan got what she'd come for, that she was satisfied with her lesbian experience. She seemed to be pretty much into it. Maybe she'd go on to be the lesbian conqueror of USC. Jaye smiled to herself. Am I okay with that? she asked herself. She had to be. It was just the way things were, and they had both known that. Best of luck to her.

Jaye focused her gaze on the road and forced her thoughts back to the subject of Willie. In an hour, it could all be over.

"You told them not to shoot anybody, didn't you?" she asked Delgado. "If they don't have to, they won't shoot?"

Without turning around, Delgado said, "It is standard police practice. We do not go in with guns blazing and ask questions later. But my officers will protect themselves. And they will protect your Willie too. If the kidnappers resist, they will be stopped."

Jaye sighed and looked out the window, knots in her stomach. They were following two other police cruisers. The lead cars carried the agents who would conduct the operation.

After they had turned over Eddie's location to the police, they had pinpointed the building using satellite images. It was a small, ordinary-looking house. Paloma didn't recognize it or the area and had no idea what her brother would be doing there. Even before they had left the clinic, Eddie Marra's phone quit transmitting its location. He might have simply turned it off or the battery might have died, but Jaye worried there was more to it. It seemed like too much of a coincidence that the phone went offline so soon after the police started tracking it.

Jaye tried to keep disturbing images out of her mind, of Willie being held in that house with three ruthless men, and of the firestorm that might soon take place there. Even though she knew turning him in had been the right decision, she was sick over it. If Paloma's brother really was one of the kidnappers and if he were killed, Jaye knew she could never look Paloma in the eye again.

Delgado unwrapped a stick of gum and popped it in her mouth. Then she held the pack up and said, "Juicy Fruit, anybody?" There were no takers.

"Thank you for letting me come," said Jaye.

Delgado laughed. "What choice did I have? You would not take no for an answer."

They continued south on Highway 9 toward the village of Salado. It was a two-lane road. On either side was low vegetation covering the shoulder, then a dense growth of trees beyond that. There were telephone poles strung with wire at regular intervals, but no other sign of human habitation. Soon they came to a green sign announcing the town of Salado. Side roads and structures appeared, concrete buildings and adobe houses with thatched roofs. There were lines of clothes hung out to dry. They passed a girl in a yellow shirt, a boy sitting on a stone wall, two men at the side of the road talking. Jaye had never been here before. This village looked a lot like Tocamila, she thought. For some reason, she had expected something much more sinister. People watched them go by with curiosity. It was a caravan of police with no sirens, no lights flashing, but clearly on the way to something important.

The lead car honked to warn a dog out of the road, and all three cars sped through town until they came to a stop sign at a T intersection. On the corner was a Mini Super with an orange three-wheeled bike parked out front. The cars turned left and they were soon out of town and back in the jungle. Was this the route they had taken Willie on that horrible day? Jaye wondered.

"How much farther?" she asked.

"Just a few minutes," said Delgado. Then she got on the radio to tell the other cars they were breaking off.

When they approached a dirt pullout on the side of the road, she told Santos to park. Then she got out of the car with the radio and waited, chewing her gum furiously. Jaye got out of the car to join her.

"We're not going in?" she asked.

"Did you think I was going to give you an AK-47 and tell you to cover the back door?" Delgado laughed her throaty chortle, then held the radio slackly, waiting for a message. A few minutes later her contact announced that they had arrived and were surrounding the building.

Santos leaned against the car and Jaye stood beside him, both of them staring at the radio, waiting for it to give them information.

They waited for an excruciating length of time to nothing but silence, standing in the hot sun, insects buzzing around their heads, tense and uncomfortable. Santos lit a cigarette and stepped away to smoke it, the back of his shirt wet and stuck to his skin. Finally, there was a report.

"They're inside," Delgado said. "No sign of anybody."

After another ten minutes, Delgado ushered them back to the car. "All clear," she said.

Jaye's hopes crumbled. She wanted to cry.

They arrived at the house to find the other police cars parked nearby. The uniformed officers were moving in and out of the building, a small white house with security bars on the windows, its exterior walls covered in graffiti. One of the officers met Delgado as she exited the car and gave her the details of their investigation. Someone had been here recently. There were dirty dishes, food scraps in the trash and sink, empty beer bottles. In the bedroom, there was a mattress with a recent bloodstain.

"Blood!" Jaye shouted. She dashed toward the front door of the house.

"Don't go in there!" Delgado shouted after her.

But Jaye couldn't stop herself. She had to see. She ran through the open door and into the front room. The house smelled so bad she tried not to inhale. She quickly found the bedroom on the left side of the hallway and stepped inside. There was a light fixture in the ceiling with no bulb in it. In one corner was a plastic bucket. On the floor was a bare mattress. She knelt beside the mattress to get a closer look at the blood. It was a patch about two inches in diameter. Not that much. Was that Willie's blood? Had they injured her? Tortured her?

Beside the mattress on the floor were strips of duct tape. It was the tape more than anything that confirmed that this was the place. Willie had been here. But where was she now? Jaye stood, staring into space.

A police officer took hold of her arm and silently led her back outside, delivering her to Delgado, who narrowed one eye at her with displeasure. "I hope you did not touch anything."

Jaye shook her head. She moved back toward the road and leaned against the car, watching the police activity. Then she called Megan to give her the news.

"Willie was here," she said. "But they must have taken her away. The place is empty."

"It's been less than two hours since they were there," Megan said.

"I know. It's like they knew we were coming." Jaye felt angry and frustrated. "Can you tell Paloma so she won't worry about her brother? I'll see you soon." She ended the call and stepped purposefully up to Delgado. "Did they know we were coming?" she demanded. "Is that why they're gone?"

Delgado pursed her lips, but said nothing, and the two women stood face-to-face staring defiantly at one another while Jaye felt the pressure rising in her body. The inspector's expression was cool and unapologetic. But her nonanswer was practically an admission.

"Son of a bitch!" Jaye hissed, stamping the ground. She turned swiftly back to Delgado and moved in close. "The national police can't keep a secret for two hours? Did you even try? Do you even care? Am I supposed to pay you off? Is that how this works? If I pay you, will you then conveniently find Willie? Because if that's how it works, I'll figure out how to pay." Jaye clenched her fists. "But somebody's got to tell me how the fuck this works!"

Delgado chewed her gum slowly, unruffled, which made Jaye even more angry.

"The one lead you had," she said, gesturing in Delgado's face, "was what we gave you. And you completely blew it. You let her slip right through your fingers."

Delgado did not back away, nor did her expression change. She was coolly unfazed by Jaye's accusations. "We will be here a while longer gathering evidence," she said calmly. "You will wait by the car." She walked away.

"Evidence," Jaye said to herself. "You wouldn't know a piece of evidence if it bit you in the ass." She sat on the side of the road in the shade to wait for her ride home.

A half hour later, Delgado approached her to say they were ready to return to Tocamila. In the meantime, Jaye had gotten over being angry and felt simply sad. Delgado must have realized her mood had softened.

"Señorita Northrup," she said, "the tip you gave us this morning was not the only piece of information we had. We knew the kidnappers were in this area. We had a witness who saw the Jeep come through Salado on Sunday. So when you gave us this location, we knew it was good information. Yes, they have moved, but being on the move makes them more visible, no? I too am very disappointed we did not find Dr. Willett this morning."

Jaye couldn't bring herself to answer.

"I have other news," Delgado said. "This is good news. The kidnappers have made another call and designated the place and time for the ransom to be delivered."

"When?"

"This afternoon at four o'clock in San Vicente. Nathan Willett will be going there soon."

"Did anybody talk to Willie?"

"Her father asked to speak to her, but the kidnappers refused."

"Refused? Why? Why would they do that?"

Delgado hesitated, looking somber. "There are several possibilities."

Jaye felt her throat tighten, remembering the blood on the mattress. "Oh, my God! No, you can't be saying…"

"I am saying nothing," Delgado cut her off. "I am saying only what I know."

"But why didn't he demand to talk to her?" Jaye asked. "Why didn't he say he wouldn't pay them unless they proved she was safe?"

"He did say that. And they refused. They said she was alive. They said they would kill her at four o'clock if the money wasn't delivered. We have no choice. Who has the upper hand, you see?" She raised one hand level with her forehead.

Jaye put her head in her hands. Everything was out of control and the situation was spiraling down toward disaster. Taking a deep breath, she looked at Delgado and said, "What are the other possibilities?" She clenched her teeth. "Other than that she's dead?"

Delgado wagged her head. "The other possibilities are all better news than that. She might be unconscious. They might have put her somewhere that they cannot easily access. We have seen this. They hide a victim in one location and they themselves are somewhere else. That can be a very smart strategy, as long as the hiding place is secure. It could be that they no longer trust her to talk on the phone. Maybe she has become violent and uncooperative and they are afraid of what she will say. And there is also the possibility that she has escaped."

"Escaped?" Jaye grabbed onto the hopefulness of that explanation.

"So, you see, there is no reason to think she is dead."

"Except the blood."

"It is a very small amount of blood. A razor and a razor blade were found in the room. The blade has blood on it. It could have been from one of the kidnappers who cut himself shaving. Or the blade might have been used to cut the tape and accidentally cut Dr. Willett's skin. Based on the amount of used tape we found, we think they bound her and cut her free several times."

Ever since Jaye had seen the room where Willie had been held, she'd felt a sense of doom, and every additional detail that added to the vividness of Willie's desperate reality made it worse.

"Señorita Northrup, please try not to worry. The information network, it is full of leaks. We have seen how that works already. But the leaks flow both directions." She passed her hands across her chest in opposite directions. "It is often true that they know what we know. But it is also true that we know what they know. If they had killed her, I believe we would be hearing something about it. I believe she is still alive."

Jaye looked into Delgado's eyes and saw nothing but compassionate sincerity. She swallowed hard and tried to hold on to hope.

CHAPTER TWENTY-FOUR

"Hand me that socket wrench," Megan said to Perez. He had been leaning over the fender of the van, watching her for the last twenty minutes as she set the points and put in a new rotor and distributor cap. She wasn't sure how much English he understood, but her request, accompanied by a jerk of her head, seemed to do the trick. He handed her the wrench.

"*Gracias*," she said, placing one of the new spark plugs in its hole. She spun it around until it threaded in, then used the wrench to snug it down.

While she put in the other five plugs, she thought about Jaye and how incredible she was. Megan had never felt like this before. Happiness was bubbling over in her. She kept catching herself smiling. She tried to stop herself because her giddiness was causing Perez to smile nearly every time she looked at him. Pretty soon he's going to think I'm flirting with him, she realized.

Unfortunately, she and Jaye weren't on the same page at the moment. During their brief phone conversation a few minutes earlier, it had been clear that Jaye was angry and disappointed, anything but happy. Megan didn't blame her. She knew Jaye had built up her hopes of rescuing Willie. Too bad for everybody that hadn't worked out.

When they returned, Delgado was taking Megan back to Punta Larga. There didn't seem to be any way out of that. Delgado threatened that if Megan didn't come willingly, she'd arrest her and take her by force. She didn't seem to be bluffing. And so far Megan had not come up with a plan that would allow her to stay. Leaving Jaye right now was the last thing on earth she wanted.

Perez's phone rang and he stepped away to take the call. With the new plugs in, Megan started putting back the wires. She pushed the lead down until it snapped in place, then went on to the next one.

"Delgado," Perez reported, returning to his post at the van's fender. He attempted to give her a message, struggling with each word. "The, uh, ransom?"

"Ransom? Yes, what about it?"

"*Cuatro*," he said, then shook his head and held up four fingers.

"Four o'clock?"

"*Sí.*" He smiled.

"The ransom will be paid at four o'clock. Today?"

He nodded. That was good news, Megan thought. The sooner the better. By this evening, Willie would be home, Jaye would be happy and she would be free to join Megan in Punta Larga for a blissful end to this odd vacation. Megan closed her eyes momentarily, assailed by a sensation of Jaye's smooth, silky body pressed close to her own.

She roused herself to open her eyes. Perez had unwrapped the air filter from its packaging and was holding it out to her. The air cleaner was perched on the engine frame next to him. She pointed to it and said, "Go ahead. You do it."

He seemed to understand. He put the filter inside the air cleaner and placed it where it belonged. She reached into her pocket and found the wing nut, which she spun down over the bolt.

"I think that's it," she said, looking around to make sure there was nothing she had forgotten.

He nodded encouragingly. She got into the van and turned the key. It started right up and ran smooth. She revved the engine. It sounded good. Perez gave her a thumbs-up. She turned off the engine.

"*Bueno!*" he declared.

She nodded. "*Bueno.*" She put the wrench back in the toolbox and picked it up.

"No, no," Perez said, smiling. He took the box from her.

Megan wondered if he'd already gotten the wrong idea. As he walked off to return the tools to the shed behind the house, Megan pulled the hood down and slammed it shut.

What happened next happened fast.

Someone rushed at her from the jungle, grabbing her from behind. She managed to get out a partial yell before a hand clamped over her mouth. A man appeared in front of her and grabbed both of her ankles, lifting her off the ground. The two men, holding her like a rolled-up carpet, fled back into the jungle and carried her down a slope. She heard Perez shout in the distance. "Megan!" he called, but she couldn't answer. All she could do was squirm ineffectively. She was whisked to the main road where a black Camaro was parked. The men put her on the ground. While one of them held her mouth, the other wrenched her arms behind her and taped them together. Then they taped her mouth shut. She was then lifted off the ground again and rolled into the trunk of the car. They slammed the trunk lid down and everything went dark.

"*Alto!*" she heard. "*Policia!*" It was Perez. He sounded close. He must have run down the road.

Car doors slammed. The engine started.

"*Alto! Alto!*" Perez yelled again, his voice loud and anxious.

Then a shot rang out just as the car lurched, tires squealing.

Hell, don't shoot me, Megan thought, picturing Perez firing at the back of the car.

They were picking up speed and there were no more shots. Megan realized all of her muscles were tensed up. She willed herself to relax. The trunk was big enough for her, but far from comfortable. It was sweltering and the car fumes were terrible. She rolled over, trying to find a place with better air. For several minutes she tried to loosen the tape around her wrists, but made no progress. Finally, sapped by heat, she quit trying. She had no idea where they were taking her, but hoped it wasn't far. Between the tape over her mouth, the fumes and the confinement, she was finding it hard to breathe.

CHAPTER TWENTY-FIVE

During the night, Willie had been thankful for the cover of darkness, which had produced its own kind of dread, but it had allowed her to stay more easily hidden without going deep undercover. She had kept to the thick vegetation, making her way parallel to the road, heading, she hoped, homeward. She was certain that at least one patrol was out looking for her. A Jeep had been passing by in one direction or the other all night. She hadn't dared to close her eyes to rest, had kept moving, and she was exhausted. She had been too frightened to stop— frightened of being caught and frightened of the creatures in the jungle, especially snakes.

Now that it was daylight, she was even more cautious, staying deeper in the brush and, consequently, moving more slowly. But she had not seen the Jeep all morning. Maybe she had somehow gotten turned the wrong way and they were looking for her on the correct route. They would expect her to be headed back to the clinic. Until she got sight of a road sign, it would be impossible to know for sure.

From her knees down, her pants were wet and muddy. She had tripped several times over vines. The more tired she got, the less sure-footed she became. Every time her movement caused a rustling nearby, she wanted to run, but she somehow managed to keep herself from losing her mind.

She was tempted to go out to the road and flag somebody down, but was too afraid of happening on the wrong person. If there was a price on her head, nobody could be trusted. Besides, they had brought her here, to this place, for a reason. Maybe it was their home turf. Maybe the people who lived around here were their family and friends.

At the pace she was traveling, she was beginning to worry that it could take her several days to get back to safety, to the only people she knew for sure would protect her, Jaye and Paloma. She didn't think she could get through another sleepless night in the jungle without going insane. Her face was scratched and bloody, her exposed skin covered with mosquito bites. She was dirty, thirsty and hungry. She didn't want to drink any standing water, but had taken advantage of some leaves filled with dew earlier in the day. She had eaten a couple of mangoes, but they weren't ripe enough to taste good, and the same was true of a bunch of bananas she found. Starchy and mealy, but at least it was something to put in her stomach. She thought back to the plate of beans she had left untouched the night before. She was a very poor planner, she knew, never thinking things through properly, but normally it didn't matter that much. Normally, every decision wasn't a matter of life or death.

She kept imagining life back at the clinic, a place that had never seemed quite so comfortable as it did now, despite its lukewarm showers, cramped living spaces and dry rot.

She had arrived at a village, and was carefully keeping out of sight, staying in the jungle on the outskirts of town, but was tempted by glimpses of ordinary life on the streets. People were walking around, talking to neighbors, going to the market, hanging out the laundry and cooking meals. She could smell tortillas scorching on an open flame.

She hesitated for a long time outside a house, hidden in the brush behind it, seeing the silhouettes of adults and children through the lace curtains. The presence of children gave her hope that the people inside were honest and good. She could knock on their door and within minutes be rescued.

Still she waited, finding it hard to give up her freedom for the chance of a meal and a life-saving phone call. She had already made too many mistakes. She had left the house without the car keys and without a phone. Both of those treasures had probably been lying on the kitchen counter. She had no doubt walked right past them. She wanted to kick herself.

A woman walked into the frame of the window and leaned down to a small child, cradling the child's face between her hands. Then the child ran away from the window. She could hear him laughing. In the end, she decided it was too much of a risk. The occupants of this house, or any house, could be friends of the kidnappers or somebody willing to sell her back to them for a few pesos. She was free now and she had to stay that way by avoiding any more dumb mistakes.

As she sat on a moss-covered stone, exhausted and miserable, there was nothing in the world she wished more than that she could quit running, quit fighting. In a way, she almost wished for Grady or Eduardo to show up, wrap tape around her wrists, and lead her back to her cell. At least then she could sleep.

She had no energy left. Several times she determined to stand up and move on, but couldn't muster the strength. She realized she was probably dehydrated. She finally persuaded herself to leave her resting place and went in search of a faucet out of sight at the back of a house. Water was her top priority. Then, after that, a telephone.

"I have to find a way to call Jaye," she said to herself. "Then everything will be okay." Jaye would know what to do. Jaye would save her.

CHAPTER TWENTY-SIX

A few minutes after the Camaro had reached its destination, Megan was pulled out of the trunk by one of her assailants and shoved through a doorway into a cinder block building. The second man stayed outside while the first one pulled her across a concrete floor stained with oil, tightly gripping one of her bound arms. The interior of the building was open and the ceiling was high above them. There were windows, but they too were high, letting in sunlight, but not allowing a view of the outside. Parked on one side of the space was an old Ford pickup with faded green paint. There were two doors in the front of the building, a regular personnel door and a large corrugated metal sliding door that opened and closed on wheels. Both doors were shut and the building appeared empty.

This was the first time Megan had gotten a good look at her kidnapper. He was in his thirties, short and stocky, Hispanic with a Carlos Santana-style mustache. He held a handgun in his left hand, aimed imprecisely at her torso. As he pulled her further into the room, his body language and the perspiration on his forehead made it clear that he was nervous. He wasn't on his own turf, she decided.

"*Hola!*" he yelled, his voice echoing upward toward the high ceiling.

He swung her around as he turned, anxiously watching for movement, his gun ready.

"*Tengo la dentista,*" he announced to the blank walls.

La dentista? Megan silently contemplated. This guy thought she was the other Megan Willett? So he wasn't one of Willie's kidnappers, she concluded. Maybe he was here to meet them.

A silent moment passed before two men appeared, one of them from behind the pickup and the other from a glassed-in office near it. The first was a teenager, lank and handsome, with attractive dark eyes, wearing a Bob Marley T-shirt. Observing his features, Megan guessed he was Paloma's brother Eddie. The other man was older, overweight with a scar across his face and dull-looking brown eyes.

Her Santana wannabe walked her up to the other two, and the four of them stood face-to-face. Eddie and Scarface stared at her, looking stunned and confused. They too had apparently expected to see Willie.

"*Tengo la dentista,*" Santana said again, smiling and looking very pleased with himself.

Oh, buddy, Megan thought, you screwed up big-time!

When the scar-faced man overcame his shock, he started angrily berating Megan's kidnapper. He, in turn, argued back, gesturing with his gun hand. Everything was in Spanish, so Megan was nearly at a loss, but she began to get the idea that the guy who had grabbed her from the clinic was trying to sell her to these other two for some kind of reward. The name "Megan Willett" came up a few times, confirming her conclusions. That could mean only one thing—that Willie had escaped from these goons and they were trying to get her back. Good for her!

Scarface was completely disgusted, making hand gestures that indicated he wanted Megan out of his sight.

Suddenly Megan realized the gun was next to her temple and the dude holding it looked like he was going to use it. She stiffened, trying to think of a way out.

But then they began arguing again until Paloma's brother approached her and pulled the tape off her mouth, causing her to cry out in pain. She was sure it had taken off her entire upper lip. The other two men fell silent and watched, seeming interested in what she had to say.

"What is your name?" Eddie asked, his voice soft and low.

"Megan Willett."

"Shit!" Scarface uttered.

Eddie narrowed his eyes at her. "You will tell the truth."

Megan indicated the man with the gun. "What did he say my name was?"

"Megan Willett."

"There you go."

"But he is lying. We know Megan Willett. You are not her."

"I've heard that a lot the last couple of days. But that is my name. There are two of us. People can have the same name, you know. I'd be willing to bet you're not the only Eddie Marra in the world."

His eyes widened in surprise, then he turned to Scarface with a questioning look.

"How do you know his name?" he demanded.

Okay, she thought, maybe identifying one of the kidnappers wasn't the smartest thing I've ever done. Maybe they hadn't known the police were onto Eddie after all.

Scarface waved his hand dismissively. "It doesn't matter. You, little girl, have just committed suicide." He laughed, then grabbed the gun out of Santana's hand, handing it to Eddie.

Everything after that was in Spanish as Scarface gave instructions to Eddie and then took a set of keys from Santana-stache, who reluctantly surrendered them. Then Scarface grasped him by the back of the neck and walked him across the floor to the door. A moment later they were both gone. She heard vehicles start and drive away outside.

As far as she could tell, she was now alone with Eddie. She sized him up. Slightly built, he didn't look very tough, but he was the one with the gun and she had her hands taped behind her back.

"Are you going to kill me?" she asked.

"*Sí*, we are going to kill you. Whoever you are, Americana, you are not the one we want." He pointed the gun at her. "How do you know my name?"

"Your sister Paloma."

He stared, close-lipped, then finally said, "You know my sister?"

"Yes."

He seemed both reluctant and tempted to speak at the same time. He finally asked, "How is she?"

"You mean how badly injured? After your amigo roughed her up?" Megan let her eyes wander the walls of the building, looking for anything that could help her. "You must know she's alive because she's been texting you. Not that you cared enough to answer."

There wasn't much of anything in this building: a table and two chairs against one wall and a cage-like office with an open doorway about thirty feet behind Eddie. She couldn't see what was inside the office. She didn't know if the doors to the outside were locked, but if she made a run for the door, Eddie would have no trouble picking her off before she could get out. Unless he missed. It was a chance, maybe not a good one, but if there was nothing else...

"She's out of the hospital," Megan said, seeing no advantage to withholding information. "She has a fractured sternum, but she'll be okay."

"What is that? What is sternum?"

"Breastbone."

Eddie seemed to relax a little. She wanted to keep him talking and maybe learn how he ticked so she could find some psychological advantage.

"Another thing you should know is that the police are out there looking for your Jeep. As soon as you hit the road, they'll nail you."

"We're not using the Jeep anymore. That imbecile who brought you here has given us his car." Eddie laughed, looking truly tickled. "That was his payment for bringing you. Stupid amateurs. Sucks for you, right?" He laughed again.

Megan didn't want to die, especially today of all days, right after finally finding out what love was all about. There must be some way out of this.

"Why are you going to kill me?" she asked. "If I'm not who you want, you can just let me go."

"You know too much. You even know my name."

"Since you're in the kidnapping business, I'd think you would at least try to get something for me before you kill me. I can give you my parents' number. I may not be the Megan Willett you want, but my family has a little money. I'm like a bonus."

He smiled knowingly, seeming to understand that she was trying to bargain for her life. "We don't have time to mess with you."

"Because you're too busy fucking up your other kidnapping?"

Anger flashed across his face. "Time to kill you now."

God, Megan thought, when will I ever learn to keep my mouth shut?

Eddie approached her, aiming his gun at her head. "On your knees!"

CHAPTER TWENTY-SEVEN

Jaye sat in the front room with her head in her hands. Delgado, Santos and Perez were all there, but all she could think about was how useless they were. Megan had been kidnapped right under Perez's nose. Two men in a black Chevy Camaro had taken her. They didn't match the description the Salado witness had given of Willie's kidnappers. So that meant a whole new group of kidnappers?

"Why did this happen?" Jaye asked, not really expecting an answer. "What's going on around here?"

"We've been hearing some chatter," Delgado said.

Jaye looked up. "Chatter?"

"*Sí*, that's what the FBI calls it. Chatter. Bits and pieces of information picked up here and there."

"What's it about?"

The inspector looked reluctant to speak, pressing her lips tightly together. Her expression was cool.

"Look," Jaye said, "I'm sorry about what I said earlier. I trust you. I do."

Delgado seemed satisfied. "It started last night. A reward was offered. We believe it has come from Señor Olivos. He is well known to us. About a year ago, he moved his headquarters from Colombia to this island, and things have not been the same here since."

"A drug lord?"

"He has offered a fifteen thousand peso reward for the capture of Dr. Megan Willett."

"This chatter started last night? I don't understand."

Delgado nodded knowingly. "It can mean only one thing, no?"

Jaye waited impatiently for Delgado to explain.

"Your Dr. Willett must have escaped, you see? The kidnappers are desperate to get her back, so they offer a reward and spread the word. Then everybody is out looking for Dr. Willett. She is on the run. They cannot let her reach her destination before four o'clock this afternoon or they will lose the ransom money."

"Oh, my God!" Jaye uttered. "Do you really think so?"

Delgado nodded. "I also think that is why we found the hideout empty. After she escaped, they abandoned it."

Jaye glanced at the wall clock. It was nearly one in the afternoon. Three hours until the payoff. Imagining desperate bands of greedy fortune hunters scouring the land for Willie, she closed her eyes, filled with dread. When she opened them, she observed Delgado's thoughtful expression, then asked, "If she escaped last night, why hasn't she called? Why isn't she here? Why hasn't anyone seen or heard from her?"

"I cannot answer that."

Jaye imagined Willie lost, maybe injured, out in the jungle somewhere. "Oh, God, this is a nightmare!" Then she thought of Megan, nightmare number two. "What about Megan?"

"That is why we believe Dr. Willett escaped and that the reward offer is legitimate. Somebody took Señorita Willett, thinking she was Dr. Willett, to turn her in for the reward."

"But how could anybody make a mistake like that? The kidnappers know what she looks like."

"*Sí*, the kidnappers do, but everybody out to collect the fifteen thousand pesos does not. You understand?"

Jaye nodded morosely. She looked up at Delgado, who attempted a reassuring smile, but it was an utter flop.

"So they take Megan to the kidnappers," Jaye said, "hoping for the reward. The kidnappers know she's the wrong woman. What then? What happens to Megan?"

Delgado glanced around the room, first at Perez, then at Santos, and all of them looked uneasy. Jaye bounded out of her chair. "What the hell are you all doing standing around here? You should be out looking for them."

"I'm waiting for my ride," Delgado said. "It should be here any minute."

"What about these guys?"

"We can't leave the clinic unprotected."

"I don't need any protection. There aren't any more Megan Willetts left to kidnap, so go! All of you, go! You have to find them."

Delgado seemed to reconsider. She nodded curtly to her men. "Join the other teams," she said. "If you hear anything at all, Señorita Northrup, call me immediately."

Within two minutes, Jaye was alone. She sat at Willie's craft table and rested her head on her arms, rolling a thin dowel between her fingers. The dowels fit just under the opening in the birdhouses, serving as perches. The birdhouse beside her on the table was painted white with brown patterns intended to look like birch bark. That was funny, she thought. It was camouflaged to blend in with a birch tree, but there were no birches on Santuario. This birch-like paint job would stand out strikingly against the deep greens of the local flora. Chances were good that whoever ended up with this birdhouse would have no idea what the pattern was meant to resemble.

She pushed the dowel into the hole Willie had drilled for it. When Willie returns, she'll coat the end of the dowel with glue and secure it in place, she thought. Maybe that would be tonight. Just like that, it now seemed that Willie was potentially safer than Megan. What Delgado wasn't willing to say was easy enough to guess. The kidnappers didn't want Megan. She was just a mistake, and expendable. Jaye prayed silently to the ancient Taino gods to keep both of her women safe.

CHAPTER TWENTY-EIGHT

Megan knelt on the concrete floor, the surface gritty against her bare knees, her hands still bound.

Eddie stood behind her. She assumed he was aiming at the back of her head. He didn't seem entirely comfortable with the task of killing her. Maybe he'd never done it, or even witnessed it before. This was a tremendously important line he was about to cross. The point of no return. He was taking his time, maybe trying to work up the courage. She was glad for the delay, but knew it wouldn't last indefinitely.

Okay, Megan, she said to herself. This is the moment of truth. You've got to go it or blow it and no second chance.

"By the way," she said, casually, "if you want to visit your sister during her recuperation, she's not home with your family. She's staying with a friend."

She could sense him moving uneasily behind her, then suddenly he was in front of her, the gun in one hand, slack against his side.

"What friend?" he asked.

"Sofia. Her lesbian lover. You know who she is, right?"

Megan swore she saw flames shoot out of his eyes.

"You've seen them together," she continued. "You've been spying on them. Maybe you've even seen them…you know." She winked.

Here it comes, she thought, tensing up. His lips pressed so tightly together they disappeared, Eddie reeled back, raising his gun hand over his head, preparing a blow. As soon as he rocked his weight onto his back foot, Megan sprang up and exploded into the center of him with all her strength. He lost his footing, stumbling back. She kept pushing, running him into the cinder block wall where his head hit a steel pipe. He closed his eyes and slid down the wall into a seated position, his head slumped over, the pistol on the floor between his legs.

That couldn't have gone better, she congratulated herself.

She kicked the gun away from Eddie, across the floor through the open office doorway, then she followed it into the small room. Inside she found a desk, electric fan, a file cabinet and desk chair. She backed up to the desk and pulled open the center drawer. Jackpot! There were two pairs of scissors inside. She selected the shorter one, thinking it would be easier to use with limited mobility. Then she started the time-consuming process of cutting the tape binding her hands. As long as Eddie stayed out and the other goons stayed away for a few more minutes, she'd be free.

Once she was able to wriggle one hand out, she used it to remove the rest of the tape. Then she picked up the pistol and stuck it in her waistband. She checked to make sure Eddie was still breathing and, reassuring herself that he was, searched through his clothes, locating his cell phone. Since the GPS signal had shut down earlier, she was surprised to see the phone was on and the battery wasn't near dead. But there were no bars, no signal. So the kidnappers didn't know they were being tracked by this phone after all. When it had gone dark right after the police started tracking it, it had just been a coincidence. It had moved with Eddie into this dead zone.

She ran to the door and found it unlocked. Outside was an old asphalt parking area, severely cracked and sprouting grass. This used to be some kind of garage or gas station, she concluded, noting a faded Texaco sign on the side of the building. There was nobody on the road. Her problem was, she didn't know where she was, and with the phone not working, she couldn't call for help or get her location. What did people do when they didn't carry phones, she wondered, cringing at the thought. She noticed the compass app icon on the phone and tapped it. Watching the dial, she rotated her body to point north. Now she knew north from south, but that wasn't much help. Locked in the trunk of a car on the way here, she had no idea which way they'd come. Clicking back to the main screen, she saw there was still no signal.

She went back inside to consider her course of action. Eddie was still out. She could wake him up, she thought, and force him to draw her a map. Too risky. She liked him the way he was. But just in case he woke up on his own, she decided to tie him up. She found a roll of duct tape in the office and taped his feet together, then his hands behind his back. She stood over him, both feet planted firmly on concrete, arms akimbo, and said, "Threat neutralized." Then she knelt beside his limp body and took a selfie on his phone. Viewing it, she giggled involuntarily.

She looked around, her eyes landing on the old pickup. It didn't look like much, but all four tires were aired up. Maybe it ran. She looked in the ignition. No key. She checked the glove compartment and under and behind the seat, finding a toolbox, but no keys. She went into the office and looked through the desk drawers and the filing cabinet. Just when she realized she could hotwire the truck, she spotted a set of keys hanging on a nail. "Ford" was clearly stamped on one of them.

Back at the truck, she hopped into the driver's seat and turned the ignition. The vehicle started right up and ran smoothly, not what she had expected based on its looks. "Sweet!" she said. She jumped out and ran to the rolling door and pushed it open. An empty, open road lay before her, and the truck had a quarter tank of gas.

She backed the vehicle out of the building and onto the road. She checked Eddie's phone again. Still no signal. She set the phone beside her on the seat. She needed to get out of the dead zone so she could call for help. She looked down the road to the left, then to the right. Same diff, she said to herself. Just gotta pick one. She turned right and headed out, then turned on the radio and tuned into an English language pop station. Eventually, she thought, I'll see a road sign showing the way to somewhere, hopefully before I run out of gas. Her wallet was back at the clinic on the table beside Willie's bed.

But for now, everything was cool. She was free and safe and the song on the radio was one she knew, so she could sing along.

After ten minutes of driving through nothing but green, she was dismayed to see that Eddie's cell phone still had no signal. She was beginning to think there was something wrong with the phone. Or maybe the plan. Or maybe the network just didn't cover remote parts of Santuario. Her coverage in Punta Larga had been perfect, less so in Tocamila. Road signs so far had been useless to her. They contained the names of places she'd never heard of.

If she was going in the wrong direction, she knew she was wasting valuable time. Somehow, she needed to figure out where she was.

She saw a four-way intersection ahead with stop signs. On one corner was a run-down building. A sign on the roof, made of weathered wooden planks, said Mercado Elsa. There were no vehicles parked there and it didn't look open for business. In fact, the building looked abandoned. Of more interest to Megan was the Teléfono sign by the road. She looked around and located the public phone in front of the store. She had no idea what the state of public phones was in Santuario. Maybe mobile phones were less common here and the public phones were still in operation. Even in the States there were still a few, and she had heard somewhere that you could always make an emergency call on a public phone, even without money. It was worth a try.

She rolled up to the side of the store, parked and got out. She saw no one and heard nothing but a far-off bird call. She realized she didn't know the emergency number here in Santuario. Traveling 101, she chided herself. Maybe the phone had emergency numbers listed on it. She reached into her pocket for some coins. In the palm of her hand were a few pesos and one firecracker. She'd forgotten that, picking up a firecracker last night. Thinking about last night, she remembered Jaye and smiled to herself. She put the firecracker back in her pocket and walked up to the phone. Though she'd put Jaye's number in her phone, she hadn't memorized it, so she couldn't call Jaye. Maybe she had enough change to call Mickey or Nicole. She could tell them it was an emergency and have them call her back. All she'd need is enough time to get that message through.

She looked for a coin slot like she'd seen in old movies. There wasn't one. She picked up the receiver and examined the antique machine, feeling like an alien. There was a slot, a thin opening about the size of a credit card. Calling cards! she realized. That's what it takes. She placed the receiver back on its hook, then stood helplessly in front of the phone, realizing there was no way she could use it. Man, this sucks!

Then she heard a car door slam. She spun around to see somebody inside the pickup, in the driver's seat. Oh, hell no! she thought, flying toward it. Just as she reached the vehicle, she heard a click coming from under the hood. Then another. Through the windshield, she saw that the would-be driver was a fair-skinned, wild-haired woman who kept turning the key with the same result: click, click, click.

Megan pulled the gun out of her waistband, held it in both hands and aimed it at the windshield. She sidestepped to the side of the vehicle with the gun pointed continuously at the woman's head, feeling like she was in a *Mad Max* movie. But, yeah, this was a desperate situation. After what she'd been through, there was no way some pirate chick was going to steal her ride.

"Get out of my truck!" she yelled. She had no idea how to say that in Spanish, but she hoped the gun would convey her meaning. "Get out or I'll blow your head off!"

The woman screamed and flung up her hands, waving them frantically. She looked like some kind of maniac. Her hair was tangled and had twigs in it. Her face was covered with red welts. Do they have lepers here, Megan momentarily wondered. And do I even want this truck now? But she did want it, she decided, because it was her lifeline. And Eddie's phone was in the front seat.

"Get out!" Megan gestured with the gun. "I swear I'm gonna shoot you if you don't get out right now!"

"Don't shoot me!" the woman pleaded in perfect American English. She opened the door and emerged from the cab where Megan got a better look at her. Her clothes, a short-sleeved shirt and tan pants, were dirty all over, and the pants were mud brown from the knees down. Her nervous eyes were ringed with dark circles, and her face was covered with a network of surface scratches. She looked like a refugee from *Survivor*. Despite all of that, she looked familiar. The shape of her face and her eyes, especially, looked like…

"You're an American?" the woman breathed, sounding hopeful.

"Yep," said Megan tentatively, still pointing the gun at her.

"Me too," the woman said. "What's your name?"

"Megan. Megan Willett."

The woman dropped her hands to her side and looked defeated. She shook her head and said, "I think I'm losing my mind. I haven't slept for so long. Whatever your name is, please help me."

The woman seemed to be in despair. Her body language was all about reconciliation. There was clearly no fight in her. Megan relaxed, lowering the gun.

"Willie?" she asked, mentally forcing this woman into the form she was familiar with from the photos. "Is it you?"

The woman looked up, surprised. "That's my name. Do you know me?"

"Yes. We've never met, but I know who you are. You're Megan Willett, the dentist."

Willie nodded rapidly, a smile forming on her face. Then quite suddenly she looked afraid and glanced about as if she were looking for an escape route.

"No, no," Megan said. "I'm a friend."

Willie looked suspicious, her eyes like those of a frightened animal.

"I know this is confusing," Megan said, "but that's my name too. I'm Megan Willett from San Diego. We have the same name. I will help you." Megan reached a hand toward Willie, who hunkered backward in fear. "I know you've been through hell the last couple of days, but you can trust me. I'm a friend of Jaye's." At the sound of Jaye's name, Willie caught her breath, but still looked like she was about to make a break for it. "Look, Willie, you've got to trust me. We need to get back before somebody comes by and sees us. The kidnappers are all over the place looking for you."

"Do you think I don't know that?" She seemed to calm down. "So you're really a friend of Jaye's? Why don't I know you?"

"We just met. It's kind of a long story and we don't have time right now. Are you okay? Are you hurt? There was something about some blood found in the room they were holding you."

"Self-inflicted." Willie laughed and held up her wrist to show a small cut. "A little slip in the escape plan."

Megan nodded. "I stopped to use the phone. I don't suppose you have a calling card."

Willie shook her head, not grasping that Megan was joking. "Do you know where we are?"

"Yes. Once I got to this intersection, I knew."

"Come on. Let's go. We need to get back so we can stop your brother from making the drop. That's scheduled to go down at four o'clock."

"The truck won't start."

Megan climbed in and tried the key herself just to be sure. Again, nothing but a click.

"It sounds like the battery's dead," Willie said.

Megan looked at Eddie's phone, trying to will it to display a couple of bars, but it remained stubbornly off the grid. Now that she'd found Willie, she could be a hero. She could drive back to Tocamila and deliver her, only slightly damaged, to Jaye. Then this whole kidnapping affair would be over and she could have Jaye to herself for two whole days.

"Maybe it's just a loose cable," Megan said, trying to persuade herself.

She popped the hood and tested the terminals for tightness. They were both snug. "Maybe they're not getting good contact. Lots of humidity around here. If I can find a wrench, I can clean them up and reseat them."

"We don't have time for that," Willie objected.

"Every other plan I can think of will take longer than that."

"Out here in the open, we're sitting ducks."

At that moment, an eighties model Chevy rolled up to the intersection. Both women flew around the vehicle to the side facing away from the road and knelt out of sight.

"It's not a Camaro," Megan whispered.

"What? Why does that matter?"

"They're driving a Camaro. They've ditched the Jeep."

The Chevy went on its way and they both heaved a sigh of relief. Being this close to Willie, Megan got a whiff of her less than appetizing odor. She smelled of sweat and swamp and who knew what else. Megan stopped breathing for a moment before moving to the other side of the truck to look behind the cab seat for the toolbox. She took out a crescent wrench and went to work loosening the battery cables.

"Do you know what you're doing?" Willie asked.

"I know I'm taking off the battery cables. Whether or not that will do any good is up for grabs."

Willie leaned over the engine to watch. "What's wrong with that phone?"

"No signal." Megan looked in the toolbox to find a folded piece of sandpaper. She wiped the cable terminals and battery posts with a rag, cleaning off grease and dirt. Then she lightly sanded the inside of the cable terminals before pushing them back over the posts.

She tightened the bolts, then stood up and looked around. Willie was sitting on the ground with her head in her hands. Off in the distance, Megan saw the glint of metal. Another vehicle was coming…fast. She jumped in the driver's seat and turned the key. As she heard a click, her spirits fell, but immediately after, to her tremendous relief, the engine turned over and started. She jumped back out and slammed the hood down. Looking again at the approaching vehicle, she thought it looked suspiciously Camaro-like.

"Get in the truck!" she screamed at Willie.

As soon as the door shut, Megan hit the accelerator. The tires spun, then threw up gravel as she made a tight U-turn in the parking lot, then shot out to the road.

"What's the quickest way to the clinic?" she asked Willie.

"Turn right!"

Without stopping at the intersection, Megan hooked a right and put her foot to the floor. The Camaro came up fast. It appeared to have two occupants. In the rearview mirror, Megan saw the passenger lean out the window, then pull out an automatic rifle.

"That's them!" Willie screamed, terrified.

"I sort of figured that," Megan replied.

Gunfire rang out from behind them. She didn't hear anything hit the truck. Warning shots?

"Keep your head down," she told Willie as they dipped into a low spot across a ravine. The few hills on this stretch would work to their advantage, but Megan was afraid she would not be able to keep far enough ahead of the Camaro to keep them safe. And for all she knew, they would follow right up to the clinic and come out firing at everybody. With that thought, she realized they couldn't head for the clinic. There were innocent people there—Paloma, Sofia. Maybe patients. And Jaye was there. She couldn't lead a firefight right to their door. But where else?"

"Where's the closest police station?" she asked Willie.

"San Vicente."

"Where is that?"

"It's on the other side of Tocamila. It's farther."

They would never be able to stay in the lead that long, Megan knew, even if they did avoid getting shot. This was not going to end well, she concluded. The only real hope they had was that the kidnappers would lose control of their vehicle and crash. At this speed, that was certainly possible. For either of them.

Willie was bent over her knees, her hands over her head, bouncing on the seat as they flew over potholes and dips. She occasionally peered over the dash with one wild eye.

"Next road you come to, turn left. Please don't roll the truck." She sounded terrified.

"Don't worry. I'm a great driver."

As she slowed to take the turn, the pop, pop, pop of an assault rifle rang out. This time she heard the zing of a bullet hit the truck, at least one. Willie screamed. Not a warning shot this time. They made it around the corner and she sped up again. But now the Camaro was closing the gap between them and she knew they weren't going to make it. An oncoming car swerved onto the shoulder to be fully clear of the chase. Megan passed it, then watched in the side mirror to see if, by some fortunate twist of fate, the other car interfered somehow with the Camaro. But it sailed past the car without slowing.

Megan gripped the wheel with both hands so hard her fingers hurt. She was about to die, she realized. Any second a bullet could pierce her skull and it would be over. Lights out. Forever. She was going to die in a car chase in Isla Santuario, fleeing assault rifle-wielding crooks while trying to save the life of…what had they called her…a true American hero, a stinky true American hero. That wasn't so bad, if you thought about it. Then she thought of her parents and grandparents and siblings. Her brother Rick, her Wrestlemania partner, would take it hard. They all would. Going out in a blaze of glory might be okay for her, but it would be lousy for her family. She glanced at Willie, who was still doubled up beside her.

"Do you have any brothers and sisters other than Nathan?" she asked.

Willie turned her head, revealing a scowl of incomprehension. "You're not seriously trying to have a chat with me right now, are you?"

As Megan flew over the next hummock, Willie bounced off the seat, nearly hitting the roof.

"Slow down!" Willie pleaded. "You have to turn left at the next road."

Megan did not slow down, nor did she turn left.

"You missed it!" Willie screamed. "That's the road to Tocamila."

"Look," Megan said, "we can't lead these goons back to the clinic. We could get everybody there killed. And if we just keep running, they'll eventually hit us or overtake us. The way it looks to me, we have two choices. We can stop and surrender and hope for the best or we make a U-turn and hit them head-on. That should strike them a serious blow or take them out altogether."

"And us! Are you crazy?"

"So you want to surrender?"

"They'll kill us. That was the plan all along. They never would have let me go. As soon as they had the ransom money, I was a goner. That's why I had to get away. And now you'll be a goner too because they don't want any witnesses." Willie's speech was punctuated with her teeth banging together as they hit a bump. She winced.

"Oh, they already tried to kill me," said Megan. "I vote for ramming them."

Willie sat up and stared. "Oh, my God! You're a maniac!"

"I don't want to die either. If you have a better idea, tell me quick because they're catching up."

As if to confirm that, gunfire rang out again. They both ducked as a bullet shattered the window behind them and glass flew through the cab.

"Okay," Willie said, tears coming to her eyes. "Let's give up. At least we'll have another hour to breathe."

Even giving up was going to be tricky. Personally, Megan liked the idea of ramming them, but she felt sorry for Willie, who had already been through so much. She tried to think of a way to surrender where it would be obvious to the kidnappers what was happening. Maybe if she turned on her flashers and gradually eased off the road, they would understand the deliberation of her act. Or maybe Willie could hold her shirt out the window like a white flag.

"Take off your shirt!" she barked at Willie.

Willie stared at her, her mouth open. "I know I didn't hear what I just thought I heard."

Megan was about to explain when she heard the loveliest sound she had ever heard in her life: a siren. Two sirens. She had already eased up on the gas pedal in anticipation of surrender, but now she floored it again, heading toward that beautiful, beautiful noise.

Willie looked up, an expression of tentative wonder on her face.

"Head down!" Megan warned.

More gunfire and another bullet ripped through the window, zinging over Willie's head and going out a clean hole in the windshield. Glass pebbles fell into her hair. All those dudes wanted now was to kill them, Megan concluded, worried that the next bullet would rip open a tire and send them hurtling off the road. She knew she couldn't control the truck at this speed with a blown tire.

But maybe she wouldn't have to, she realized, seeing the flashing lights ahead. The Camaro, she saw, was falling back. They were going to turn around and make a run for it. She reached over and slapped Willie triumphantly on the back.

"We made it! We made it!"

Willie sat up as Megan braked the truck. They rolled up to a National Police car parked across the road, two officers standing behind it with guns drawn, their faces set and eyes obscured by sunglasses. Another car, sirens blaring, went through the dust on the shoulder to chase after the Camaro. Megan turned off the engine, then both women got out with their hands up.

"God, I hope these really are the good guys," Willie said in a shaky voice.

Inspector Delgado, her mane of ebony hair glowing in the sun, walked out between the armed officers and grimaced.

"They are," Megan assured her, lowering her hands.

CHAPTER TWENTY-NINE

"It was Eddie's phone," Jaye explained, walking over to Willie's bed. "It started transmitting its location. That's how they knew where you were. Actually, the police thought they were going after the kidnappers. Nobody knew you had the phone."

Willie smiled wearily. "I can't believe it's over."

The doorbell rang again.

Jaye rolled her eyes. "They just keep coming. Everybody wants to see Willie and leave her food offerings."

"I'm just not up to it yet," Willie said. She sat on the edge of her bed in a clean T-shirt and shorts. She looked and smelled so much better already after just a shower and a sandwich.

"They understand," Jaye said, sitting beside her and holding her hand. "Perez is on door duty, letting everybody know you're home safe and sound."

Megan stood near Jaye's bed, leaning against the wall, observing this reunion with curiosity. Up until today, Willie had been more of an idea than a real person, built up into a legend. But the woman sitting on her bed with slightly hunched shoulders, wearing purple flip-flops and bobby pins in her hair, looked surprisingly ordinary and unimpressive. Her knee bounced unconsciously up and down with nervous energy. Jaye sat next to her, looking stunning as usual. Megan was impatient. She wanted to get this homecoming over with so she could have Jaye to herself. She was especially irritated at the way the two of them kept hugging one another and holding hands.

"I've just been sick to my stomach ever since that day," Jaye told Willie. "It was so hard not to be able to do anything and imagining what terrors you were enduring."

Willie patted her hand. "It could have been a lot worse, Jaye. To set your mind at ease, I will tell you that they didn't hurt me. But I'm sure they would have once they got the money."

"Try not to think about it," Jaye said. "You're safe now."

Willie looked suddenly worried. "Did somebody tell Nathan? He didn't pay them?"

"No. Don't worry. They didn't get anything. In fact, the police met the guy in San Vicente who was going to take the money and arrested him."

Willie smiled with relief. "I couldn't be happier to be here." She turned to Megan. "Thanks to the other Megan, it all turned out okay."

"A while ago you said I was a maniac," Megan observed with a laugh.

"I want to hear everything," Jaye urged.

"Sure, no problem," Willie said, "but I have a feeling there's an even more interesting story here." She looked from Jaye to Megan with a smile. "I still want to know how a woman named Megan Willett ended up coming to my rescue."

Jaye looked sheepish.

"Well," Megan said, moving away from the wall, "it all started with an itsy bitsy teeny weenie black and white bikini."

"Oh," Willie looked bewildered and turned to Jaye for an explanation.

"She doesn't need to hear that part," Jaye said.

Megan was about to contradict her when a deep female voice barreled down the hallway. "Where are you, Señorita Willett?"

"Which one?" Willie asked.

"I think she means me," Megan said, then hollered back, "we're all in the bedroom, Inspector."

Delgado appeared in the doorway and surveyed the three women. "Ah, Dr. Willett, you are looking much better. Feeling better too, I hope."

"Yes, much better."

"I just got word the suspects are in custody. One of them is in the hospital. He has a concussion. He will recover."

Megan raised her hand. "I can take credit for that."

"Which one?" Willie asked.

"Eduardo Marra," answered Delgado.

Willie looked confused. "Marra?"

"Willie," said Jaye, "Eduardo Marra is Paloma's brother Eddie."

Willie looked stunned. "Oh, my God! Paloma's brother! How is that possible? He was just an informant, she said."

"Apparently he was bucking for a promotion," Jaye suggested.

"He said I deserved to die for...I don't understand. I've done nothing but help Paloma. I gave her training, experience and friendship."

"He obviously thinks you...or maybe you and I...were a bad influence. He might have jumped to a conclusion about us."

Willie looked as confused as ever.

"Oh, Jaye!" Megan intervened impatiently. "Just tell it to her straight. Look, Willie, Paloma has a girlfriend. Eddie found out about it, and he blames you and Jaye because he assumed you two were lovers."

Willie opened her mouth to speak but said nothing, apparently stunned into silence.

"He fingered you for a kidnapping," Jaye explained, "killing two birds with one stone."

"Sí, sí!" Inspector Delgado said excitedly. "Two birds, one stone. He catches a big fish for his employer and moves up the ladder." She walked her fingers up the air. "And he gets revenge on you, Dr. Willett, his sister's mentor who has led her down the wrong path, or so he believes."

"Paloma's going to be devastated," Willie said.

"He's a minor," Delgado intervened. "They might go easy on him. Right now, he is in the hospital, but in police custody."

"Will Paloma be able to visit him?"

"I will encourage it. This boy is like a bird in a cage in the hospital, and he will be unable to escape the outraged sister. It will, perhaps, do some good that his grand scheme ended in failure."

"Let's hope so," said Jaye.

"I have other news for you." Delgado held up a finger. "Your amigo Carlos Baza is out in the van. I have just arrested him."

The three women all looked at one another, then back at Delgado for an explanation. "His wife called us. She wants to press charges. We will want your records as evidence."

"Wow," Jaye said. "I can't believe it."

Delgado grinned. "Señora Baza, she has apparently grown a pair of *cojones*. Speaking of *cojones*, Señorita Willett, Señora Baza said to tell you she likes your style."

Megan laughed, remembering the pleased look on Maria Baza's face after Megan took her husband down.

"I am ready to go back to the city and get down to the business of interrogations." Delgado rubbed her palms together in anticipation, then addressed Megan. "Are you ready to go?"

"I'm packed, but before we go, I need to talk to Jaye."

"Okay. I will be outside. Do not be too long."

After Delgado was well out of hearing, Megan turned to Jaye. "Can we go somewhere and talk privately?"

Willie jumped up. "You know what? I'm starving again. I think I'll go take a look at some of those food offerings you were talking about." She glanced uneasily from one to the other of them, then left the room quickly.

Megan closed the door after her, thankful she could take a hint. "I'm really glad everything turned out okay," she said. "It was wild, it really was. But it sounds like there's no more danger, right? The kidnappers are in jail. Willie's home."

Jaye nodded. "All back safe and sound. I hope you know how thankful I am to you for what you did. It was very brave."

Megan sashayed over to where Jaye was sitting. "How thankful are you?" she asked coquettishly.

Jaye looked nervous. She stood up and paced across the room. Megan could tell something was wrong.

"Since everything's good here," Megan said, "maybe you can take a couple of days off from the clinic. We could spend the entire time together. We could snorkel and kayak and have a blast. It can't hurt to take a couple of days off, can it?" Megan approached Jaye and slung her arms loosely around her waist. "Two whole days together. And two whole nights."

"And then what?" Jaye asked.

Megan shrugged. "Another two more nights with you and I don't think I'll ever want to leave."

"Come on, Megan, be serious."

"I am serious."

"No, you're not. You know you're going home in two days." Jaye pulled away from her.

"Right, I am. But what I meant was that I think this could be the real thing. Maybe we could make it work…somehow." Megan pulled Jaye around to face her and kissed her. "I want to see where this goes. I want more of you, a lot more. I'm not ready to say goodbye."

"What about what I want?"

"What do you want, Jaye?"

Jaye looked pained. "I want to be realistic. I want more than fantasies and fun."

"You're not hearing me, Jaye. I know you think I just wanted to do it with a lesbian, that it was a sexual experiment. But I just had the most incredible night of my life with you. You don't just walk away from that. I'm serious. I think I'm falling in love with you." Megan touched Jaye's face gently.

Jaye's expression began to remind her of how she was before their night together, cynical.

"Oh, Megan, that's just the afterglow. You barely know me."

Megan felt frustrated. "Why do you have to believe you'll get married someday to have a second date? I was into you the minute I met you. And I've liked you more every minute after that. After forty-eight hours more, who knows? Why can't we just see where it goes?"

Jaye uttered a bitter little laugh and moved a short distance away. "It goes nowhere. What kind of dream are you in? You're going back to California in two days. I'm staying here. And I really don't want to be in a long-distance relationship."

"I could stay. I mean, I could come back after graduation and stay here with you until your year is up. We'd have a blast here. Then we can go wherever we want, wherever I get into medical school. I can do my internship in the same hospital you're working! We could meet in the janitor's closet and make out." She giggled involuntarily. "See, we can make it work. No long-distance relationship."

Jaye sighed deeply. "No, that's impossible. I can't even imagine that. To tell you the truth, I don't want to be in any kind of relationship. I never did. I didn't want anything to happen between us because I knew what it would be, a one-night stand. As nice as it was, it was never going to be more than that. I'm not looking for anything serious." She shook her head. "Megan, I really hope you find the right person to make you happy. You're a beautiful young woman and I feel grateful to have known you for a couple of days. But now you go back to your life and I go back to mine. That's the only thing that makes sense here."

"You can't be serious. You're giving me the kiss-off? You don't even want to take advantage of the next two days? You don't even want to give it a chance?"

Jaye shook her head. "No. I really don't. We never should have started this because it had no future, and getting in deeper would just make it harder to say goodbye."

Megan ran to her, embraced her and hung on. "We don't have to say goodbye. Have some faith in love, Jaye. We could make it work if we wanted to."

"I don't want to. That's what I'm trying to tell you." Jaye wriggled out of Megan's grasp. "Last night was incredible, but that's it. I like my life here. I'm happy here. I don't want anything else. I don't want to change my life."

Megan began to feel desperate. "Why not? Who doesn't want to fall in love?"

Jaye stared, her lips pressed tightly together. Sometime between this morning and now, Jaye must have made up her mind. She appeared resolute. It was over. But why? They were so good together. It was so worth pursuing. What can I say, Megan thought, that I haven't said already?

The sound of dishes in the kitchen momentarily caused both of them to look in that direction. Willie making herself a snack, Megan remembered.

"I'm sorry," Jaye said quietly. "I didn't want to hurt you. I'm sure you'll be okay with this in a few days and you'll get it, why I'm sending you away. We'll both get back to our normal lives and it will be a nice memory. For both of us."

Megan felt annoyed at Jaye's condescending words. "I'm beginning to get it already. You keep saying how much you like your life here and I keep wondering why. I've been listening and watching and trying to figure that out. What's so freaking awesome about it? So you get a lot of satisfaction out of helping people who really need help. There are people like that everywhere. There are tons of people like that in Southern California. But, then, it hits me. And I'm like, uh, yeah, what's changed between this morning and this afternoon? There's only one thing that you've only got here." Megan felt heat rushing into her face. "Willie."

Jaye stared in surprise.

"It's not me that wanted a one-night stand," Megan continued. "It's you. Now you want to go back to your regular life, your life with *her*. You can't imagine me here because three's a crowd. You don't want to fall in love with me because you're already in love with her."

"You're nuts. Why are you saying that?"

"It's obvious you're in love with her."

Jaye shook her head and said emphatically, "Megan, you're just wrong. We're good friends. Friendships in a place like this are close and special. Maybe you're just reaching for an explanation that makes sense to you instead of the truth. You won't listen to me. I don't want to run off like some teenager chasing a crazy maybe. When you're a few years older, with some heartbreak under your belt, you'll understand. It gets harder to take a leap of faith when you've been through it before."

Megan felt her lip quiver. "I already have some heartbreak under my belt, thanks to you!"

She grabbed her bag and ran from the room, sprinting outside to where Delgado was waiting, chewing on a wad of gum.

"Ready?" she asked.

"Totally," Megan said, tossing her bag in the car and fighting back tears. "I'm so out of here!"

CHAPTER THIRTY

From the numerous offerings brought by the locals, Jaye took a dish at random from the refrigerator to prepare dinner. She set two place settings as usual. In no time at all, everything would be back to normal. And she couldn't wait to get back to normal. It seemed like the last few days had been complete chaos, and she hated chaos. She'd had plenty of that in her life. Perhaps the best thing about Tocamila was how predictable her life was from one day to the next. She and Willie stuck to a regular schedule and slept peacefully at night because they knew what tomorrow would be like.

Not knowing what tomorrow might be like was terrifying. She knew all about that. Not knowing where you would be living or with whom. Not knowing where or when your next meal would be served. Not knowing if a stranger would drive up to your house and take you away in a strange car to a strange place. And it could happen any day, any time. You would never know it was coming. Nobody ever warned you. A car would just suddenly be there and people would grab at you and put you in it and take you away. You would have no idea where you were going or what your life was about to be like.

Jaye leaned against the counter and wiped at her eyes. She heard Willie enter the room and quickly tried to recover.

"Is something wrong, Jaye?" Willie asked gently.

Jaye turned to face her, observing the numerous light scratches across her face. "There's never any guarantee," she said, "that tomorrow will turn out like you planned."

"What do you mean?"

"I was just thinking about something that happened to me when I was six years old. I thought I'd never feel like that again once I was an adult and in charge of my own life. I'd call the shots then, you know? But things happen. You can't predict. You can't plan everything."

Willie shook her head and took her place at the table. "That's absolutely true. I'm still surprised I'm alive this evening. I was surprised I was about to die. Now I'm surprised I'm not going to die. You're right. You can't predict."

Jaye sighed and sat across from Willie. "I like my predictable life here."

"Do you? Not too boring for you? From what I've heard, you used to raise quite a bit of hell."

Jaye chuckled and said nothing.

"It's always hard to reconcile the Jaye of those stories with the Jaye I've known the last six months."

"Those stories are about a younger woman."

"It's not like you're sixty, Jaye. You're still a young woman. What's been going on around here anyway? I just saw Megan run out of here. It looked like she was upset. Now here you are standing in the kitchen crying."

"I wasn't crying," Jaye lied.

"Okay, if you say so."

Jaye sighed again. "I'm afraid I let myself get carried away a little bit with Megan. God, Willie, it was so unexpected."

"What happened?"

Jaye bit her lip. "We spent the night together, actually."

Willie looked startled. She had clearly not imagined that. Eventually, she recovered her poise and said, "I see. I'm sure she has her good points." She grinned. "She's got good teeth."

Jaye stared, perplexed at Willie's tone. "Yes, there's that. And she's cute and fun. She made me laugh."

"I can see why you'd be attracted to her. But I hope you're not considering going any further with it. She doesn't seem like the most responsible, mature person. In fact, from the short time I was around her, she seemed kind of nuts."

Jaye laughed. "Yeah, maybe a little. There's a lot of life in her. But nuts, like you said. I'll tell you how nuts she is. She thinks I'm in love with you."

Willie's hand flew to her throat. "Oh, dear!"

"I know! Crazy, right?"

"Well, maybe not entirely crazy. I can sort of understand how she'd get that impression. You explained to her, right, that we're not…"

"Of course. I don't think she believed me. That's the only thing that makes sense to her, to explain why I don't want to just chuck everything and run away with her."

"What about because you have a good life here and you love your work and you're happy here?"

"Exactly!" Jaye tossed up her hands. "But she thinks it's true love with me, so…"

"True love." Willie shook her head with an amused smile. "She's still young enough to believe in that."

Jaye had never asked Willie if she believed in true love. Her scoffing tone suggested she did not.

"Yes," Jaye said. "It's infatuation. I tried to tell her that. It's not enough to reroute our lives for. It won't last."

"No, it won't last. It's all sex. Hormones. It clouds your reason…for a while. Then you wake up one day and you're sitting across the breakfast table with somebody who's a virtual stranger making gross smacking sounds with her lips, and you think, what the heck am I doing here?"

"And this is the voice of experience speaking?" Jaye asked.

Willie grinned. "Just something I read in a book once. It seemed kinda funny, but also true. I mean, you can imagine it would be true."

Jaye got up and stood by the window, staring out at the backyard and remembering watching shooting stars with Megan.

"How did you leave it with her?" asked Willie.

"Over." Jaye turned to face her friend, who looked concerned and not completely convinced. "It's over. I've come to my senses. I wasn't myself. The kidnapping made me kind of…I was so upset and…yes, it's over."

Willie nodded. "And you're good with that?"

"Totally. What else? She'll be going home. I'm staying here."

"Good. Then it's all over and no harm done."

"Right. It was just one of those things. Spring fling. It's not like I haven't done that before."

"Not since I've known you."

"No, not since a long time ago, actually. Before Lexie." Jaye shrugged. "She'll be fine. She got what she wanted."

"And what did you get, Jaye?" Willie's expression was thoughtful and concerned.

Jaye swept the uncertainty from her mind and grinned. "Another toaster oven." She left the kitchen, leaving Willie with a puzzled look on her face.

CHAPTER THIRTY-ONE

Megan and her four friends sat in a circle around a fire pit near the beach with their hands around steaming mugs of hot chocolate. By now, even Mickey had had enough alcohol. Clouds had come in during the afternoon and the night smelled like rain, but so far, the skies held onto their payload. Lisa tucked newspaper under a pile of kindling, preparing to start the fire. The sun dipped beneath the sea, leaving a palette of purple and midnight blue above the watery horizon.

Megan had just told the story of her kidnapping and rescue of the beloved jungle dentist, omitting the part of the story that was most important to her, that she had fallen in love with the gorgeous jungle nurse. Her friends were suitably impressed. She had had to repeat herself on certain points, like when bullets came through the windows, because at first they simply didn't believe her. Even though it had happened only hours earlier, she too found it a little hard to believe.

"That was one bitchin' ride, girl. Sweet!" Mickey whistled.

"I could have been killed," she objected. "I almost was killed. Two bullets went right over my head."

"Word!" Mickey fist-bumped Gavin, biting his lower lip.

"Exactly," Gavin agreed, pulling the brim of his Trojans cap around to the back. "I can't believe we missed out on that."

Megan shook her head, glancing at Lisa and Nicole, whose expressions silently agreed with her that the boys were idiots. She pulled up a photo on her phone, the selfie she'd taken with an unconscious Eddie Marra. Before surrendering his phone to the police, she'd forwarded this to herself. It made a good souvenir. She passed it around the group so they could admire her handiwork.

"You should get a medal," Gavin said. "Or a reward. A nice thick slice of the ransom money. How much was it?"

"A hundred thousand."

"American?" Lisa asked.

Megan nodded, observing the boys with their open-mouthed amazement. Gavin whistled.

"I don't want a reward," she said. "It really felt good, maybe not at the time, but after. It made me feel amazing, actually. So did the other stuff."

"What other stuff?" Nicole asked.

"Working in the clinic. Helping those people. I could really see doing that…for real. When I'm a doctor, I mean."

"Uh-oh." Mickey grinned. "Is our Megan turning into a philanthropist?" He held his hands up to his eyes as if shielding them from a bright light. "Look, she's glowing all over, glowing from her shiny heart of gold."

"Shut up!" she ordered. "What do you know about it? It feels good to help people. Like, you should try it sometime."

"I have," he said in self-defense. "I volunteer every other Sunday at the homeless shelter, serving meals and stuff like that."

"Then what are you going on at me for?"

"Yeah!" Nicole added. "Shut up, you red-headed slut!"

He shrugged, sufficiently rebuked, and handed back her phone. He might never escape that new nickname, especially if Nicole had her way, but Megan could tell he sort of liked it.

Lisa put a match to the newspaper under the kindling and a small flame shot up, growing as the paper burned and drawing everyone's attention to the fire.

A message came through on her phone. From Jaye? A rush of adrenaline surged through her. But the text was from her mother. She wasn't happy about Megan's venture into the Santuarian wilds. She'd even used a frowny face. She didn't know the half of it! She would tell her parents the whole story someday, but not for a while, not until they'd gotten over the original scare.

She brought up the photo she had taken of Jaye at the fiesta. She wished she'd taken a dozen, but how could she have realized it would end so soon? This was all she had to remember her by. In the photo Jaye was smiling self-consciously, her hair falling forward, unhinged from her ear. Megan shook her head, marveling at what had happened to her over the last few days. She had fallen in love. She had finally figured out what she wanted from life. And then she had lost it. She gulped down a sob and stuck her phone in her pocket as Lisa crab-walked on her long legs away from the fire pit to sit beside her.

"Hey," said Megan, "what happened to the chick you were all hot for?"

"Rita?" Lisa shook her head. "Her girlfriend, that's what happened. Big and mean. So I said no, thank you, and got the hell outta there." She poked at the fire with a stick, then sat back and asked quietly, "Is something wrong with you?"

"No."

"Are you sure? Ever since you came back, you seem unhappy or something. It sounds like you were in deep shit out there, so I can understand if you're upset about what happened."

Megan shrugged. She couldn't talk about it. Not here anyway. "No, I'm okay. It was just a lot of stuff. A lot of stuff happened in the last couple of days. It's going to take some time to process it."

That answer seemed to satisfy Lisa. "I really can't imagine. It must have been terrifying. The whole thing is so unreal." She tossed a couple more sticks on the fire.

She was right. It all seemed like a dream. But one thing remained completely real to her, the way she felt about Jaye. She so badly wanted to call and hear her voice. But she'd always been a believer in ripping the tape off fast. If Jaye didn't want her, a phone call would just be awkward and unwelcome. Besides, she had said some stupid stuff before storming out. She didn't really believe Jaye and Willie were lovers or that Jaye was in love with Willie. Not in a sexual way. But they were obviously close and Megan was jealous of that. Even with the bonus of sex, Jaye didn't want to be with her, didn't want her enough to disrupt any part of her life, not even the last two days of spring break.

"I fell in love," she said impulsively, just loud enough for Lisa to hear.

Lisa turned to stare at her. "You did? When?"

"Monday. Tuesday. I don't know." My mother was so right, Megan said to herself. I cannot keep my mouth shut!

Lisa was clearly confused. "Then what are you doing here with us? Believe me, if it had worked out with Rita, I wouldn't be here right now, as much as I love all you nuts."

Mickey and Gavin were arguing about a girl and Nicole was on the other side of the fire, too far away to notice the quiet conversation between Megan and Lisa.

"It's a one-way thing," Megan explained. "You know, unrequited."

"Oh! I'm so sorry. But who is it? One of the policemen you told us about? A handsome young stranger in the village? The guitar player at that fiesta you went to?"

"It doesn't matter. It wasn't meant to be."

Lisa put her arm around Megan's shoulders and squeezed her.

"Thanks," Megan said, then took a long drink from her mug. The taste of the spicy chocolate reminded her of Jaye. Everything reminded her of Jaye. She wanted to cry. "I think I'll go back to the hotel."

"Are you sure, Megan? Don't you want to be around friends?"

"Thanks, but I'm just gonna bring the mood down. See you later."

Megan said a quick goodbye to the group and walked up the loose sand to the road. She stopped under a streetlight and pulled out her phone to look at Jaye's photo again. She knew she shouldn't make herself look pathetic, but she couldn't help it. She sent a text to Jaye: *I miss you so much.*

CHAPTER THIRTY-TWO

Jaye left Willie in the kitchen and went to the bedroom to be alone. She checked her phone, not surprised to see a text from Megan. *I miss you so much*, it said. Jaye pressed her lips together, pushing back a sudden upwelling of emotion. *I miss you too*. She put the phone down and picked up a wilted plumeria blossom from the dresser. She put it to her nose, breathed in its perfume and thought of Megan's unabashed grin and mischievous eyes. Then she closed her eyes and remembered the touch and smell and taste of her body. The memory left her light-headed.

But Willie agreed that it was foolish and irresponsible, completely absurd to give up a home, work, a life you loved for such an uncertain chance at...*true love*? Or disaster? Maybe they were the same thing. As for Megan's wild idea that she could come live here, Jaye couldn't even imagine it. Willie would never be okay with that. There was no place for Megan in their life here.

It had been a beautifully sweet interlude. But it was over and real life would now resume. She crushed the bloom in her hand and dropped it in the wastebasket.

A pounding on the front door interrupted her thoughts.

She went to the front room and opened the door to Nathan Willett. He was dressed more casually than the last time she had seen him, in khakis and a polo shirt. He smiled, then looked past her to see his sister, and his smile bloomed.

"Nathan!" Willie called gleefully. She ran to his arms. They held one another for a long time.

"I've missed you," Nathan said, his voice full of emotion. "Are you all right? Look at your face. It's all scratched up. What on earth happened?"

"Oh, nothing. Just brambles. I'm fine."

Looking over Willie's head, Nathan said, "How about you, Jaye? Are you all right?"

"I'm just fine," she answered.

"Nate," Willie said, looking up at him, "let me show you around. Do you want anything? Something to drink?"

"Ice water would be nice."

"I'll get it," Jaye offered, and left them together. She filled a glass with ice and water, listening to Willie's animated voice as she led Nathan around the premises.

"This is our kitchen," Willie said, sweeping into the room with Nathan in her wake. "You know I don't cook much. We eat very simply, just cereal for breakfast, but we get a few fresh fruits and vegetables from the garden. Look, you can see the garden out the window."

Nathan leaned over the sink to oblige.

"And people bring us food all the time," Willie said. "Since they don't have to pay for services, they feel compelled to bring gifts. Today, for instance, we must have taken in a dozen meals. There are handmade blankets and furniture and…oh, we've had several offers of goats, but I had to turn those down." Willie's grin threatened to break out of her face and fly around the room. She seemed to be overwhelmed by her brother's presence. "We were about to have dinner. Will you stay for that? Can you stay the night? You have to stay the night. You won't want to drive back in the dark."

He nodded. "Yes, I'll stay for dinner, for the night, whatever you two divine women have to offer."

"We can fix you up with a cot," Jaye said, handing him the water.

As he drank, his sister watched him with unrestrained joy on her face. It was disconcerting to Jaye to see this familial attachment after the months she had spent thinking that Willie, like herself, was permanently estranged from her family. But these two seemed ecstatic at seeing one another again, and whatever the affronts of the past had been, they had obviously been forgotten. Though she was happy for Willie, a part of her felt like she had suddenly been pushed into a more distant orbit, further from the warm sanctuary of Willie's affections. Yes, they were like sisters, but they had known one another only a short time. Nathan had been there her whole life. Having been out of her life for two years, he could still step right into it again without missing a beat. She realized she was a little jealous. She'd had Willie to herself for six months. Maybe that was why Willie hadn't been happy to hear about Megan. Maybe she was jealous too. They had both gotten very comfortable with this arrangement.

Jaye opened a plastic bag she'd selected from the refrigerator. Inside was baked chicken. Perfect, she thought. That would work for the three of them. She went through the refrigerator again to find a side dish while Willie showed her brother the pantry, explaining how the Nutella was a special order the grocer made just for Jaye. "She can't live without her Nutella," she proclaimed with a laugh.

"Well, there's your Arizona iced tea," he countered, pointing at her stash. "And what's this, hey?" He pulled a plastic container out and held it up with a grin. "Homemade granola, isn't it?"

Willie nodded sheepishly.

Nathan laughed and put the container back.

Jaye rummaged through the bags and found something that looked like a corn casserole. That would do. When she emerged from the refrigerator, she saw Nathan and Willie in a tight embrace. Nathan was stroking Willie's hair and she seemed to be sobbing. Nathan smiled at Jaye over his sister's shoulder. "It's okay," he said, to both of them, it seemed. "It'll take you a while to come down from this."

Willie lifted her head. "Oh, Nate, it was the most harrowing experience! From beginning to end, it was a nightmare, and the entire time I was sure I was going to die. Especially after I got in the truck with that lunatic."

"Lunatic?" he asked.

"The other Megan Willett."

"Oh, her. Where is she?" He glanced around the room as if expecting to see her.

"She's back in Punta Larga," Jaye said, "enjoying the rest of her vacation."

"It was all so surreal, this wild girl with her death wish. Bullets flying over my head, glass shattering, and she's as calm as can be, like this happens every day in her world. She's very strange."

"I liked her," Nathan said. "She was fun."

"Fun? Not my idea of fun!"

He nodded with understanding. "No. I'm sure it was horrible."

"I'll get dinner ready," Jaye said. "So you'll have to get out of the kitchen because there's not enough room in here for all of us."

"Let's go outside and sit on the porch," Willie suggested. "Nate, I want to tell you everything!"

Nathan put his arm around Willie and walked her from the room. Jaye set the table and heated up the dishes one at a time in the microwave. Images of Megan kept invading her consciousness and she kept pushing them back out. Nathan was right. She was fun. They'd had such a good time at the fiesta. It seemed like Jaye had smiled the entire evening. She shook herself and put water glasses on the table. It was going to take time to get past this, she knew. She was glad she hadn't made it worse by spending two more days with Megan.

When the food was hot, she put it in serving dishes on the table and went out front to get Willie and Nathan.

"Jaye!" Willie called excitedly. "Jaye, you can't guess what we've been talking about. The ransom money. The hundred thousand. My father's going to give it to us!"

Jaye was puzzled. "And you're going to take it?"

"Yes!" Willie jumped out of her chair. "Imagine all the illegal drugs and bullets that money would have bought. Then imagine what we could do with it. A new X-ray machine to begin with. And we could pay for Mrs. Alvaro's cancer treatments. We could actually save her life! Do you see?"

"And Luna? What about Luna? Megan's mother might have found a doctor to help her."

"Yes! And Luna. We can pick up all the expenses."

"That's wonderful!"

Willie nodded gleefully.

"But I don't understand. Couldn't you have gotten this kind of money at any time?"

Willie rolled her eyes. "Yes! So I should kick myself, right? I don't know what I was thinking before. It was so short-sighted." Willie flung her arms around Jaye's neck. "We make an unbeatable team, don't we, Jaye?"

Jaye held Willie at arm's length, observing the joy flashing in her eyes. "We do, yes. By the way, dinner's ready."

Nathan stood, so composed in contrast to his sister. He took Willie's arm and walked inside with her. "You know, Willie," he said with a chuckle, "this place is just as I would have imagined it. Your personal stamp is everywhere, from the arrangement of furniture to the wall décor. There's the austere bedroom with its two twin beds and your little garden in back of the house so you can have your organic vegetables." Jaye followed them into the kitchen. "Then there's the two of you sitting here at the shop-worn table every morning with your homemade granola. It's all very predictably Willie, I have to say. Very orderly and calm. The outward contrast to your mind's inner turmoil." He laughed shortly. "It makes me think of a convent, you know, like two Sisters of Mercy living in a grim little place with no luxuries, just your mission and your faith to hang your hat on." He looked back toward Jaye with an apologetic smile. "Sorry, Jaye. I know it's not like that at all. At least you're not. Willie has always wanted to live like a monk. You, however, I could tell when I met you, are a different case. Yeah." He pulled a chair out for Willie. When she was seated, he did the same for Jaye. Then he seated himself and surveyed the simple meal before them. "This looks great!"

* * *

Jaye was the first one up Thursday morning. She didn't know what time Willie had come to bed, but by two in the morning when she woke up, Willie was sound asleep nearby. That's when Jaye had been lying awake thinking about her future, troubled and torn by her conflicting desires.

She turned on the coffeepot and stood staring into space while it sputtered. What Nathan had said about this place being just as he would have expected had been eating at her ever since last night. He was right. It was Willie through and through. Everything looked exactly as it had six months ago when Jaye arrived. She had changed nothing. She hadn't hung a picture on a wall. She hadn't bought a new set of towels, despite her loathing of aqua in bathrooms. She had adapted completely to Willie's routine, her tastes, her habits, even her damned granola. She had never eaten granola in her life before coming here. She ate shredded wheat. And yet, there had never been a box of shredded wheat in this house. Why? Why had she subjugated herself so completely to Willie's lifestyle?

Because Willie had been here first. That was part of it. Jaye wasn't going to come in and boss her around. But it was more than that. When Jaye had come here six months ago, she'd been broken. Her will had been shattered. She didn't care about much of anything, let alone the color of the towels or what she ate for breakfast. None of it was because Willie was a tyrant, but simply because Jaye didn't assert her desires. And that wasn't really like her. Not the person she had been before.

Willie had taken her in and taken care of her. Willie had given her meaningful work, a home and friendship. She had given her a sanctuary in which to heal. And like it had always been, Jaye had been a sucker for a woman who was concerned about her welfare. Maybe she *was* a little in love with Willie.

But not like Megan thought. It was Miss Ingalls all over again. She adored someone who was completely inappropriate and unavailable for a relationship. A chaste infatuation. Which was a safe position to be in whether you're twelve or twenty-seven. It was safe, yes, but it wasn't enough for her now. Not anymore. She knew that now, and Nathan's alarming image of the two of them living like nuns had driven it home.

The coffeepot beeped, signaling that it was finished. Jaye filled her mug, leaned against the counter and took a swallow, then her gaze panned slowly around the room. I've been content here, she thought. It was exactly what I needed…for a while.

She gulped some more coffee, feeling a rising sense of urgency in her chest.

Willie came in, yawning. She wore her pale blue bathrobe, her hair haphazardly pulled back into a rubber band.

"Good morning," she said, then poured herself a cup of coffee.

"How late were you up?" asked Jaye, pushing aside her uneasiness. She sat in her usual place at the table.

"I don't know. It was after midnight anyway. Nate's still asleep." She set her cup on the table.

"What'd you talk about?"

"Old times. And the other thing."

"The other thing?"

"The money, what we can do with the money. And maybe a monthly allowance from my parents' trust fund. Nate thinks I can have that if I want it." She narrowed her eyes at Jaye. "What are you smiling at?"

"You. This complete reversal on the money issue."

Willie shrugged and went to the pantry. "What can I say? I've seen the light." She opened the granola container and scooped her usual half cup into a bowl, the green one, the one she always used. Jaye knew she would then peel a banana and slice half of it on the granola. Normally, Jaye would use the other half. "Have you eaten?" Willie asked. "Do you want me to give you a scoop?"

"No," Jaye replied a little too forcefully.

Willie didn't seem to notice. She put the banana and milk in her bowl and returned to the table, sitting opposite Jaye.

"The last few days have been mind-blowing," Jaye said.

Willie nodded, then put a spoonful of granola in her mouth.

"I mean, we've both had a lot to think about." Jaye put her hand over Willie's to get her attention. "So I've been thinking. I'd like to make a few changes around here."

Willie set her spoon in the bowl, giving Jaye her complete attention. "What do you want?"

Jaye pulled her hand back. "I want shredded wheat."

Willie stared, looked at her bowl, then looked back at Jaye. "Okay. I think that can be arranged. Not immediately, but by tomorrow anyway. Is that it? That's the change you want to make?"

Jaye shook her head. "No. That's not really it at all. Willie, you and I aren't the same person. I admire you and I love you, but I don't want to be you or live like you. I don't want to be a philanthropist, for instance. I don't want to wade through swamps to save people. I'm more selfish than you are. I just want to be a nurse, an ordinary nurse, and I want more in my life than my work. Much more. I want a wife, a family, a comfortable home with one of those rulers on the kitchen wall where I mark off the heights of my kids through the years. I want a permanent address."

Willie looked stunned and was silent for some moments, then blinked and said, "The shredded wheat, I can accommodate, Jaye, but I'm not sure I know what to do about…"

Jaye shook her head. "No, I'm not saying I have to have all those things right now. I mean that's what I want out of life, eventually. This time in Santuario has been wonderful for me. I love it here. But I'm beginning to realize this is not only temporary, but unique for me. This is your kind of life. For me, it's just a respite. Do you see?"

Willie looked hurt. "I never asked you to be like me."

"No, I know. You've done nothing wrong. You've been incredibly good to me. You gave my life structure. I really needed that when I first got here. But things are different now.

I didn't even realize that I've been coming into my own again. I'm feeling better about life, stronger. And that means wanting things again, wanting the things that make me happy. I guess I've put some of the negative shit behind me."

Willie cringed.

"Sorry." Jaye reconsidered. "No, I'm not sorry. I'm not going to apologize for being myself. I'm sorry it bothers you, but I'm not sorry for the way I am."

"No, I'm sorry. After all the shit I've just been through, you'd think the word 'shit' wouldn't bother me."

Jaye blinked, never having heard Willie utter that word before.

"I'm going to work on that language thing. I know, it's juvenile to react that way to words." Willie smiled fatalistically and held Jaye's gaze. "I know you've been hurting all these months. I know you just wanted to hide somewhere and curl up into a tight knot and not let anybody touch you. That's never been what I wanted for you, Jaye. I love our life here together, but I never loved it that you were grieving. I'm glad you're feeling better, feeling more alive. I want you to have all those things, the wife and the kids and a permanent address… eventually."

Jaye patted her hand. "You're a good friend, Willie."

"Maybe we've both seen the light. This has been a really transformative experience, hasn't it?" Willie smiled affectionately.

"It has."

"This is your home too, Jaye, for now. You can make any changes you want. We can repaint, get new furniture, new appliances, whatever you want. We've got a little extra cash now, and a few dollars can certainly go toward making this place more suitable for you."

"There are just a few small things. We don't need to bring in a bulldozer." Jaye smiled reassuringly at Willie, then got up and rinsed out her mug. Standing at the sink, she took a deep breath. She was no longer thinking about new towels in the bathroom. She realized quite suddenly that she'd made a decision. She spun around to face Willie. "What are your plans for today?" she asked. "Do you need the van?"

"I'm taking Nate to the museum in San Vicente. We can take his rental. Of course, you're welcome to come along." She narrowed her eyes, as if looking at something unfamiliar. "But, no. You've got other plans, don't you?"

Jaye nodded. "Thanks anyway."

Willie's expression turned pensive. It was obvious where her mind had gone. She knew shredded wheat wasn't going to keep Jaye here forever. But, then, Jaye had never planned on being here forever. Neither had Willie, for that matter. She'd been talking about Africa ever since Jaye arrived, a keen wanderlust in her eye for the challenge of living in mosquito nets and boiling her drinking water. The fact was, Isla Santuario was just too much luxury for Willie. It was only her first adventure, and Jaye knew she would go on to have many more. This small, quirky, unremarkable-looking woman, Jaye thought, is going to have one hell of an interesting life.

"Don't worry," she said, approaching Willie and squeezing her shoulders. "I'm not running away from home. I'll be back tomorrow night. Then we'll talk some more. But I've really got to get going."

Willie grabbed her by the wrist, halting her exit. "Jaye, I really am happy for you, you know?"

Jaye nodded, then kissed her cheek before leaving the room.

CHAPTER THIRTY-THREE

After an interminably long drive into Punta Larga, made bearable only by the exceptionally smooth-running engine of the van, Jaye found a parking spot and nearly ran to the front desk of the Fiesta Royale Resort. She asked the clerk for Megan Willett's room number. The young woman facing her said, "I'm sorry, we can't give out room numbers. But I can ring her room and tell her you're here. What is your name, please?"

She gave her name and waited impatiently while the woman pressed keys on a computer keyboard. Jaye glanced around the lobby, thinking she might catch Megan by chance. She noticed the column near the lounge that Megan had hidden behind Monday afternoon. That seemed so long ago now. In terms of emotions, a lifetime ago.

A boy and an unusually tall girl stood between Jaye and the front doors talking. The boy, olive-skinned and handsome, wore swimming trunks and an open shirt. On his head was a red and gold baseball cap, worn backward.

"Ms. Northrup," the clerk said, drawing her attention back. "Ms. Willett checked out this morning."

"What? No, no, that's not possible. She doesn't leave until tomorrow."

The young woman looked irritated. "I'm sure this is correct."

Jaye glanced again at the boy and girl in the lobby, convinced that they were Megan's friends, two of the ones who had been with her Sunday night.

"Never mind," she told the clerk. She walked over to the pair and said, "Excuse me. You're friends of Megan Willett's, aren't you?"

The boy turned to her and smiled, but the girl looked suspicious. Jaye tried to remember the boy's name. He was the one who had kissed Megan that night.

"Gavin, isn't it?" she asked.

He nodded.

"I'm Jaye."

"You're the nurse!" he said, shaking her hand. "Hey, Lisa, it's the nurse Megan told us about. At the clinic."

Lisa nodded, the suspicious expression dropping away.

"She said you were smoking hot," Gavin said, ogling her.

"Gavin, shit!" said Lisa. She turned to Jaye. "Sorry. He's not house-trained."

"Can either of you tell me what room she's in?"

Lisa shook her head. "Oh, sorry. She's gone."

"Gone?"

"She decided to go home early," Lisa explained.

Jaye's heart fell.

"She was seriously bummed about something," Gavin said, shrugging. "Personally, I didn't get it. After being kidnapped and that way cool car chase and all, I'd be stoked. She should've been too. Nothing gets to Megan. She's the coolest."

"I know what she was bummed about," Lisa said self-importantly.

"What time did she leave?" Jaye interrupted. "When was her flight?"

"I think she said seven thirty or something like that," offered Gavin.

"Yeah," confirmed Lisa. "She left before any of us were up."

Jaye knew exactly what time it was, but she looked at her watch anyway, confirming that it was just past nine. Megan was well on her way home already. *Oh, God! How could I have let this happen?*

"Was it something important?" Lisa asked.

Jaye laughed ironically.

"If you have something to give her," Gavin said, "you could give it to Nicole. They're roommates."

Jaye closed her eyes and choked back her disappointment, then said, "No. I…I just had something to say to her."

Lisa's expression was thoughtful. She regarded Jaye as if she were trying to figure something out. "You know what was bothering her, don't you?" she asked. "You know what happened?"

Jaye nodded, no longer caring what Lisa and Gavin had to say.

"Then you must know who it is," Lisa prodded.

"Who what is?" Gavin asked.

"Thanks for the information," Jaye said, ignoring Lisa's expectant look. "I guess I was just too late."

"Well, you can call her in about five hours," Gavin said brightly.

Jaye forced a smile. "Thanks."

She turned and moved toward the doors, stopping to lean against a sofa. What should she do now? Gavin was right, she could call Megan in five hours, but could she possibly make her case over the phone? Worse than that, she had been longing so much to see Megan again, to hold her and kiss her. She had anticipated that moment every mile of the drive in. She'd been so determined to be with Megan again, she was having a hard time giving up the idea.

I could go to San Diego, she thought. I could leave now and be with her tonight. She thought about Willie and the clinic and her obligations there. She'd go just for the weekend, she decided. She'd be back Monday. She just needed a little time with Megan to tell her and show her what was in her heart. Then it would be okay if they were apart for a while.

Willie would think she was insane. But she didn't believe in true love only because it had never happened to her. If it had, she'd go after it like anybody else. As Megan had said, who doesn't want to fall in love? Love is what life is all about.

She hadn't wanted to fall in love. She hadn't thought it was possible. Even yesterday when she'd sent Megan packing, she had been certain of herself and what she wanted. But having Megan actually gone had left such a painful void. So, yes, it had happened in spite of herself. She didn't want to let go. She couldn't let go!

She opened the web browser on her phone and started looking up flight schedules.

When she heard the whoosh of the hotel doors, she automatically looked up and was surprised to see the familiar figure of Inspector Delgado, her shirt snug across the chest and her halo of hair as impressive as ever.

"Inspector…"

"*Buenos días*, Señorita Northrup!" Delgado flashed her hideous grin. "I am surprised to see you here. Why are you not in Tocamila? And how is Dr. Willett?"

"She's fine. Her brother is there. They're having a great visit."

Delgado nodded, not seeming to notice Jaye hadn't answered her other question about what she was doing in Punta Larga. But the inspector was distracted, frowning back toward the hotel doors. She muttered something unintelligible, then turned abruptly and returned to the doors. Whoosh! they opened again and in walked Megan pulling a suitcase. She wore sunglasses, sky-blue shorts above her shapely, tanned legs and a crinkly green blouse with ruffles on cap sleeves. She looked absolutely delicious. Over her shoulder she carried a large tote bag. Jaye stared, frozen in place and not believing her eyes.

"Come along," Delgado urged, then fell in behind Megan, who was preoccupied by her suitcase, which was insisting on going sideways instead of straight ahead. When she looked up and saw Jaye, she abruptly stopped, causing Delgado to run into her suitcase and yelp, grabbing her shin.

But Megan didn't even turn around. She didn't seem to be aware of the collision in her wake. She released the handle of the suitcase and it popped upright behind her. She removed her sunglasses and gazed into Jaye's eyes. Her tote bag fell to the floor with a thud.

"Megan…" Jaye uttered.

It seemed they both overcame their amazement at the same instant, breaking into smiles, and falling toward one another. They embraced tightly. Jaye buried her face in Megan's hair and pulled her in even tighter. Megan pulled away slightly, her eyes brimming with tears of joy. Jaye kissed her, lingering and enjoying her sweet mouth, tuning out the rest of the world until a guttural throat-clearing interrupted them. Jaye roused herself to see that Inspector Delgado was standing beside them looking deadly serious. Just a few feet away were Gavin, Lisa and a couple of other students, a girl in glasses and a red-headed boy, all four of them staring open-mouthed.

"Oh, my God," said Lisa in a low tone. "It's *her*."

Megan looked slightly self-conscious as she noticed her whole gang standing there watching. The pale redhead was the first to address her.

"What happened to your flight, dude?" he asked.

Delgado stepped forward authoritatively. "I'm afraid Señorita Willett nearly caused an international incident at the airport."

They all looked at Megan, who slipped her hand into Jaye's between them.

"She tried to carry an explosive device onto the plane," Delgado explained.

"No shit?" Gavin said, scratching his head through the ball cap.

"Because of her recent involvement in the Willett kidnapping," Delgado continued, "airport security called me."

"Were you going to blow up the plane?" Gavin asked.

"Of course not," said Megan. "It was a mistake."

Delgado held up a firecracker for everyone to see. "This is the explosive device. It was hidden in her pocket." She tucked the firecracker in her own pants pocket to illustrate. "It set off the alarm and she was taken into custody."

Megan shrugged. "I forgot it was there."

"Inspector," Jaye objected, "she didn't mean anything by it. It was an innocent mistake. She picked up that firecracker the other night at the fiesta in Tocamila. Everybody had them."

Delgado held up her hand. "No need to plead this case. We've already resolved the issue and I have filed my report. Señorita Willett is free to go on the next flight to San Diego. And I hope she does so." She stared pointedly at Megan. "This one is trouble."

Delgado turned and strode out of the hotel, the doors parting for her with their customary whoosh.

Jaye took Megan by the shoulders. "Megan," she pleaded, "please don't go on the next flight. Please stay. I was so wrong to let you go. I love you, and all I want is to be with you."

"Oh, Jaye! I love you too!" Megan threw her arms around Jaye's neck. "I'll stay here forever."

Jaye laughed. "That may be a little extreme. But we'll find a way to be together eventually. We'll take it one day at a time. And today we can be together here in Isla Santuario." She smiled into Megan's joyful, trusting face. "We can make it work."

They kissed again, and Jaye heard Lisa say, "Quit staring, you pervs. Let's go, and I'll fill you in."

Jaye heard nothing after that except Megan's breathing and her contented sigh as she rested her head on Jaye's shoulder.

"We have the entire day together," Jaye said, stroking the back of Megan's head. "What do you want to do? Snorkeling? Kayaking?"

Megan nuzzled into Jaye's neck and said, "Let's go shoe shopping."

Jaye laughed. "Okay."

Jaye realized she had no idea what the day after tomorrow would be like, what promises or plans would have been made, or where this journey would lead them. But it was okay with her. She wasn't afraid of the uncertainty, of not knowing where she would end up. She had never had a place to call home for very long. But one thing she had learned was that home could be anywhere, that the place didn't matter, as long as there was love. Holding Megan in her arms, her eyes closed, she could be anywhere in the world. It just didn't matter. This felt so right. This felt like home.

Bella Books, Inc.

Women. Books. Even Better Together.

P.O. Box 10543
Tallahassee, FL 32302

Phone: 800-729-4992
www.bellabooks.com